BOOKS BY CRAIG RICE

My Kingdom for a Hearse
Knocked for a Loop
45 Murderers
Innocent Bystander
The Fourth Postman
The Lucky Stiff
Home Sweet Homicide
The Thursday Turkey
    Murders
Having Wonderful Crime
Sunday Pigeon Murders
The Big Midget Murders
Trial by Fury
The Right Murder
The Wrong Murder
The Corpse Steps Out
8 Faces at 3

With Ed McBain:
    The April Robin
    Murders

BOOKS BY STUART PALMER

Unhappy Hooligan
Monkey Murders
    and Other Stories
Riddles of Hildegarde Withers
Cold Poison
Nipped in the Bud
The Green Ace
Four Lost Ladies
Before It's Too Late
Miss Withers Regrets
Omit Flowers
Puzzle of the Red Stallion
Puzzle of the Blue Banderilla
Puzzle of the Happy Hooligan
Puzzle of the Silver Persian
Puzzle of the Pepper Tree
Murder on the Blackboard
Murder on Wheels
Penguin Pool Murder
Ace of Jades

STUART PALMER/ CRAIG RICE

People
VS.
Withers
&
Malone

LIBRARY OF CRIME CLASSICS®

MISTER E'S™

INTERNATIONAL POLYGONICS, LTD.
NEW YORK CITY

Contents

An Informal Introduction by Ellery Queen   7

Preface by Stuart Palmer   13

ONCE UPON A TRAIN   17

CHERCHEZ LA FRAME   49

AUTOPSY AND EVA   81

RIFT IN THE LOOT   115

PEOPLE VS. WITHERS & MALONE   151

WITHERS AND MALONE, BRAIN-STORMERS   203

. . . from E.Q.'s Uncommonplace Book

An Informal Introduction

NOTES ON CRAIG RICE

Portrait parlous　　　　When a full-color portrait of Craig Rice, painted by Artzybasheff, appeared on the January 28, 1946, issue of "Time," Craig Rice achieved a position and status peculiarly fitting to her ambitions. The portrait was parlous (and perilous) in all its meanings. A purple background showed a smoky ghost with six arms (a sextopus?) rising gruesomely out of typewriter keys; the wraith was blackmasked and his (or her) six hands grasped, reading from left to right, a dagger, a rope (held nooselike in two hands), a bottle of poison, an automatic, and a hypodermic syringe. (What, no blunt instrument?)

According to "Time," Craig Rice was virtually the only woman writer of the distinctively American type of mystery, the tough, hard-boiled school that combines hard drink, hilarity, and homicide; she was also (said "Time") an exponent of the so-called detective farce, "investing unholy living and heinous dying with a high atmosphere of mixed excitement and amusement." Parlous, indeed!

Did you know   that Craig Rice was once a crack publicity woman? She blew the trumpet and drove the band-wagon for no less a client than Gypsy Rose Lee.

Alas, alas   One of Craig Rice's literary ambitions was to write a detective novel using all the mystery clichés in a single story—including "the hard-boiled private eye who starts out broke and invariably gets a beautiful blonde client who pays off in hundred-dollar bills (updated, these would be thousand-dollar bills); the heiress bride who wonders, until almost too late, why her shifty-eyed husband spends so much time digging in the basement; the girl who knows something that will give the murderer away, but can't think what; identical twins; a homicidal butler; and, for full measure, an old lady in a wheel chair who walks around when everybody is asleep. . . . I'll bet (her stake—"all the rice in Craigland") it would be a best seller!" Alas, the mistress of the detective farce never got around to it.

Portrait parle   Oh, how she is missed these unfunny days: she was a wild, wacky, wonderful woman; she was gay, impulsive, generous, often reckless; she was fearful and courageous; and she was foolish and wise beyond her years.

NOTES ON STUART PALMER

Incunabula   Stuart Palmer wrote his first story at the age of six—a little tale called "Shag, My Dog" (out of print); he sold his first short story to "College Humor" at the age of nineteen—and has been writing and selling in almost every conceivable field ever since.

Portrait particular   The creator of Hildegarde Withers has had a crazy-quilt background of vocations and avocations: iceman, supercargo, apple picker, taxi driver, newspaper reporter, publicity man, editor, teacher, treasure hunter, private investigator. . . . He replaced Thorne Smith, who invented Topper, as chief copy writer for Doremus and Company, New York advertising agency (a desk previously held by Richard Lockridge, co-inventor of Mr. and Mrs. North); he was editor of Brentano's; he wrote screenplays in Hollywood, including flickers about Gay Falcon, The Lone Wolf, and Bulldog Drummond (but did he ever write any of the Hildegarde Withers movies?); he played polo with Darryl Zanuck and Spencer Tracy and Jimmy Gleason; he was a major in the U.S. Army in World War II; he has covered famous murder trials for Los Angeles newspapers, worked as special investigator for Los Angeles defense attorneys; he has a collection of penguin statuettes rivaled only by his collection of classic purple limericks.

And did you know that Stuart Palmer was once a clown with Ringling Brothers and Barnum & Bailey, under the big top?

Oscar The trained penguin that appeared in the movie version of Stuart Palmer's first great success, "The Penguin Pool Murder," was named Oscar. Palmer recalls that Oscar had a tendency to faint in the glare of the klieg lights and finally had to be given a stand-in—a duck! The name of the duck is not recorded for posterity: was it perhaps the great Donald himself, incognito, playing a sort of Caliph of Bagdad in true Hollywood style?

'Tec tintype Miss Hildegarde Withers is an equine-visaged spinster schoolteacher whose hats resemble nothing so much as fallen soufflés, and her creator often refers to her affectionately as "that meddlesome old battle-ax." Among those who played Hildy on the pre-TV screen were Edna May Oliver (wasn't she magnificent in the role?—Hildy to a T), Helen Broderick, and Zasu Pitts—and did you know it was once rumored in Hollywood that Mae West was being considered? No, we are not spoofing . . .

9

but, as Robert Browning did not say in "Pippa Passes": When Hildy's in her heaven, all's right with the world.

Toothsome twosomes "Once Upon a Train" was the first story in which the ever-battling Miss Withers and the ever-bibulous Mr. Malone appeared as a 'tec team, and also the first story, to the best of our recollection, in which two well-known mystery writers combined their chief characters —in this case, a dipsodetective and a spinstersleuth. It makes one wonder: suppose there were other manhunting mergers . . .

Imagine, if you will, A. Conan Doyle's misogynous Sherlock Holmes being consulted by Baroness Orczy's Lady Molly of Scotland Yard, instead of by G. Lestrade or Tobias Gregson, and forming a ferreting fellowship which might have elevated Lady Molly to the rank of The Woman II . . .

or R. Austin Freeman's austere Dr. Thorndyke in criminological cahoots with Anna Katharine Green's vivacious Violet Strange . . .

or G. K. Chesterton's mystical Father Brown as half of a sleuthing syndicate with Agatha Christie's mundane Miss Marple . . .

or the Lockridges' Mrs. North breezing past the breezy Archie Goodwin to become Rex Stout's Nero Wolfe's Girl Friday . . .

or a private-eye partnership between Dashiell Hammett's rough, tough Sam Spade and Nigel Morland's rough, tough Mrs. Pym . . .

or a detective duo of Ellery Queen's E.Q. and . . . our imagination fails us!

On the nature of collaboration Until her death in 1957, Craig Rice worked with Stuart Palmer on the Malone-

and-Withers (mis)adventures, and in this active collaboration the two writers produced four stories. After Craig Rice's death, two more stories appeared—all six were first published in "Ellery Queen's Mystery Magazine." Which raises an interesting question: How were the last two stories possible?

Well, the collaboration between the two mystery authors had been largely through correspondence; from existing letters and notes there was enough for Stuart Palmer to pick out a starting point (or, perhaps, an ending point) or find a plot inspiration in some Craigean scrap or Ricean fragment. The main line had been established in the stories created and written jointly: the great John J. Malone, a rowdy, raffish legal beagle with an irrepressible fondness for wine, women, and song, wiggles and wriggles himself into a seemingly impossible predicament, whereupon the prim and prudish super-duper snooper Hildegarde Withers extricates the perennially hungover John J.—with the extricating process always rife with risk and full o' fun. . . .

L'envoi   If only there were more mad capers from those two madcappers!

ELLERY QUEEN

11

Preface

How it started, nobody really knows. Craig always insisted it had been *my* idea; Our Favorite Editor, once said he thought the inspiration came from Craig; I myself am sure that it was OFE himself who suggested a teaming-up of the unlikely combination of John J. Malone and Miss Hildegarde Withers.

Craig and I had been friends since the time—over twenty years ago—when we were both assigned to the same script (I think it was one of the Falcon series) at R.K.O., where for three weeks we kept each other thoroughly amused, if not our producer. After that we corresponded spasmodically, mostly in the exchange of unprintable limericks or stories. Craig was absolutely unique as a storyteller, anywhere, any time. No matter what befell her in her dizzy life as newspaper sob sister, poetess, radio writer, author or whatnot, she could send her listeners into stitches with her account of the disaster. She was, when at her best, absolutely the funniest woman I have ever known.

The first story, "Loco Motive" (published as "Once Upon a Train") was supposed to be *it*, but the two characters seemed to complement each other and one thing led to another. Soon two of the stories were sold to M-G-M, resulting finally in "Mrs. O'Malley and Mr. Malone," a starring vehicle for James Whitmore, in which Miss Withers mysteriously changed into Ma Kettle. But Whitmore was a brilliant Malone, and I like to think that the role prepared him for his present stardom as a crusading attorney in the delightful television show "The Law and Mr. Jones."

The collaboration between Craig and me (almost entirely by letters since we were usually at opposite ends of the country) continued until her untimely death, and after. It was certainly the happiest and least controversial of collaborations in all literary history. We never once had an argument, though she did once remark, when I had a line in a story about Malone talking of his "sainted mother" (actually he was left on the steps of a foundling home at an early age), something to the effect that: "Well, Malone *did* have a mother and a normal childhood, I think—in some of the early books. But let it *stet;* on thinking it over it's somehow more *right* this way."

She always allowed me complete leeway with her beloved Malone, perhaps because of a feeling she expressed in a letter I still have: "You know, Stu, if you weren't so tall and if you had a law degree, you'd *be* Malone. You wear expensive suits and dribble cigar ashes over the lapels, you follow the races and sit up all night playing poker, your secretaries all adore you, you have Malone's taste in women and usually his bad luck with them, and when you get high you always try to form a barbershop quartet!" Without admitting any of the fond impeachment, I might say that this was Craig's highest compliment, and I felt flattered.

Craig's real contribution to the stories, apart from the unique character of Malone (and the faithful Maggie), was in the gimmicks, the gadgets, the slant—a beginning or an ending or a line or two of dialogue. After her death I had enough notes left over, and bits and pieces from her letters, to concoct the last two stories in the series. Oddly enough, it is in the last one we did—"Withers & Malone—Crime-

14

Busters"—that Craig had most to say about it all. Months before her last illness she had written me: "Let's have one with Malone in a hospital with his leg in traction, no bottle, and the heavy after him. Miss Withers has to disguise herself as a head nurse to get in to see him, and she says, 'Lie still, Malone, and smell the pretty flowers,' which of course are poison ivy or henbane or something . . ."

I discovered some years ago that Craig Rice and Stuart Palmer appeared together in quite another volume than this present one—an anthology of regional verse entitled *Poetry Out of Wisconsin,* circa 1937. Craig's poem, "The Immeasurable," had these lines:

> *What do I want of you, what am I seeking?*
> *Nothing to keep.*

In a sense it was always true. Craig wanted to experience everything, and to keep nothing. She was, like Scaramouche, "born with the gift of laughter, and a sense that the world was mad." I am glad that I was privileged to be one of her several thousand most intimate friends.

STUART PALMER

*

Once Upon a Train

TTTTTTTTTTTTTTTTTTTTTTTTTTTTTTTTTTTTTTTTT

"It was nothing, really," said John J. Malone with weary modesty. "After all, I never lost a client yet."

The party in Chicago's famed Pump Room was being held to celebrate the miraculous acquittal of Stephen Larsen, a machine politician accused of dipping some thirty thousand dollars out of the municipal till. Malone had proved to the jury and to himself that his client was innocent—at least, innocent of that particular charge.

It was going to be a nice party, the little lawyer kept telling himself. By the way Larsen's so-called friends were bending their elbows, the tab would be colossal. Malone hoped fervently that his fee for services rendered would be taken care of today, before Larsen's guests bankrupted him. Because there was the matter of two months' back office rent. . . .

"Thank you, I will," Malone said, as the waiter picked up his empty glass. He wondered how he could meet the redhead at the next table, who looked sultry and bored in the midst of a dull family party. As soon as he got his money from Larsen he would start a rescue operation. The quickest way to make friends, he always said, was to break a hundred-dollar bill in a bar, and that applied even to curvaceous redheads in Fath models.

But where *was* Steve Larsen? Lolly was here, wearing her most angelic expression and a slinky gown which she overflowed considerably at the top. She was hinting that the party also celebrated a reconciliation between herself and Stevie; that the divorce was off. She had hocked her bracelet again, and Malone remembered hearing that her last show had closed after six performances. If she got her hand back into Steve's pocket, Malone reflected, goodbye to his fee of three grand.

He'd made elaborate plans for that money. They not only included the trip to Bermuda which he'd been promising himself for twenty years, but also the redhead he'd been promising himself for twenty minutes.

Others at the table were worrying too. "Steve is late, even for him!" spoke up Allen Roth suddenly.

Malone glanced at the porcine paving contractor who was rumored to be Larsen's secret partner, and murmured, "Maybe he got his dates mixed."

"He'd *better* show," Roth said, in a voice as cold as a grave-digger's shovel.

The little lawyer shivered, and realized that he wasn't the only guest who had come here to make a collection. But he simply had to have that money. $3,000—$30,000. He wondered, half musing, if he shouldn't have made his contingent fee, say, $2,995. This way it almost looked like . . .

"What did you say about ten per cent, counselor?" Bert Glick spoke up wisely.

Malone recovered himself. "You misunderstood me. I merely said, 'When on pleasure bent, never muzzle

18

the ox when he treadeth out the corn.' I mean rye." He turned to look for the waiter, not solely from thirst. The little lawyer would often have been very glad to buy back his introduction to Bert Glick.

True, the City Hall hanger-on had been helpful during the trial. In fact, it had been his testimony as a prosecution witness that had clinched the acquittal, for he had made a surprise switch on several moot points of the indictment. Glick was a private detective turned bail-bondsman, clever at tapping wires and dipping his spoon into any gravy that was being passed.

Glick slapped Malone on the back and said, "If you knew what I know, you wouldn't be looking at your watch all the time. Because this ain't a coming out party, it's a surprise party. And the surprise is that the host ain't gonna be here!"

Malone went cold—as cold as Allen Roth's gray eyes across the table. "Keep talking," he said, adding in a whisper a few facts which Glick might not care to have brought to the attention of the district attorney.

"You don't need to be so nasty," Glick said. He rose suddenly to his feet, lifting his glass. "A toast! A toast to good ol' Stevie, our pal, who's taking the Super-Century for New York tonight, next stop Paris or Rio. And with him, my fine feathered friends, he's taking the dough he owes most of us, and a lot more too. Bon voyage!" The man absorbed the contents of his glass and slowly collapsed in his chair.

There was a sudden hullabaloo around the table. Malone closed his eyes for just five seconds, resigning himself to the certainty that his worst suspicions were true. When he opened his eyes again, the redhead was gone. He looked at his watch. There was still a chance of catching that New York train, with a quick stop at

19

Joe the Angel's bar to borrow the price of a ticket. Malone rushed out of the place, wasting no time in farewells. Everybody else was leaving too, so that finally Glick was left alone with the waiter and with the check.

As Malone had expected, Joe the Angel took a very dim view of the project, pointing out that it was probably only throwing good money after bad. But he handed over enough for a round trip, plus Pullman. By the time his cab had dumped him at the I.C. station, Malone had decided to settle for one way. He needed spending money for the trip. There were poker games on trains.

Suddenly he saw the redhead! She was jammed in a crowd at the gate, crushed between old ladies, noisy sailors, and a bearded patriarch in the robes of the Greek Orthodox Church. She struggled with a mink coat, a yowling cat in a traveling case, and a caged parrot.

Malone leaped gallantly to her rescue, and for a brief moment was allowed to hold the menagerie, before a Redcap took over. The moment was just long enough for the lawyer to have his hand clawed by the irate cat, and for him and the parrot to develop a lifelong dislike. But he did hear the girl say, "Compartment B in Car 10, please." And her warm grateful smile sent him racing off in search of the Pullman conductor.

Considerable eloquence, some trifling liberties with the truth, and a ten-dollar bill got him possession of the drawing room next to a certain compartment. That settled, he paused to make a quick deal with a roving Western Union boy, and more money changed hands. When he finally swung aboard the already moving train, he felt fairly confident that the trip would be pleasant and eventful. And lucrative, of course. The minute he got his hands on Steve Larsen . . .

Once established in the drawing room, Malone studied himself in the mirror, whistling a few bars of "The Wabash Cannonball." For the moment the primary target could wait. He was glad he was wearing his favorite Finchley suit, and his new green-and-lavender Sulka tie.

"A man of distinction," he thought. True, his hair was slightly mussed, a few cigar ashes peppered his vest, and the Sulka tie was beginning to creep toward one ear, but the total effect was good. Inspired, he sat down to compose a note to Operation Redhead, in the next compartment. He knew it was the right compartment, for the parrot was already giving out with imitations of a boiler factory, assisted by the cat.

He wrote:

Lovely lady,
Let's not fight Fate. We were destined to have dinner together. I am holding my breath for your yes.
Your unknown admirer,

J.J.M.

He poked the note under the connecting door, rapped lightly, and waited.

After a long moment the note came back, with an addition in a surprisingly precise hand.

Sir, You have picked the wrong girl. Besides, I had dinner in the Pump Room over an hour ago, and so, I believe, did you.

Undaunted, Malone whistled another bar of the song. Just getting any answer at all was half the battle. So she'd noticed him in the Pump Room! He sat down and wrote swiftly:

Please, an after-dinner liqueur with me, then?

This time the answer was:

My dear sir: MY DEAR SIR!

But the little lawyer thought he heard sounds of feminine laughter, though of course it might have been the parrot. He sat back, lighted a fresh cigar, and waited. They were almost to Gary now, and if the telegram had got through . . .

It had, and a messenger finally came aboard with an armful of luscious *Gruss von Teplitz* roses. Malone intercepted him long enough to add a note which really should be the clincher.

To the Rose of Tralee, who makes all other women look like withered dandelions. I'll be waiting in the club car. Faithfully, John J. Malone.

That was the way, he told himself happily. Don't give her a chance to say *No* again.

After a long and somewhat bruising trip through lurching Pullman cars, made longer still because he first headed fore instead of aft, Malone finally sank into a chair in the club-car lounge, facing the door. Of course, she would take time to arrange the roses, make a corsage out of a couple of buds, and probably shift into an even more startling gown. It might be quite a wait. He waved at the bar steward and said, "Rye, please, with a rye chaser."

"You mean rye with a beer chaser, Mr. Malone?"

"If you know my name, you know enough not to confuse me. I mean beer with a rye chaser!" When the drink arrived Malone put it where it would do the most good, and then for lack of anything better to do fell to staring in awed fascination at the lady who had just settled down across the aisle.

She was a tall, angular person who somehow suggested a fairly well-dressed scarecrow. Her face seemed faintly familiar, and Malone wondered if they'd met before. Then he decided that she reminded him of a three-year-old who had winked at him in the paddock at Washington Park one Saturday and then run out of the money.

Topping the face—as if anything could—was an incredible headpiece consisting of a grass-green crown surrounded by a brim of nodding flowers, wreaths and ivy. All it seemed to need was a nice marble tombstone.

She looked up suddenly from her magazine. "Pardon me, but did you say something about a well-kept grave?" Her voice reminded Malone of a certain Miss Hackett who had talked him out of quitting second-year high school. Somehow he found himself strangely unable to lie to her.

"Madam, do you read minds?"

"Not minds, Mr. Malone. *Lips,* sometimes." She smiled. "Are you really *the* John J. Malone?"

He blinked. "How in the—oh, of course! The *magazine!* Those fact-detective stories *will* keep writing up my old cases. Are you a crime-story fan, Mrs.—?"

"Miss. Hildegarde Withers, schoolteacher by profession and meddlesome old snoop by avocation, at least according to the police. Yes, I've read about you. You solve crimes and right wrongs, but usually by pure ac-

23

cident while chasing through saloons after some young woman who is no better than she should be. Are you on a case now?"

"Working my way through the second bottle," he muttered, suddenly desperate. It would never do for the redhead to come in and find him tied up with this character.

"I didn't mean that kind of a case," Miss Withers explained. "I gather that even though you've never lost a client, you have mislaid one at the moment?"

Malone shivered. The woman had second sight, at least. He decided that it would be better if he went back through the train and met the Rose of Tralee, who must certainly be on her way here by this time. He could also keep an eye open for Steve Larsen. With a hasty apology he got out of the club car, pausing only to purchase a handy pint of rye from the bar steward, and started on a long slow prowl of mile after mile of wobbling, jerking cars. The rye, blending not unpleasantly with the champagne he had taken on earlier, made everything a little hazy and unreal. He kept getting turned around and blundering into the long-deserted diner. Two or three times he bumped into the Greek Orthodox priest with the whiskers, and similarly kept interrupting four sailors shooting craps in a men's lounge.

But—no redhead. And no Larsen. Finally the train stopped—could it be Toledo already? Malone dashed to the vestibule and hung over the step, to make sure that Steve didn't disembark. When they were moving again he resumed his pilgrimage, though by this time he had resigned himself to the fact that he was being stood up by the Rose of Tralee. At last, he turned mournfully back toward where his own lonesome cubicle ought to be—and then suddenly found himself back in the club car!

No redheaded Rose. Even The Hat had departed, taking her copy of *Official Fact Detective Stories* with her. The car was deserted except for a bridge game going on in one corner and a sailor—obviously half-seas over—who was drowsing in a big chair with a newspaper over his face.

The pint was empty. Malone told the steward to have it buried with full military honors, and to fetch him a cheese on rye. "On second thought, skip the cheese and make it just straight rye, please."

The drink arrived, and with it a whispered message. There was a lady waiting down the corridor.

Malone emptied his glass and followed the steward, trying to slip him five dollars. It slipped right back. "Thanks, Mr. Malone, but I can't take money from an old classmate. Remember, we went through the last two years of Kent College of Law together?"

Malone gasped. "Class of '45. And you're Homer—no, *Horace* Lee Randolph. But—"

"What am I doing here? The old story. Didn't know my place, and got into Chicago Southside politics. Bumped up against the machine, and got disbarred on a phony charge of subornation of perjury. It could have been squared by handing a grand to a certain sharper at City Hall, but I didn't have the money." Horace shrugged. "This pays better than law, anyway. For instance, that lady handed me five dollars just to unlock the private lounge and tell you she's waiting to see you there."

The little lawyer winced. "She—was she a queer old maid in a hat that looked like she'd made it herself?"

25

"Oh, no. No hat."

Malone breathed easier. "Was she young and lovely?"

"My weakness is the numbers game, but I should say the description is accurate."

Humming "But 'twas not her beauty alone that won me; oh, no, 'twas the truth . . ." Malone straightened his tie and opened the door.

Lolly Larsen exploded in his face with all the power of a firecracker under a tin can. She grabbed his lapels and yelped: "Well, where is the dirty ———?"

"Be more specific. Which dirty ———?" Malone said, pulling himself loose.

"*Steve,* of course!"

"I don't know, but I still hope he's somewhere on this train. You joining me in the search? Nice to have your pretty face among us."

Lolly had the face of a homesick angel. Her hair was exactly the color of a twist of lemon peel in a glass of champagne brut, her mouth was an overripe strawberry, and her figure might have inspired the French bathing suit, but her eyes were cold and strange as a mermaid's. "Are you in this with Steve?" she demanded.

Malone said, "In simple, one-syllable words that even you can understand—No!"

Lolly suddenly relaxed, swaying against him so that he got a good whiff of brandy, nail polish and Chanel Number 5. "I'm sorry. I guess I'm just upset. I feel so terribly helpless—"

For Malone's money, she was as helpless as an eight-button rattlesnake. "You see," Lolly murmured, "I'm partly to blame for Steve's running away. I should have stood by him at the trial, but I hadn't the courage. Even afterward—I didn't actually promise to come back to him, I just said I'd come to his party. I meant to tell him

26

—in the Pump Room. So, please, please help me find him—so I can make him see how much we really *need* each other!"

Malone said, "Try it again, and flick the eyelashes a little bit more when you come to 'need each other.'"

Lolly jerked away and called him a number of things, of which "dirty little shyster" was the most complimentary. "All right," she finally said in a matter-of-fact tone. "Steve's carrying a hundred grand, and you can guess how he got it. I happen to know—Glick isn't the *only* one who's been spying on him since he got out of jail yesterday. I don't want Steve back, but I do want a fat slice for keeping my mouth shut. One word from me to the D.A. or the papers, and not even you can get him off."

"Go on," Malone said wearily. "But you interest me in less ways than one."

"Find Steve!" she told him. "Make a deal and I'll give you ten per cent of the take. But work fast, because we're not the only ones looking for him. Steve double-crossed everybody who was at that party this afternoon. He's somewhere on this train, but he's probably shaved off his mustache, or put on a fright-wig, or—"

Malone yawned and said, "Where can I get in touch with you?"

"I couldn't get a reservation of any kind." Her strange eyes warmed hopefully. "But I hear you have a drawing room?"

"Don't look at me in that tone of voice," Malone said hastily. "Besides, I snore. Maybe there'll be something available for you at the next stop."

He was out of there and back in the club car before Lolly could turn on any more of the charm. He decided to have one for the road—the New York Central

Road, and one for the Pennsy too. The sensible thing was to find Steve Larsen, collect his own hard-earned fee, and leave Lolly alone. Her offer of ten per cent of the blackmail take touched on a sore spot.

Malone began to work his way through the train again, this time desperately questioning porters. The worst of it was, there was nothing remarkable about Larsen's appearance except curly hair, which he'd probably had straightened and dyed, a mustache that could have been shaved off, and a briefcase full of money, which he'd probably hidden. In fact, the man was undoubtedly laughing at everybody from behind a false set of whiskers.

Such were Malone's thoughts as he suddenly came face to face again with the Greek Orthodox priest, who stared past him through thick, tinted spectacles. The little lawyer hesitated and was lost. Throwing caution to the winds, he yanked vigorously at the beard. But it was an orthodox beard, attached in the orthodox manner. Its owner let loose a blast which just possibly might have been an orthodox Greek blessing. Malone didn't wait to find out.

His ears were still burning when he stepped into a vestibule and ran head on into Miss Hildegarde Withers. He nodded coldly and started past her.

"Ah, go soak your fat head!"

Malone gasped.

"It's the parrot," Miss Withers explained, holding up the caged monstrosity. "It's been making such a racket that I'm taking it to the baggage car for the night."

"Where—where did you get that—bird?" Malone asked weakly.

"Why, Sinbad is a legacy from the aunt whose funeral I just went back to attend. I'm taking him back to New York with me."

"New York!" Malone moaned. "We'll be there before I find that—"

"You mean that Mr. Larsen?" As he stood speechless, she went briskly on. "You see, I happened to be at a family farewell party at the table next to yours in the Pump Room, and my hearing is very acute. So, for that matter, is my eyesight. Has it occurred to you that Larsen may be wearing a disguise of some sort?"

"That it has," admitted Malone sadly, thinking of the Greek priest.

The schoolteacher lowered her voice. "You remember that when we had our little chat in the club car some time ago, there was an obviously inebriated sailor dozing behind a newspaper?"

"There's one on every train," Malone said. "One or more."

"Exactly. Like Chesterton's postman, you never notice them. But somehow that particular sailor managed to stay intoxicated without ordering a single drink or nipping at a private bottle. More than that, when you suddenly left he poked his head out from behind the paper and stared after you with a very odd expression, rather as if he suspected you had leprosy. I couldn't help noticing—"

"Madam, I love you," the lawyer said fervently. "I love you because you remind me of Miss Hackett back in Dorchester High, and because of your hat, and because you are sharper than a tack."

Miss Withers sniffed, but it was a mollified sniff. "Sorry to interrupt, but that same sailor entered our car just as I left it with the parrot. I just happened to look back, and I rather think he was trying the door of your drawing room."

Malone clasped her hand fondly. Unfortunately it was the hand that held the cage, and the parrot took advantage of the long-awaited opportunity to nip viciously at his thumb. "Thank you so very much—some day I'll wring your silly neck" was Malone's sincere but somewhat garbled exit line.

"Go boil your head in lard!" the bird screamed after him.

The maiden schoolteacher sighed. "Come on, Sinbad, you're going into durance vile. And I'm going to retire to my lonely couch, drat it all." She looked wistfully over her shoulder. "Some people have all the fun!"

But twelve cars, ten minutes, and four drinks later, Malone was lost again. A worried porter was saying, "If you could only remember your car number, sah?" A much harassed Pullman conductor added, "If you'd just show us your ticket stub, we'd locate you."

"You don't need to locate *me,*" Malone insisted. "I'm right here."

"Maybe you haven't got a stub."

"I have so a stub. It's in my hatband." Crafty as an Indian guide, Malone backtracked them unerringly to his drawing room. "Here's the stub—now where am I?"

The porter looked out the window and said, "Just coming into Altoona, sah."

"They lay in the wreck when they found them, They had died when the engine had fell . . ." sang Malone happily. But the conductor winced and said they'd be going.

"You might as well," Malone told him. "If neither one of you can sing baritone."

The door closed behind them, and a moment later a soft voice called, "Mr. Malone?"

He stared at the connecting door. *The Rose of Tralee*, Malone told himself happily. He adjusted his tie, and tried the door. Miraculously, it opened. Then he saw that it was Miss Hildegarde Withers, looking very worried, who stared back at him.

Malone said, "What have you done with my redhead?"

"If you refer to my niece Joannie," the schoolteacher said sharply, "she only helped me get my stuff aboard and rode as far as Englewood. But never mind that now. I'm in trouble."

"I knew there couldn't be two parrots like that on one train," Malone groaned. "Or even in one world."

"There's worse than parrots on this train," snapped Miss Withers. "This man Larsen for whom you were looking so anxiously—"

The little lawyer's eyes narrowed. "Just what is your interest in Larsen?"

"None whatever, except that he's here in my compartment. It's very embarrassing, because he's not only dead, he's *undressed!*"

"Holy St. Vitus!" gulped Malone. "Quiet! Keep *calm*. Lock your door and *don't* talk!"

"My door is locked, and who's talking?" The schoolteacher stepped aside and Malone peered gingerly past her. The speed with which he was sobering up probably established a new record. It was Larsen, all right. He was face down on the floor, dressed only in black shoes, blue socks, and a suit of long underwear. There was also a moderate amount of blood.

At last Malone said hoarsely, "I suspect foul play!"

"Knife job," said Miss Withers with professional coolness. "From the back, through the *latissimus dorsi*. Within the last twenty minutes, I'd say. If I hadn't had some difficulty in convincing the baggage men that Sinbad should be theirs for the night, I might have walked in on the murderer at work." She gave Malone a searching glance. "It wasn't *you*, by any chance?"

"Do you think I'd murder a man who owed me three thousand dollars?" Malone demanded indignantly. He scowled. "But a lot of people are going to jump to that conclusion. Nice of you not to raise an alarm."

She sniffed. "You didn't think I'd care to have a man —even a dead man—found in my room in this state of undress? Obviously, he hasn't your money on his person. So—what is to be done about it?"

"I'll defend you for nothing," John J. Malone promised. "Justifiable homicide. Besides, you were framed. He burst in upon you and you stabbed him in defense of your honor . . ."

"*Just* a minute! The corpse was *your* client. You've been publicly asking for him all through the train. I'm only an innocent bystander." She paused. "In my opinion, Larsen was lured to your room purposely by someone who had penetrated his disguise. He was stabbed, and dumped here. Very clever, because if the body had been left in your room, you could have got rid of it or claimed that you were framed. But this way, to the police mind at least, it would be obvious that you did the job and then tried to palm it off on the nearest neighbor."

Malone sagged weakly against the berth. His hand brushed against the leather case, and something slashed viciously at his fingers. "But I thought you got rid of that parrot!" he cried.

"I did," Miss Withers assured him. "That's Precious

32

in his case. A twenty-pound Siamese, also part of my recent legacy. Don't get too close, the creature dislikes train travel and is in a foul temper."

Malone stared through the wire window and said, "Its father must have been either a bobcat or a buzz saw."

"My aunt left me her mink coat, on condition that I take both her pets," Miss Withers explained wearily. "But I'm beginning to think it would be better to shiver through these cold winters. And speaking of cold— I'm a patient woman, but not very. You have one minute, Mr. Malone, to get your dead friend out of here!"

"He's no friend of mine, dead or alive," Malone began. "And I suggest—"

There was a heavy knocking on the corridor door "Open up in there!"

"Say something!" whispered Malone. "Say you're undressed!"

"You're undressed—I mean, I'm undressed," she cried obediently.

"Sorry, ma'am," a masculine voice said on the other side of the door. "But we're searching this train for a fugitive from justice. Hurry, please."

"Just a minute," sang out the schoolteacher, making frantic gestures at Malone.

The little lawyer shuddered, then grabbed the late Steve Larsen and tugged him through the connecting door into his drawing room. Meanwhile, Miss Withers cast aside maidenly modesty and tore pins from her hair, the dress from her shoulders. Clutching a robe around her, she opened the door a crack and announced, "This is an *outrage!*"

The train conductor, a Pullman conductor, and two Altoona police detectives crowded in, ignoring her protest. They pawed through the wardrobe, peered into every nook and cranny.

Miss Withers stood rooted to the spot, in more ways than one. There was a damp brownish-red spot on the carpet, and she had one foot firmly holding it down. At last the delegation backed out, with apologies. Then she heard a feeble, imploring tapping on the connecting door, and John J. Malone's voice whispering "Help!"

The maiden schoolteacher stuck her head out into the corridor again, where the search party was already waiting for Malone to open up. "Oh, officer!" she cried tremulously. "Is there any danger?"

"No, ma'am."

"Was the man you're looking for a burly, dark-complexioned cutthroat with dark glasses and a pronounced limp in the left leg?"

"No, lady. Get lost, please, lady."

"Because on my way back from the diner I saw a man like that. He leered, and then followed me through three cars."

"The man we're looking for is an embezzler, not a mental case." They hammered on Malone's door again. "Open up in there!"

Over her shoulder Miss Withers could see the pale, perspiring face of John J. Malone as he dragged Steve Larsen back into her compartment again.

"But, officer," she improvised desperately, "I'm sure that the awful dark man who followed me was a distinct criminal type—" There was a reassuring whisper of "Okay" from behind her, and the sound of a softly closing door. Miss Withers backed into her compartment, closed and locked the connecting door, and then sank down on the edge of her berth, trying to avoid the blankly staring eyes of the dead man.

Next door there was a rumble of voices, and then suddenly Malone's high tenor doing rough justice to "Did Your Mother Come from Ireland?" The schoolteacher heard no more than the first line of the chorus before the Jello in her knees melted completely. When she opened her eyes again, she saw Malone holding a dagger before her, and she very nearly fainted again.

"You were so right," the little lawyer told her admiringly. "It was a frame-up all right—but meant for me. *This* was tucked into the upholstery of my room. I sat on it while they were searching, and had to burst into song to cover my howl of anguish."

"Oh, dear!" said Miss Withers.

He sat down beside her, patted her comfortingly on the shoulder, and said, "Maybe I can shove the body out the window!"

"We're still in the station," she reminded him crisply. "And from what experience I've had with train windows, it would be easier to solve the murder than open one. Why don't we start searching for clues?"

Malone stood up so quickly that he rapped his head on the bottom of the upper berth. "Never mind *clues*. Let's just find the murderer!"

"Just as easy as that?"

"Look," he said. "This train was searched at the request of the Chicago police because somebody—probably Bert Glick—tipped them off that Larsen and a lot of stolen money were on board. The word has got around. Obviously, somebody else knew—somebody who caught the train and did the dirty work. It's reasonable to assume that whoever has the money is the killer."

There was a new glint in Miss Withers' blue-gray eyes. "Go on."

"Also, Larsen's ex-wife—or do I mean ex-widow?—is aboard. I saw her. She is a lovely girl whose many friends agree that she would eat her young or sell her old mother down the river into slavery for a fast buck." He took out a cigar. "I'll go next door and have a smoke while you change, and then we'll go look for Lolly Larsen."

"I'm practically ready now," the schoolteacher agreed. "But take *that* with you!"

Malone hesitated, and then with a deep sigh reached down and took a firm grasp of all that was mortal of his late client. "Here we go again!"

A few minutes later Miss Hildegarde Withers was following Malone through the now-darkened train. The fact that this was somebody else's problem never occurred to her. Murder, according to her tenets, was everybody's business.

Malone touched her arm as they came at last to the door of the club car. "Here is where I saw Lolly last," he whispered. "She only got aboard at the last minute, and didn't have a reservation." He pointed down the corridor. "See that door, just this side of the pantry? It's a private lounge, used only for railroad officials or bigshots like governors or senators. Lolly bribed the steward to let her use it when she wanted to have a private talk with me. It just occurred to me that she might have talked him into letting her have it for the rest of the night. If she's still there—"

"Say no more," Miss Withers cut in. "I am a fellow passenger, also without a berth, seeking only a place to rest my weary head. After all, I have as much right in there as she has. But you will be within call, won't you?"

"If you need help, just holler," he promised. Malone watched as the schoolteacher marched down the corridor, tried the lounge door gently, and then knocked. The door opened and she vanished inside.

The little lawyer had an argument with his conscience. It wasn't just that she reminded him of Miss Hackett, it was that she had become a sort of partner. Besides, he was getting almost fond of that equine face.

Oh, well, he'd be within earshot. And if there was anything in the inspiration which had just come to him, she wasn't in any real danger anyway. He went on into the bar. It was half-dark and empty now, except for a little group of men in Navy uniforms at the far end, who were sleeping sprawled and entangled like a litter of puppies.

"Sorry, Mr. Malone, but the bar is closed," a voice spoke up behind him. It was Horace Lee Randolph, looking drawn and exhausted. He caught Malone's glance toward the sleeping sailors and added, "Against the rules, but the conductor said don't bother 'em."

Malone nodded, and then said, "Horace, we're old friends and classmates. You know me of old, and you know you can trust me. *Where did you hide it?*"

"Where did I hide what?"

"You know what!" Malone fixed the man with the cold and baleful eye he used on prosecution witnesses. "Let me have it before it's too late, and I'll do my best for you."

The eyes rolled. "Oh, Lawdy! I knew I shouldn't a done it, Mista Malone! I'll show you!" Horace hurried on down through the car and unlocked a small closet filled with mops and brooms. From a box labeled *Soap Flakes* he came up with a paper sack. It was a very small sack to hold a hundred thousand dollars, Malone thought, even if the money was in big bills. Horace fumbled inside the sack.

"What's *that?*" Malone demanded.

37

"What would it be but the bottle of gin I sneaked from the bar? Join me?"

The breath went out of John J. Malone like air out of a busted balloon. He caught the doorknob for support, swaying like an aspen in the wind. It was just at that moment that they both heard the screams.

The rush of self-confidence with which Miss Hildegarde Withers had pushed her way into the lounge ebbed somewhat as she came face to face with Lolly Larsen. Appeals to sympathy, as from one supposedly stranded fellow passenger to another, failed utterly. It was not until the schoolteacher played her last card, reminding Lolly sharply that if there was any commotion the Pullman conductor would undoubtedly have them both evicted, that she succeeded in getting a toehold.

"Oh, *all right!*" snarled Lolly ungraciously. "Only shut up and go to sleep.'

During the few minutes before the room went dark again, Miss Withers made a mental snapshot of everything in it. No toilet, no wardrobe, no closet. A small suitcase, a coat and a handbag were on the only chair. The money must be somewhere in this room, the schoolteacher thought. There was a way to find out.

As the train flashed through the moonlit night, Miss Withers busily wriggled out of her petticoat and ripped it into shreds. Using a bit of paper from her handbag for tinder—and inwardly praying it wasn't a ten-dollar bill—she did what had to be done. A few minutes later she burst out into the corridor, holding her handkerchief to her mouth.

She almost bumped into one of the sailors who came lurching toward her along the narrow passage, and gasped, "What do you want?"

He stared at her with heavy eyes. "If it's any of your business, I'm looking for the latrine," he said dryly.

When he was out of sight, Miss Withers turned and peeked back into the lounge. A burst of acrid smoke struck her in the face. Now was the time. *"Fire!"* she shrieked.

Thick billows of greasy smoke flooded out through the half-open door. Inside, little tongues of red flame ran greedily along the edge of the seat where Miss Withers had tucked the burning rags and paper.

Down the corridor came Malone and Horace Lee Randolph, and a couple of startled bluejackets appeared from the other direction. Somebody tore an extinguisher from the wall.

Miss Withers grabbed Malone's arm. "Watch her! She'll go for the money—"

The fire extinguisher sent a stream of foaming chemicals into the doorway just as Lolly Larsen burst out. Her mascara streaked down her face, already blackened by smoke, and her yellow hair was plastered unflatteringly to her skull. But she clutched a small leather case.

Somehow she tripped over Miss Withers' outstretched foot. The leather case flew across the corridor to smash against the wall, where it flew open, disclosing a multitude of creams, oils, and tiny bottles—a portable beauty parlor.

"She must have gone to sleep smoking a cigarette!" put in Miss Withers in loud clear tones. "A lucky thing I was there to smell the smoke and give the alarm—"

But John J. Malone seized her firmly by the arm and propelled her back through the train. "It was a good try, but you can stop acting now. She doesn't have the money." Back in her own compartment he confessed about Horace. "I had a wonderful idea, but it didn't pay off. The poor guy's career as a lawyer was busted by a City Hall chiseler. If Larsen was the one, Horace might have spotted him on the train and decided to get even."

"You were holding out on me," said Miss Withers, slightly miffed.

Malone unwrapped a cigar and said, "If anybody finds that money, I want it to be me. Because I've got to get my fee out of it or I can't even get back to Chicago."

"Perhaps you'll learn to like Manhattan," she told him brightly.

Malone said grimly, "If something isn't done soon, I'm going to see New York through those cold iron bars."

"We're in the same boat. Except," she added honestly, "that I don't think the Inspector would go so far as to lock me up. But he does take a dim view of anybody who finds a body and doesn't report it." She sighed. "Do you think we *could* get one of these windows open?"

Malone smothered a yawn and said, "Not in my present condition of exhaustion."

"Let's begin at the beginning," the schoolteacher said. "Larsen invited a number of people to a party he didn't plan to attend. He sneaked on this train, presumably disguised in a Navy enlisted man's uniform. How he got hold of it—"

"He was in the service for a while," said the little lawyer.

"The murderer made a date to meet his victim in your drawing room, hoping to set *you* up as the goat. He stuck a knife in him and then stripped him, looking for a money-belt or something."

"You don't have to undress a man to find a money-belt," Malone murmured.

"Really? I wouldn't know." Miss Withers sniffed. "The knife was then hidden in your room, but the body was moved in here. The money—" She paused and studied him searchingly. "Mr. Malone, are you sure you didn't—?"

"We plead not guilty and not guilty by reason of insanity," Malone muttered. He closed his eyes for just five seconds' much-needed rest, and when he opened them a dirty-looking dawn was glaring in at him through the window.

"Good morning," Miss Withers greeted him, entirely too cheerfully. "Did you get any ideas while you were in dreamland?" She put away her toothbrush and added, "You know, I've sometimes found that if a problem seems insoluble, you can sleep on it and sometimes your subconscious comes up with the answer. Sometimes it's even happened to me in a dream."

"It does? It *has?*" Malone sat up suddenly. "Okay. Burglars can't be choosers. Sleep and the world sleeps —I mean, I'll just stand watch for a while and you try taking a nap. Maybe you can dream up an answer out of your subconscious. But dream fast, lady, because we get in about two hours from now."

But when Miss Withers had finally been comfortably settled against the pillows, she found that her eyelids stubbornly refused to stay shut.

"Try once more," John J. Malone said soothingly. She closed her eyes obediently, and his high, whispering tenor filled the little compartment, singing a fine old song. It was probably the first time in history, Miss Withers thought, that anyone had tried to use "Throw Him Down, McCluskey" as a lullaby, but she found herself drifting off. . . .

Malone passed the time by trying to imagine what he

would do with a hundred grand if he were the murderer. There must have been a desperate need for haste—at any moment, someone might come back to the murder room. The money would have to be put somewhere handy—some obvious place where nobody would ever think of looking, and where it could be quickly and easily retrieved when all was clear.

There was an angry growl from Precious in his cage. "If you could only say something besides 'Meeerow' and 'Fssst'!" Malone murmured wistfully. "Because you're the only witness. Now if it had been the parrot . . ."

At last he touched Miss Withers apologetically on the shoulder. "Wake up, ma'am, we're coming into New York. Quick, what did you dream?"

She blinked, sniffed, and came wide awake. "My dream? Why—I was buying a hat, a darling little sailor hat, only it had to be exchanged because the ribbon was yellow. But first I wore it out to dinner with Inspector Piper, who took me to a Greek restaurant, and the proprietor was so glad to see us that he said dinner was on the house. But naturally we didn't eat anything because you have to beware of the Greeks when they come bearing gifts. His name was Mr. Roberts. That's all I remember."

"Oh, *brother!*" said John J. Malone.

"And there wasn't anyone named Roberts mixed up in this case, or anyone of Greek extraction, was there?" She sighed. "Pure nonsense. I guess a watched subconscious never boils."

The train was crawling laboriously up an elevated platform. "A drowning man will grasp at a strawberry," Malone said suddenly. "I've got a sort of an idea. Greeks bearing gifts—that means look out for somebody who

42

wants to give you something for nothing. And that something could include gratuitous information."

She nodded. "Perhaps someone planned to murder Larsen aboard this train and wanted you aboard to be the obvious suspect."

The train shuddered to a stop. Malone leaped up, startled, but the schoolteacher told him it was only 125th Street. "Perhaps we should check and see who gets off." She glanced out the window and said, "On second thought, let's not. The platform is swarming with police."

They were interrupted by the porter, who brushed off Miss Withers, accepted a dollar from the gallant Malone, and then lugged her suitcases and the pet container down to the vestibule. "He'll be in your room next," she whispered to Malone. "What do we do now?"

"We think fast," Malone said. "The rest of your dream! The sailor hat with the wrong ribbon! And Mr. Roberts—"

The door burst open and suddenly they were surrounded by detectives, led by a grizzled sergeant in plain clothes. Lolly Larsen was with them. She had removed most of the traces of the holocaust, her face was lovely and her hair was gleaming, but her mood was that of a dyspeptic cobra. She breathlessly accused Miss Withers of assaulting her and trying to burn her alive, and Malone of engineering Steve Larsen's successful disappearance.

"So," said Malone. "You wired ahead from Albany, crying copper?"

"Maybe she did," said the sergeant. "But we'd already been contacted by the Chicago police. Somebody out there swore out a warrant for Steve Larsen's arrest . . ."

"Glick, maybe?"

"A Mr. Allen Roth, according to the teletype. Now, folks—"

But Malone was trying to pretend that Lolly, the sergeant, and the whole police department didn't exist. He faced Miss Withers and said, "About that dream! It must mean a sailor under false colors. We already know that Larsen was disguised in Navy uniform . . ."

"Shaddap!" said the sergeant. "Maybe you don't know, mister, that helping an embezzler to escape makes you an assessory after the fact."

"*Acc*essory," corrected Miss Withers firmly.

"If you want Larsen," Malone said easily, "he's next door in my drawing room, wrapped up in the blankets."

"Sure, sure," said the sergeant, mopping his face. "Wise guy, eh?"

"Somebody helped Larsen escape—escape out of this world, with a shiv through the—through the—?" Malone looked hopefully at Miss Withers.

"The *latissimus dorsi*," she prompted.

The sergeant barked, "Never mind the double-talk. Where is this Larsen?"

Then Lolly, who had pushed open the connecting door, let out a thin scream like tearing silk. "It *is* Steve!" she cried. "It's Steve, and he's dead!"

Momentarily the attention of the law was drawn elsewhere. "Now or never," said Miss Withers coolly. "About the Mr. Roberts thing—I just remembered that there was a play by that name a while back. All about sailors in the last war. I saw it, and was somewhat shocked at certain scenes. Their language—but anyway, I ran into a sailor just after I started that fire, and he said he was looking for the *latrine*. Sailors don't use Army talk—in *Mister Roberts* they called it the *head!*"

Suddenly the law was back, very direct and grim about everything. Miss Withers gasped with indignation as she found herself suddenly handcuffed to John J. Malone. But stone walls do not a prison make, as she pointed out to her companion-in-crime. "And don't you see? It means—"

"Madam, I am ahead of you. There was a *wrong* sailor aboard this train even after Larsen got his. The murderer must have taken a plane from Chicago and caught this train at Toledo. I was watching to see who got off, not who got on. The man penetrated Larsen's disguise—"

"In more ways than one," the schoolteacher put in grimly.

"And then after he'd murdered his victim, he took Larsen's sailor suit and got rid of his own clothes, realizing that nobody notices a sailor on a train! Madam, I salute your subconscious!" Malone waved his hand, magnificent even in chains. "The defense rests! Officer, call a cop!"

The train was crawling into one of the tunnels beneath Grand Central Station, and the harried sergeant was beside himself. "You listen to Mr. Malone," Miss Withers told their captor firmly, "or I'll hint to my old friend Inspector Oscar Piper that you would look well on a bicycle beat way out in Brooklyn!"

"Oh, no!" the unhappy officer moaned. "Not *that* Miss Withers!"

"That Miss Withers," she snapped. "My good man, all we ask is that you find the real murderer, who must still be on this train. He's wearing a Navy uniform . . ."

"Lady," the sergeant said sincerely, "you ask the impossible. The train is full of sailors. Grand Central is full of sailors."

"But this particular sailor," Malone put in, "is wear ing the uniform of the man he killed. *There will be a slit in the back of the jumper*—just under the shoulder blade!"

"Where the knife went in," Miss Withers added. "Hurry, man! The train is stopping."

It might still have been a lost cause had not Lolly put in her five cents. "Don't listen to that old witch!" she cried. "Officer, you do your duty!"

The sergeant disliked being yelled at, even by blondes. "Hold all of 'em—her too," he ordered, and leaped out on the platform. He seized upon a railroad dick, who listened and then grabbed a telephone attached to a nearby pillar. Somewhere far off an alarm began to ring, and an emotionless voice spoke over the public address system. . . .

In less than two minutes the vast labyrinth of Grand Central was alerted, and men in Navy uniforms were suddenly intercepted by polite but firm railroad detectives who sprang up out of nowhere. Only one of the sailors, a somewhat older man who was lugging a pet container that wasn't his, had any real difficulty. He alone had a narrow slit in the back of his jumper.

Bert Glick flung the leather case down the track and tried vainly to run, but there was no place to go. The container flew open, and Precious scooted. Only a dumb Siamese cat, as Malone commented later, would have abandoned a lair that had a hundred grand tucked under its carpet of old newspapers.

"And to think that I spent the night within reach of that dough, and didn't grab my fee!" said Malone.

But it developed that there was a comfortable reward for the apprehension of Steve Larsen, alive or dead. Before John J. Malone took off for Chicago, he accepted an invitation for dinner at Miss Withers' modest little apartment on West 74th Street, arriving with four dozen roses. It was a good dinner, and Malone cheerfully put up with the screamed insults of Sinbad and the well-meant attentions of Talley, the apricot poodle. "Just as long as the cat stays lost!" he said.

"Yes, isn't it odd that nobody has seen hide nor hair of Precious! It's my idea that he's waxing fat in the caverns beneath Grand Central, preying on the rats who are rumored to flourish there. Would you care for another piece of pie, Mr. Malone?"

"All I really want," said the little lawyer hopefully, is an introduction to your redheaded niece."

"Oh, yes, Joannie. Her husband played guard for Southern California, and he even made All-American," Miss Withers tactfully explained.

"On second thought, I'll settle for coffee," said John J. Malone.

Miss Withers sniffed, not unsympathetically.

*

Cherchez la Frame

TTTTTTTTTTTTTTTTTTTTTTTTTTTTTTTTTTTTTTT

"Don't look at me in that tone of voice!" said John J. Malone firmly, as he emerged from the bedroom of his bungalow set among the palm gardens of the Beverly-wood. His suit was by Finchley, shirt by Brooks Brothers, but his tie was out of this or any world.

Maggie hit a typewriter key savagely. "One week in California and you go Hollywood! Is she blonde, brunette or redhead?"

"Name some other flavors. On second thought, don't bother. If you're talking about my cravat, it was a Christmas present from a feminine admirer."

"You must have it bad to actually *wear* a neon sunset like that!"

"It's from a lady I met on the train when I was mixed up in the Larsen case last year," the little lawyer admitted. "She's visiting out here now, and I asked her to meet me and go out to dinner tonight." He glimpsed himself in the mirror, and winced visibly. Then the phone rang, and Malone did a double wince.

Maggie made no move to answer it. "Probably Chicago again, for the fourth time today. *Mister* Joe Vastrelli, the guy who's paying for this junket, wants to know what, if anything, we've accomplished. Are you in or out?"

"Need you ask?" Malone gestured, dribbling cigar ashes over his lapel. "*Out!*"

But this time it was a girl on the line. When the little lawyer took the phone he heard, "Are you the Mr. Malone who's been phoning the Screen Actors' Guild and all around town trying to locate a Nina LaCosta?" The voice was silky. "Would you pay fifty dollars to know where she is right this minute?"

"Yes, my dear. Emphatically and without reservation, yes."

"Then listen. She's at Lucky's Place. That's a bar out at Canyon Cove, on the shore just north of Santa Monica. Got it?"

"Indelibly printed on my memory. But who are you, and how—?"

"Wait." She paused, and Malone could hear the door of the phone booth open, and in the distance a woman singing "Linda Mujer" to the accompaniment of a marimba band. Then the girl was back on the line, speaking cautiously. "My name's Alva—"

"Time's up!" cut in the operator. "Deposit fifteen cents for three minutes more."

"—and-I'll-come-tomorrow-to-get-my-dough," the girl finished all in one breath.

"Lucky's Place," Maggie said coldly. "A saloon. That will be handy."

But Malone was already out of the door and plunging recklessly through the hotel's tulip beds, headed toward the sunset and a taxi. It was seven-thirty on the nose

50

when his dinner date arrived, an angular spinster of un-
certain years who looked as if she had dressed hastily in
the dark. "So I'm stood up!" sniffed Miss Hildegarde
Withers.

"John J. Malone has stood up lots of people," Maggie
told her wearily. She could have added that some of
them were gorgeous, callipygous females as contrasted
with this weather-beaten battleax, whose hat looked like
an also-ran float in last year's Rose Bowl Parade.

"So disappointing," admitted the maiden schoolteacher. She had long held a sneaking admiration for the
rakish little lawyer; besides, the man semed to have a
knack for stumbling into excitement and adventure.
Her eyes brightened. "But of course, business before
pleasure. Is Mr. Malone working on a murder case?"

Maggie shook her head, and went on to explain why
they were here. It had begun on a dull afternoon in late
January, with nothing in the mail except a reminder of
overdue rent, when the phone call had come in from
Mr. Joseph Vastrelli. Back in Chicago that name meant
something. Time was when Vastrelli and his slightly
less colorful brother Jim had borne a certain dubious
repute, associated with slot machines and similar enter-
prises. But the Vastrellis had mellowed with the times.
Now Joe was head of a combination of produce firms,
eminently respectable, prominent in good works and
civic betterment, and getting a toehold in Gold Coast
society.

Maggie hadn't wanted Malone to obey the summons.
But when the lawyer had arrived at the plush uptown
apartment, he had been met with fine cognac, Uppman
cigars, and a warm handshake instead of the brass knucks
he half expected. "Why should I be sore at you?" Vastrelli had boomed. "Sure you made a monkey out of me

51

on the witness stand in that damage suit, but that was just because you are a smarter lawyer than my lawyers. I need the best and I can afford it. That's why I want you to carry out this very confidential mission for me."

And the big man let down his hair, unburdening himself of a story that proved him an arrant sentimentalist at heart. It had to do with his wife, Nina, the only woman he had ever loved. Malone was shown a photograph in a solid gold frame of a Madonna-like girl with a Delilah mouth, built like a stack of wheats. Nina had walked out, without any explanation, twenty years ago. There had been rumors about her: she was supposed to have got a quickie Mexican divorce by mail; she had taken up briefly with an orange rancher named Grimes or Gray. It was certain that she had starred in several silent movies under the name of Nina LaCosta, taking the name of the vaudeville actor who was her current inamorato. Vastrelli had seen those old films dozens of times—probably sitting in the back row, Malone thought, so nobody could see him crying.

Anyway, Nina had finally dropped out of sight—South America, someone said. Vastrelli had kept a light in the window, and her picture always in his bedroom. But he had heard nothing until this year, when at Christmas he had received a card from her—signed *Nina, remember?*—postmarked Beverly Hills, but with no return address. The bereft husband wanted Malone to locate her, to find out if she needed help. And, if she had at last broken with LaCosta, to see if she still might be the woman who could come back to Chicago and take her place beside him where she belonged.

"So Malone took the case," Maggie concluded. "He's a pushover for a sentimental story like that. I made him bring me along too—I hadn't had a vacation in four years, and I've always dreamed of seeing Hollywood. But I don't know why I'm telling you all this."

"You know very well why," said Miss Withers dryly. "You think Malone is getting into deep water, and you want an ally. Is it that you distrust Vastrelli?"

Maggie shook her head. "This Nina LaCosta—she might be a blackmailer. And she's dark and beautiful, which affects my boss like catnip."

"Say no more," said the schoolteacher, champing at the bit. "What was the name again of the dive the poor man took off for?"

Malone stood holding up the bar in the murky gloom of Lucky's, reflecting that, apart from the dusty fish nets and glass floats with which the place was decorated, it was almost like being back in Chicago. There was an aroma like that in Joe the Angel's City Hall Bar, a dusty, rich, crowded smell.

The patrons were dressed weirdly—beach togs, sweat shirts, bare midriffs, and dark glasses predominating. He surveyed them distastefully, and was about to turn back to the bar when he realized with an electric shock that ran down his spine that the woman he had come so far to seek was sitting in a booth against the farther wall. She looked very much like the photograph in his pocket, only perhaps the print had blurred a little. Malone was ready to move in, and then saw that she was having a tête-à-tête with an exceptionally handsome young man, and toying with a tall drink. This wasn't the time. He put his foot back on the brass rail and ordered beer with rye.

"Smart guy," said the bartender, whose face was a map of Madison Square Garden.

"What's wrong with my order?"

The drinks were slammed down in front of him. "I don't like slummers," said the barman. He was looking hard at Malone's hand-painted Christmas necktie.

A number of other people looked at it too, perhaps because it was the only tie being worn in the entire place. Three drinks later, a plump woman in slacks spoke frankly to the little lawyer. "You're a nice guy at heart," she said. "You shouldn't come here snooting people."

"I beg your pardon?" said Malone in bewilderment.

"That la-de-da necktie," she said, and made a primitive noise with her lips.

Malone bought her a drink, then surreptitiously slipped the offending scarf off his neck and into his coat pocket. "When in Rome," he said, "burn Roman candles at both ends." He was just about to start singing "Killarney" in hopes of getting up a quartet when he looked in the mirror and saw that Nina LaCosta was now alone.

Carefully carrying his drink, Malone crossed the room without the slightest sway in his walk, and slid into the vacant seat. Nina looked up at him and said, "Blow!"

Now that he was this near, even in the murky gloom he could see that her resemblance to the photograph was not so close after all. A walking tribute to cosmetic art, but at close range the years showed through. "Miss La-Costa—" he began.

"You want my autograph?" she asked, brightening a little.

"Why—yes. I also want a confidential chat with you."

But heavy lids were already dropping across the still-beautiful eyes. "I said, *blow!*" Nina repeated. "I don't drink with strangers."

"I'm no stranger. I'm Malone—John J. Malone."

"I don't care if you're John J. Rockefeller." She raised her voice. "Lucky!" The barman materialized out of nowhere. "Lucky, would you kindly take this fresh guy away and bring me a stale drink, or vice versa?"

"Wait!" cried Malone. But a moment later he felt the damp night air on his face.

"Don't hurry back soon," Lucky told him.

As a desperate last resort Malone scribbled the name of his hotel and bungalow number on a card, adding a five-dollar bill. "Just tell Miss LaCosta that if she'll come to see me I have news that will be to her advantage."

The man spat on the sidewalk and went back inside. Malone took out a fresh cigar and had just moved into the shelter of a nearby billboard when he looked up and saw his quarry come hurriedly out of the door and pop into a taxi that had just stopped to disgorge some frolicking customers. "212 Twentieth," came her clear soprano, as the car door slammed.

Back in Chicago Malone would have whistled for the next Yellow or Checker, but here there was no next. Not for twenty interminable minutes, and then it was only because Miss Hildegarde Withers came sailing up in one. *"You!"* he said brightly. The two friends shook hands warily, mutual respect tinctured with suspicion. "Thanks for the lovely handpainted tie," Malone told her.

Miss Withers gave him a questioning look, and his hand went to his throat and then to his pocket. "I must have lost it. A hazard of the chase. I'm hot on somebody's trail; may I borrow your cab?" He was already climbing into it.

55

"You may," she said firmly. "But I go too. I gather Miss LaCosta got away?"

"And I gather Maggie's been talking. Never mind, I'd like your expert opinion. After what happened inside, how shall I report to Joe Vastrelli?"

Miss Withers listened, and then said it was too early to pass judgment. "Not so good that she hangs out in a bar, but you say she had only one drink. Not so good that she was with a young man—"

"But a very good-looking young man. I think I've seen his picture in the papers or somewhere. And she wasn't flirting with him—he left alone."

Finally the taxi drew up beside a peeling stucco apartment house on a Santa Monica street lined with untidy palm trees, and Malone got out. But the schoolteacher was close upon his heels. "With me as chaperone, you'll not be mistaken for a wolf this time," she pointed out. A card in the lobby read *LaCosta—2B,* so they hurried up the stairs. Miss Withers rang the bell and Malone knocked, but nobody answered. "Stalemate," said the schoolma'am in a disappointed tone.

But Malone tried the knob and the door opened. Lights were on, but obviously nobody was home. Doors concealed the inevitable wall bed, a tiny bath and bare kitchenette. There was a strong smell of tobacco, perfume and mice.

"No books," observed Miss Withers, disapprovingly. "Only trashy movie magazines."

"No liquor, only empties," said Malone, who had investigated the kitchenette.

But there were both men's and women's clothing in the closet and the chest of drawers. Miss Withers shook her head disapprovingly, and went on rummaging beneath the lining of a drawer filled with lacy but much worn black underwear. She found a man's photo.

"That's him!" cried Malone. "The collegiate character she was with at Lucky's."

"Dear, dear! But one can hardly blame her—he has a lovely profile." Miss Withers bagged the photograph and edged toward the door. "Shouldn't we go?"

"This is a comfortable chair," the little lawyer said. "And Nina will be here any minute. We should have a showdown. I can't go back to Vastrelli and admit I didn't even get to talk to her. He's entitled to something for his money."

"Oh, *no!*" cried Miss Withers. Malone flushed at being so openly contradicted, and then saw that she was staring past him toward the hall door. There stood a man, tall and cadaverously thin, with an actor's mobile mouth, a bluish jaw and eyes like agates. In one arm he held a large paper sack; the other hand was lumped in his coat pocket. "Not anyone I would care to meet in a dark alley," said the schoolteacher to herself. "Or for that matter in a lighted alley." But aloud she said cheerily, "Why, this must be Mr. LaCosta! Do come in. We were just waiting for your—for Nina. This is Mr. Malone, the famous Chicago attorney—"

"From Chicago, eh?" The man set the bag of groceries down on the table so hard that it split open, scattering oranges, coffee, cornflakes, hamburger and a half pint of blended bourbon. "So Joe Vastrelli is trying to make trouble again, is he? Sending his stooges out here. You go back and tell him he can—"

"One moment," said Malone dramatically, in his best courtroom voice. "Nina has a chance to go back to her first husband, who still adores her; she has an opportunity to take up again the life for which she is fitted. He'll give her every luxury. Would you stand in her way?"

LaCosta's laugh was not pretty. "I wouldn't stand in her way, counselor. But Nina isn't going anywhere; she's happy with me in our little love nest. So *get out!*"

And, respecting the menacing bulge in his pocket, they got. "Really," said Miss Withers in the taxi, "I don't see that you have much choice in what to report to your client. Nina is still mixed up with a very unpleasant character indeed."

He nodded, a little sad. "I'll dictate the letter tonight." But the hotel bungalow was dark. Maggie had obviously retired to her little room in the main building.

As they entered, Miss Withers sniffed and said, "Your little secretary has taken to Turkish cigarettes and exotic perfumes. Chypre, isn't it?"

"Maggie must have gone Hollywood too. Back home she's more the Lily-of-the-Valley type." Malone plunged into dictating his report to Vastrelli; out of the kindness of his warm Irish heart he softened the bad news as much as he could. Then, as the schoolteacher briskly inserted paper and carbons in Maggie's typewriter, he excused himself. "I'll just brush up a bit and we'll be off in search of a cold bird and a bottle."

He was gone what seemed rather a longish time, and Miss Withers was clattering away halfway down the page when he reappeared, looking as if he had swallowed a bad oyster. "Look in there," he said, pointing to the bedroom. "Do you see what I see?"

Miss Withers looked, rubbed her eyes, looked again —and still saw Nina LaCosta sprawled across the bed. Around her still lovely neck, tied tighter than anything could be worn and live, was a certain hand-painted necktie with colors like a neon sunset. Malone, much shaken, explained that he had been trying in vain to undo it. "This is one time we're going to call the authorities," said the schoolteacher. But she had hardly picked up the instrument when there was the wolf wail of sirens outside, and then suddenly the place was swarming with uniforms.

"That's what I call *service,*" said Malone, admiringly.

The session lasted until well after midnight and finally, when they thought it must be over, a Lieutenant Lumm appeared, took over, and went through it all again. He was a bald, youngish man with glasses and a sandpaper voice. "Now, Malone," said the lieutenant, sounding for all the world like a federal income-tax examiner, "this looks pretty clear to me. You admit you got thrown out of a Santa Monica bar earlier this evening for trying to make passes at the victim. You bribed the bartender to give her your card with this address and to tell her if she dropped in she'd learn something to her advantage. That was the bait that fetched her. But she didn't want to play pattycake, and you got mad and strangled her with what you admit is your own necktie."

"I object!" said John J. Malone. "On the grounds that—"

But Miss Withers objected still more. "Mr. Malone has been with me for the past hour or more." She repeated her story.

Lumm rubbed a nutcracker jaw thoughtfully. "Okay. So he still had time to do the job while you were typing. He found her sleeping on his bed, probably passed out from working on his case of whisky while waiting for him to come home. Or maybe you're lying—as his secretary you'd be open to his bribes or threats—"

"I am only a secretary *pro tem*," she snapped, "and I don't tell lies!"

"Um hum." The lieutenant consulted his notes. "You gave your name to the officer as Hildegarde Withers, *age 38?*"

"I meant *over* 38!" she corrected swiftly. "And, young man, I suggest that Nina LaCosta was killed by somebody who wanted to frame Mr. Malone—the same somebody who took her handbag, which you'll notice is missing."

Lumm shook his head. "We found the handbag outside in a rosebush, where your boy friend tossed it after he rifled the contents."

"I object!" cried Malone. The lieutenant told him to shut up. "Exception!"

"Looks like he did it," Lumm said to Miss Withers. "And you're an accomplice or accessory if you persist in covering up for him."

"Who, pray, is covering? As soon as I saw the body I hurried to the phone—"

"Says you. The dame who tipped us off had a much younger voice."

"I have probably aged with the strain of the past few hours. Seriously, officer, shouldn't you be looking for the killer instead of badgering innocent bystanders?"

"A bird in the hand," Lumm said firmly. Then the phone rang. He snatched it up, then after a moment handed the instrument to Malone. "No tricks now," he warned. "It's long distance." He moved closer, evidently hoping to pick up information.

The voice of some female robot said tinnily, "Is this Mr. John J. Malone? Chicago is calling. Ready with Mr. Malone—go ahead."

It was Joe Vastrelli, far away but clear. "Been trying

to get you all day," he shouted. "Malone, what are you doing besides spending my money? Found Nina yet?"

"She just left," Malone said desperately, without bothering to add that she had left feet first in a wicker basket.

"Well, is she coming back to me or not?" But at this point the impatient Lumm took over. After a few questions he assured the fond husband that his long-lost bride would be returned to him after the autopsy, if he was willing to pay traveling costs for one corpse and an attendant. Then he hung up, though Vastrelli was still screaming with shock and rage. Chicago, Malone thought, must be having a major earthquake. And Vastrelli would be on the next plane with blood in his eye.

"Now this gets better and better," observed the lieutenant with professional detachment. "This case'll get written up in the true detective magazines, I shouldn't wonder. You come out here to try and locate a guy's wife and get her to return; then you fall for her and wind up bumping her off because you were afraid she'd tell her husband about your making passes. . . ."

The man had a bright-light-and-rubber-hose look in his eye, and was, Miss Withers decided, about to suggest a trip down to the station. "One moment," she interrupted, and played her ace of trumps. For a long time Lieutenant Lumm wouldn't hear of any such thing. He resisted stubbornly—and then to everybody's surprise the evil hour was postponed.

"But don't either of you try to leave town" was Lumm's final warning. "Because for my money you're both in this up to your ears." And he slammed the door.

A chill gray dawn crept into the east windows, but Miss Withers and John J. Malone sat in the bungalow living room, with Maggie nodding disapprovingly in a corner and fairly oozing, "I told you so!"

"This reminds me of the Larsen case, and that night on the Super-Century," said Miss Withers.

Malone looked into his highball glass and found it, as he had expected, empty again. "It wasn't a bad idea of yours about talking the lieutenant into phoning long distance for our character references," he admitted. "Only whether Captain von Flanagan will ever forgive me for having him yanked out of bed at four o'clock in the morning—"

"It was *five* in New York, and a wonder that Inspector Oscar Piper didn't disown me entirely. Even so, I don't think that Lumm was convinced. There is a man with a mean, suspicious nature. Probably he's just giving us rope enough to hang ourselves."

"I have worse worries than that," Malone told her. He sighed and stood up. "I'm sorry our date turned out this way." He held out his hand. "Well, goodbye."

"Goodbye? But I'm not deserting the sinking ship!"

"I am," the little lawyer told her. "Before Vastrelli gets here."

"And if you try to get away, you'll be arrested," Miss Withers reminded him. "Take a couple of aspirins and try to get some sleep. I'll be back later on."

Malone finally dozed off on the divan, waking minutes or hours later to see his secretary prowling around. Maggie said something, but he only buried his head under a pillow, muttering, "Okay, but go away, huh?"

Maggie finally went away, and he slept fitfully until a little after noon when Miss Hildegarde Withers burst in upon him, looking like the canary that ate the cat. "Good morning, merry sunshine!" the schoolteacher greeted him. "I gather that you didn't dream up a solution to our mutual problem? Neither did I, worse luck. But I've been thinking. Remember that phone call yesterday leading you to Lucky's? It was all wrong."

"It was not! Nina was there all right, because I saw her and spoke to her—"

"Of course. But the girl didn't *call* you from Lucky's —it's only a ten-cent call from Santa Monica to here, and you said the operator asked for fifteen."

The little lawyer brightened. "She did say something about its being a bar *out* at Canyon Cove, meaning she was somewhere in town. Probably a night spot, because I remember hearing marimba music and a singer. Lucky's has no floor show." Suddenly Malone felt fine again. "The girl is the key to it all. Alice? Elma?"

"Alva," spoke up Maggie, as she came in through the door with coffee. "Alva Jones. I know because she told me when she came this morning to collect her money."

"What?" Malone stared at her. "She was *here*—and you let her get away?"

"She was a foot taller than me, and outweighed me twenty pounds. I couldn't very well throw her and sit on her head. You said it was okay to take the money out of your billfold—" Maggie squared off belligerently.

But it was Miss Withers who poured oil on the troubled waters. "All is not lost that glitters," she said. "Cheer up, we all have a lunch date at La Lucia."

"La Lucia in Hollywood?" gasped Maggie. "Right around the corner from Paradox and RKO, where all the stars eat?"

"Perhaps murderers sometimes eat there too."

And the schoolteacher would say no more. But they came at last to a vine-covered one-story building crammed with people and redolent of herbs and roasting meat and expensive vintages, and before Maggie had time to recognize more than one or two of her cinema deities a headwaiter shunted them off to a large curtained booth in a far corner. "We'll order later," said Miss Withers firmly. "We're expecting a Mr. Gray."

The man bowed and left them before Malone could get in a word about a much-needed eye opener. "Just as well," said the schoolteacher. "We'll all need our wits about us when our guest of honor arrives." She produced a folded photograph.

Maggie peered over her shoulder, then cried, "Jackson Gray! *The* Jackson Gray, voted the juvenile discovery of the year! Oh, pinch me, somebody, I'm dreaming!"

Malone obligingly pinched her, but his heart wasn't in it. He looked at Miss Withers, who said, "Very simple. I noticed the studio credit stamp on the back of the photo, did a little checking this morning, then phoned Mr. Gray at Paradox, and put a flea in his ear." She looked at the old-fashioned watch pinned to her old-fashioned bosom. "He's late. Probably walking up and down outside—"

But no. The headwaiter was bringing him over now —a tall, very young man with curly hair, a dimple, and a look of having been dragged through a knothole. There were introductions all around, and Maggie almost swooned. "Haven't time to eat," Gray said. "Got to get back on the set. Now what's all this about?"

So the story hadn't hit the papers yet. Miss Withers took the bit in her teeth. "Mr. Gray, do you know a woman who calls herself Nina LaCosta?"

Brittle silence. "I know lots of women," the boy said woodenly. "Maybe I know her." His face was suddenly worldly-wise. "Is this a shakedown?"

"Don't be foolish," snapped the schoolteacher. "Nina LaCosta was strangled to death last evening in Mr.

64

Malone's bedroom. We're trying to find out who did it."

Jackson Gray said nothing, but he bit his lip hard. "You were out with her last night," Malone put in. "Wasn't she a bit old for you?"

A tumult of emotions flashed across the young man's face. "Just the right age," he said softly. "To have been my mother, I mean."

"*What?*" cried Miss Withers, Malone, and Maggie all in one breath.

"Look, I don't know who you people are or what you want," continued the young man bitterly. "I've already had about all I can stand. But you see, I was brought up as an orphan by some relatives after my father died. Nobody ever mentioned my mother. But a couple of months ago a woman got in touch with me and—well, she said she was my real mother. She said I had no right to the name of Gray because she hadn't been legally divorced when she went through the ceremony with my father. She seemed to know some of the family history, and—well, I used to meet her in that bar every pay day."

"You gave her money like a dutiful son?" asked Malone approvingly.

"If she really was my mother she never took any interest in me until I got a start in Hollywood. I got a lucky break and a lot of publicity on one picture, but a scandal right now would put a quick freeze on it. I paid to keep her mouth shut."

Miss Withers wanted to know why in this day and age anybody would worry about the possible exposure of a bar sinister. "I'm not twenty-one," the boy admitted. "If what she said was true she could have taken over as my legal guardian." He shrugged. "I'll not pretend a lot of grief I don't feel. But, Mr. Malone, you say she was killed in your room. Did anybody find her handbag? Because I gave her a hundred in cash and a check for $250 last night, and it would be worth a lot to me to have that check back with no publicity."

Maggie said quickly, "I was being questioned when the policeman came in with her handbag. There was no money or checks."

"Oh," said Jackson Gray, his shoulders sagging. He stood up. "Got to get back. But if that check should turn up, I'll gladly pay a thousand bucks—and no questions asked." He was looking at Malone pointedly as he turned away.

Maggie sighed and Miss Withers sniffed. After a moment Malone said glumly, "I wish I knew if he was insulting me or retaining me."

The schoolteacher said she wished she knew if Jackson Gray was trying to draw a red herring across a very muddled trail. Which reminded them of food, and after a fabulous lunch (still chargeable to Joe Vastrelli, Malone hoped) they returned to the hotel bungalow for a council of war.

"The trouble with this situation," observed Miss Withers, "is that we've been sitting still and letting things happen to us. Let's fix it so we happen to things."

"Whoops, take cover!" cried Maggie from the window. "We got visitors."

"Not Lieutenant Lumm?" moaned Malone. "If I take an aspirin do you think he'll go away?"

"Lumm and a portly gent in a blue suit, who must be from out of town because he wears a necktie and a hat, also a big black scowl. Boss, could it be——?"

It was. Joe Vastrelli was tense and white-lipped, rigidly self-controlled and deadly as a ticking bomb. But the lieutenant was still in charge, and he got right down to cases. "Malone, Mr. Vastrelli phoned headquarters as soon as he arrived at the airport. He's given us a new angle—"

"Fine and dandy," Malone said. "We can certainly use it."

Lumm said, unsmilingly, "It's his suggestion that perhaps at the time back in Chicago when he retained you to look for his wife, he might have given the erroneous impression that he would be just as well satisfied if something happened to her—so she couldn't carry out any possible intentions of blackmailing him. Then you could ask a big fat fee—"

"Holy St. Vitus!" cried Malone.

"Because," Lumm went on stolidly, "if you killed her thinking you were doing a favor for a wealthy and influential client—"

"Making Mr. Vastrelli the instigator of a conspiracy to commit murder, and liable to criminal prosecution," put in Miss Withers helpfully from the bleachers.

"Shut up, ma'am," said Lieutenant Lumm. "Well, Malone?"

"Look," said the little lawyer desperately. "I never laid hands on a woman except in self-defense. I didn't kill Nina LaCosta. My only idea was to locate her and make a report, a copy of which is still in that typewriter. And if I had killed her, would I do it right here and leave the body on my own bed?"

"All murderers are dumb," Lumm told him. "Or they wouldn't murder. And maybe you were just smart enough to make it look like the corpse was planted on you."

"It was! Nina was either killed by Jackson Gray, a young actor she was shaking down because she might or might not have been his mother, or by LaCosta himself, who didn't want to see her toss him overboard and go back to a life of luxury. One or the other of them knew she was coming here to see me, and he came here first and—"

"Wait!" cried Miss Withers, about to point out the flaws in that theory. But nobody was listening. Vastrelli had suddenly erupted and was aiming a Sunday punch for Malone's jaw.

"Go on, hit me in front of witnesses," said the little lawyer quickly. "I'll sue you for fifty thousand dollars charging aggravated assault—"

Vastrelli stopped, but perhaps that was only because Lieutenant Lumm's heavy hand was on his shoulder. "None of that, now!" warned the officer sharply. The big man turned away, muttering.

"You can't fire me, I quit!" Malone said.

But Vastrelli made an abrupt about-face. "No, you don't! You're in this too deep to get out now. If you killed Nina, I'll see you're hanged higher'n a kite. If you didn't, then this is your chance to get busy and find out who did. You can name your own fee if you'll just give me five minutes alone with the—"

Lumm told him that this was Beverly Hills, not Cicero, and the law would take its course. There was more of the same, and as they finally left, John J. Malone stared after them. "Baby, it's cold outside," he said, shivering. There had been a look in Vastrelli's eye that suggested somebody's feet in a cement block and the waters of the great gray green greasy Chicago River closing over that somebody's head. "Maggie, on second thought maybe we're not ever going back to Chicago. It could be unhealthy."

"Stuff and nonsense," Miss Withers cut in. "What we must do is find the real killer, and soon. After all, we're not entirely in the dark. We know that the murderer hired some girl to phone you and lure you out to Lucky's—probably the same girl who later reported to the police that there was trouble in your bungalow. The murderer himself must have been at Lucky's too, or he wouldn't have known that Nina was there—nor would he have been able to pick up the necktie you so carelessly dropped. You've seen the suspects—were any of them in the crowd at the bar last night?"

"Only Gray, and he left." Malone shrugged. "There were some men around, a whole crowd in the back room, mostly odd characters in yachting caps and bathing suits and sunglasses and so forth, but I didn't notice them much. I'm a woman-watcher myself."

The schoolteacher's sniff was monumental. "Anyway, when Alva phoned, it was a fifteen-cent call, which means it came from San Fernando to the north, Culver City to the south, or downtown Los Angeles. If we could only find what cabarets in that area were featuring a singer and a marimba band at the dinner hour last night—"

"Bingo!" cried Malone, and grabbed the phone directory. Two hours and twenty calls later he came up for air, announcing that, according to the booking agents for third-string night-club talent, the place in question must be the Casbah, on Main Street, downtown. "Not only do they have a singer and a marimba band, they have B-girls too." He smoothed down his thinning hair, and straightened his tie.

Miss Withers stood up eagerly. "Will you come with me to the Casbah?"

"If you don't mind," said the little lawyer, "he travels fastest who travels alone, especially in saloons. If I took you two respectable females down there with me I'd find out less than nothing. Besides, it's too early. If Alva does work there as a percentage girl she'd hardly be around yet. I'll have time to get the works in a barbershop and cash a check." He went out humming "Danny Boy."

"Cashing a check," commented Maggie. "Malone always says the quickest way to make friends is to break a hundred-dollar bill in a bar."

"Men have all the fun!" said Miss Withers, and in desperation went home and washed her hair. It was after eleven when she gave in and rang up the bungalow, only to hear Maggie declare that there was no news. The schoolteacher said, "Oh. But it's late, and I'm worried."

"It's never late for Malone. You don't know him."

"And he doesn't know Los Angeles' Main Street, otherwise known as Skid Row. I think a rescue party is indicated. Would you care to join me?"

"Okay," said Maggie, and ten minutes later she climbed into a taxi beside the eager schoolma'am. "But Malone's probably only in the bar at this Casbah place, leading a barbershop quartet in 'The Rose of Tralee.'"

"And he may also be putting his head in a noose. I don't yet see the picture, but I begin to see the outlines of the frame. I've been making some phone calls—to the county clerk at Santa Ana over in Orange County, who kindly looked up the old records. And to the airport, of course—though that was a letdown. Still, there's something shivery about this entire situation."

The cab finally deposited them at the Casbah, which for all its orchestra and dance floor was just another dive. A large proportion of its customers were enlisted Navy, gloomily drinking up their shore leave. Of the several houris lying in wait at the far end of the bar, none was known to Maggie. "Alva isn't here," she declared. Then she noticed that each of the girls was wearing an orchid corsage. "But I think Malone *was* here."

The flustered and overworked man behind the bar was of no help. "I know from nothing," he admitted. "But I'm only filling in for the regular bartender—he got in the middle of an argument and lost a couple of front teeth a while ago."

"Malone *was* here, indeed!" agreed Miss Withers. By the shameless pretense of being Alva's aunt from out of town, and by the judicious use of a couple of five-dollar bills, the schoolteacher secured a certain address.

Their taxi hauled them to a small and dingy hotel in the oldest section of old Los Angeles, located atop a hill which the driver called "The Angels' Flight." The two women entered somewhat gingerly, for all angels had obviously flown from this vicinity long ago. But the lobby was empty except for a man behind the desk, who was snoring quietly. They went on upstairs.

"Maybe we should have called first," Maggie said. "That girl was beautiful, in a billboard-blonde sort of way. And that type is one of Malone's weaknesses—"

"Of which he has a complete set," concluded Miss Withers dryly. She knocked on a door and they entered —then stopped short, staring.

"I'll go quietly," said John J. Malone, without looking up from his drink. The little lawyer was slumped in a chair by the window, looking as if he had just swallowed two bad oysters and an old clam. All the misery of the world was on his shoulders, but he clutched a familiar bottle of rye as if it were a talisman.

"We hardly expected to find you alone," admitted the schoolteacher.

"I am not alone," admitted the little lawyer. "She's in

71

the bathroom. Strangled, and, naturally, with another of my neckties. This is the last straw. I know when I'm licked. Get out of here while you can. Save yourselves— take to the boats!"

"Take to some black coffee!" snapped Miss Withers. She looked into the bath, and came out after a moment, somewhat pale around the gills.

"Believe it or not," continued the unhappy lawyer, "I found her this way. But everybody in the Casbah will remember that I wanted Alva's address so bad I had an argument with the bartender to get it. Would one of you call the police and make a reservation for me at the nearest gas chamber?"

"You're quite sure about the tie?" demanded Miss Withers doubtfully.

"It's a hand-painted Kelly green number that Jake and Helene Justus gave me last St. Patrick's Day. It was in my hotel closet last night."

"So was that bottle of rye!" Maggie cut in, wide-eyed. "At least it's the same brand you got a case of and that we charged off to Vastrelli as *incidentals!*"

"That," pronounced Miss Withers solemnly, "is not coincidence. It's a frame-up—a lovely, hand-painted frame!"

"You needn't look so *pleased!*" Malone said, almost peevishly.

"I was just thinking," said the schoolteacher, "that somebody wants to get you almost as badly as they wanted to get Nina LaCosta."

"Look," suggested Maggie hopefully, "we could cut off the necktie, and take it and the bottle with us, and each of us hold one of his arms and maybe we could get him away—"

"No—" said Miss Withers.

72

"Go on," Malone told them. "Sail out of here, you two ships deserting the sinking rat."

"Maggie, call the police at once," the schoolteacher decided. "Then come away."

"Goodbye!" intoned Malone theatrically. "The rest is —silence."

"The rest is a warpath, and Maggie and I are going out on it. I hope that your hours of incarceration are brief, but it may brighten them for you to know that we are going out now in search of Jackson Gray. Sit tight."

John J. Malone hiccuped gently. "That," he admitted, "will be easy."

The homicide office in the Beverly Hills police station offers hardly room enough to swing a cat. Certainly not enough for a rubber hose, John J. Malone was thinking. He was sitting on a hard chair, handcuffed, cold sober, and wrathful. "I want a lawyer," he was saying. "I want a dozen lawyers and a lie-detector test and a liverwurst sandwich with raw onions."

Lieutenant Lumm looked at him. "You know, until tonight I never really believed you were guilty. I just thought I'd put a burr under your tail and needle you into helping us solve this murder. But this Alva Jones job changes all that. Why'd you kill her, Malone? Was it because she tipped you off yesterday to where Nina LaCosta was, and therefore was in a position to blackmail you?"

"If I confess can I have a hot pastrami sandwich with a kosher dill pickle?" Malone rattled his chains. "Lieutenant, will you book me so I can get some sleep?"

Lumm slammed the desk. "Okay, you're booked!" He busied himself with certain grim formalities for a while, and then called in a subordinate. "Notify Los Angeles too, Sergeant. And have LaCosta released at once, with apologies."

"You never should have arrested LaCosta," Malone observed. "He would have been a lovely suspect, only if he had murdered Nina he'd have got the hundred dollars in cash that was in her handbag, and if he had got the money he'd never have brought home groceries for a cheap supper or bought only a half pint of whisky."

"You can talk in court," Lumm snapped at him. "And, Sergeant, phone Mr. Joseph Vastrelli at his hotel and tell him the case is closed and that if he'll stop in here and sign a statement he's free to go back to Chicago whenever he pleases."

"Vastrelli, coming here?" Malone cried. "Lock me in a cell, quick!"

"Shut up." The lieutenant turned away. "And then get hold of Jackson Gray and tell him to be here first thing in the morning. He ties into it too, and I want to know just what Malone said to him at lunch."

"Speaking of lunch—" began the little lawyer.

But the sergeant came back in a few minutes to report that while LaCosta had been turned loose, and Vastrelli was on his way down to the station, Jackson Gray could not be located. "The clerk at his hotel says he got a phone call about an hour ago and rushed out of the place."

Lumm looked blank for a moment. "No, don't worry," Malone reassured him. "It isn't Gray. He wouldn't murder a blackmailer; he'd just keep on paying. In fact, the only person who ought to be wearing these handcuffs—"

The lieutenant was on the phone, ordering a routine pickup on Hildegarde Withers and the secretary. Then

74

the door burst open and Joe Vastrelli swept in like a cyclone, his face dark with rage. "So it was you all the time, you little shyster!" And again he swung his round-house right—before Lumm could untangle himself from the telephone. John J. Malone had never been at more of a disadvantage, but in the coolness of desperation he managed to roll with the punch, and then brought his manacled wrists heavily down on the big man's head, knocking him colder than a witch's kiss.

"Your prisoner, Lieutenant," said Malone wearily. "Vastrelli waited for years for a chance to revenge himself on the woman who walked out on him. And then when I made a fool out of him in court he decided to send me out here, kill Nina, and pin it on me."

"Getting both of them at one fell swoop!" cried a confident voice from the doorway. And Miss Hildegarde Withers stalked in, like some ungainly bird of prey. "That's exactly how it happened, Lieutenant." She stepped nonchalantly over the recumbent form. "Oh, I see you've been trying to get a confession already."

"Enough is too much!" said Lieutenant Lumm with deadly calmness. "You two hooligans have been making monkeys out of me and the whole police department—"

"It was nothing, really," Malone said modestly.

Lumm hit all the buttons on his desk. "Take that man downstairs and give him first aid! And lock up these two jokers and throw away the key—"

"You'll be sorry," Miss Withers told him. "Because Vastrelli really *is* the murderer, you know."

"He is? Then just tell me this. How can a man commit a murder in Beverly Hills when he's two thousand miles away? Malone and I both talked to Vastrelli in Chicago before his wife's body was cold!"

"That does take a bit of explaining," admitted the

schoolteacher. She looked wistfully at the telephone and then at her watch. "But, Lieutenant, if you'll have your men unhand me, and all of us sit down for a quiet chat—"

"Lock 'em both up!" yelped Lieutenant Lumm, almost tearing his sparse hair.

"But you can't do this to me—to us!" cried John J. Malone.

Only they could, and did.

Iron doors clanged. "What can I order for breakfast?" asked the lawyer.

The turnkey said, "Anything you like. Only you get dry bread and coffee." He went away. Malone reminded himself that stone walls do not a prison make, nor iron bars a cage, and stretched out on the hard mattress. Yet his eyes had barely closed when there was the rattle of the lock again. "Let's go," said the turnkey.

"Shot at sunrise, without even a trial?" the lawyer cried.

But he was taken back upstairs, shoved into Lumm's office, where Miss Hildegarde Withers, looking slightly the worse for wear, was waiting. She winked at him.

Lieutenant Lumm came in, looking happy and a trifle sheepish. "Sorry I lost my temper," he said. "But I guess I made a terrible mistake—"

"Vastrelli's confessed?" cried Malone eagerly.

"He will," the lieutenant said. "When he comes to from that conk on the head and finds out that his brother just phoned me long distance from Chicago and admitted the frame-up. It seems Jim Vastrelli just read the papers and realized what he'd got mixed up in. He provided Joe with an alibi for murder, beforehand. Joe's been out here for a week, leaving his brother back in Chicago to put through phone calls in his name. It was the brother who flew out on the plane yesterday, also under Joe's name. Joe met him at the airport, changed hats and coats and luggage, and the brother took the first plane back."

"Neat," said Malone judicially. "Very neat."

"I've notified the Chicago police to pick up Jim Vastrelli and hold him for extradition," Lumm continued. "I'm going to—"

"May I say a word?" put in Miss Hildegarde Withers anxiously.

"Later," the lieutenant told her. "I want to finish telling you both how sorry I am. I feel I owe you an apology. . . ."

Malone waved his hand in a think-nothing-of-it gesture, but the schoolteacher said, "And we owe you an explanation—at least, I do. Before you go any further I must tell you that while the phone call you just received was correct in its basic information—it simply had to be, because nothing else fits the facts—it wasn't exactly from the brother of Joe Vastrelli."

Lieutenant Lumm's smile froze on his face. "I should have known!" he whispered, wide-eyed. "Of course, another phony act! Because I have a good ear for identifying voices, and I *know* that the man I just arrested was the same one I talked to over long distance the night of the murder—"

"You talked to him," Miss Withers said quickly. "But *not* over long distance. One doesn't have to be in Chicago to give the impression that he's calling from there—not if he has a young woman around to mimic the voice of the operator. Vastrelli used a B-girl he picked up in a Main Street bar to do his phoning for him, and later he murdered her when he found out that she'd been greedy enough to come to Malone for

77

her promised fifty, and thus put us on her trail. He planted a necktie and a bottle of whisky that he'd taken from Malone's room the night he killed Nina, just to make the frame tighter. Nasty character, Mr. Vastrelli."

Malone nodded placidly. "That's why I bopped him."

"A fairy story!" cried the thwarted lieutenant, wildly pressing buttons. "Sergeant! Come in here and take these——"

Suddenly the room was filled with uniforms, but amazingly enough, instead of hauling Malone and Miss Withers back to their dungeon cells, the officers were shaking Lumm's hand and patting him on the back. "Take a bow, Lieutenant!" somebody was saying. "That lug Vastrelli's confessed to both murders! Will this burn up the Los Angeles boys!"

"Words fail me," said Malone fervently, as he and Miss Withers came out into the streets of Beverly Hills, deserted and pale in the moonlight.

"We must hurry back to the hotel," said the schoolteacher. "Maggie is there alone with Jackson Gray—"

"He can always scream for help, can't he?"

"She was the operator and young Gray played the part of Jim Vastrelli, with a slight foreign accent. One of his most successful roles, I'd say. He was delighted to help—I made him very happy by discovering that his mother was really married to his father, and that she also showed proof of a divorce from Vastrelli."

"He'll be happier yet," Malone said, "when I give him his check back. It was crumpled up in Vastrelli's hand, you know—the man was evidently going to slip it into my pocket in the fracas, only I conked him first."

"Maybe Mr. Gray will even take us all out to Ciro's for dinner tomorrow night!" said Miss Withers.

The next night was a huge success. Maggie floated around the floor in the arms of Jackson Gray and once she was even asked for her autograph. Miss Withers ran into a famous screenwriter who had once been one of her grubby urchins at P.S. 38, and was embraced and feted. But inevitably John J. Malone drifted out into the bar. There was a luscious black-haired girl with bright blue eyes there for a while, and then it turned out that she was near-sighted and had mistaken him for an assistant director at Fox.

All alone, the little lawyer ordered another drink and then began to sing softly, under his breath, "Did your mother come from Ireland . . . ?" There was a man down the bar who looked like a potential baritone, but he went away.

Then someone climbed onto the stool beside Malone and ordered a lemonade. Miss Withers chimed in with a soft, true contralto—"For there's something in you Irish . . ."

*

Autopsy and Eva

ㅜㅜㅜㅜㅜㅜㅜㅜㅜㅜㅜㅜㅜㅜㅜㅜㅜㅜㅜㅜㅜㅜㅜㅜㅜㅜㅜㅜㅜㅜㅜㅜㅜ

"DON'T ANSWER IT—maybe they'll go away," called out John J. Malone hopefully as the buzzer sounded from the other room. But the bulging blonde in the wispy chartreuse dinner gown had already started to open the door; obediently she tried to shut it again but found it blocked by a stout sensible oxford.

"No matter how busy he is," said the angular female who was now pushing her way into the hotel suite, "Mr. Malone will see *me!*" Then she caught sight of the stocky little lawyer, who was just emerging from the bedroom, dressed to the teeth in a new gray-green Finchley suit and at the moment engaged in getting a perfect knot in a flaming Sulka tie already tinged with cigar ash. "Ah, there you are!" cried Miss Withers.

Malone winced, and then managed a warmish smile. "Hildegarde, I honestly did intend to give you a ring the minute I got into L.A., but I've been tied up with so many things—"

"So I see," remarked the schoolteacher, with a sideways glance.

"Sugar, wait for me in the cocktail lounge downstairs, will you?" Malone asked quickly. The blonde pouted, then grabbed up her wrap and bag and flounced out, not quite slamming the door. "My secretary," he explained hopefully.

"Goodness, how our dear Maggie has *changed*. I'd *never* have recognized her."

"You *know* it's not Maggie—"

"Yes, I know," interrupted the schoolteacher crisply. "Because I talked to Maggie yesterday in Chicago via long distance, which is how I found out where you were to be located. You were planning to leave for Honolulu tomorrow?"

"I was," Malone admitted. "I mean, I am. I just collected a fat fee and I'm on my first vacation in years and tonight I'm dancing at Mocambo where the movie stars go—"

"Correction," Hildegarde interrupted firmly. "You are staying here with *me* this evening, because I'm afraid we're thoroughly mixed up in another murder case."

The little lawyer stiffened. "*We* are? Holy Saint Paul and Minneapolis, not again!" Automatically he reached for solace in the form of a bottle and a glass.

"Try abstinence sometime," suggested Miss Withers tartly. "And go easy on that nasty stuff; tonight, unless I miss my guess, you'll need all your wits about you."

"Tonight I need a blonde about me," Malone protested. "Can't this thing wait?"

"The man—I should say men—who are coming here can't wait. The first should arrive within the hour."

"But, my dear lady, why?" Twice within the past year or so the little lawyer had been mixed up with Miss Withers on homicide cases, to the detriment of his nerves—and there hadn't been a fee in either. Enough, he thought, was enough.

"Why are they coming here? Willy-nilly to fall into my trap and give us information about the Ryan murder." She peered at him. "You read about it, of course? It happened last Saturday in a big apartment house out on Wilshire Boulevard. An Army colonel just home from Korea was found in his wife's bedroom with a bullet through his head."

Malone stared glumly at the bottom of his glass. "Yes, I read something about it in the papers back home. A sordid story. Returning hero covered with medals comes rushing back on leave, panting for the arms of his beautiful wife whom he hasn't seen in years. He unlocks the door of his apartment and finds the girl *en flagrante* with her boy friend. There is a fracas, but somehow they overpower him, then take his service pistol and shoot him dead as Kelsey. After which they get panicky and make a run for it, but the police will pick them up soon enough. It's not a case I'd care to try in court—no chance for a valid self-defense plea. Because it was the victim's own gun there might be a possibility, with luck, of cutting it to second-degree homicide, but public opinion would be so strong—"

"This time public opinion, like yours, is almost 100 per cent wrong," Miss Withers said, advancing on him with a bony forefinger wagging. "Lieutenant-Colonel Ryan was no hero; he was only in Korea on a safe staff assignment for a few months, and most of his time in the Pacific—which dates from just before the fall of Japan—was spent in the Judge Advocate General's office in Tokyo, in charge of the sequestered assets of the Japanese government. The only medal he ever got—

83

according to my informant in the Pentagon, a major who learned geography at my knee years ago—was the Legion of Merit, which I understand desk officers award to one another for not forgetting to lock up the files when they leave the office at five. Nor was Ryan exactly rushing home to the arms of his wife; the record shows that he landed at March Field some thirty-six hours before he showed up at the apartment."

"Yes," said Malone, interested. "But who else would have any motive?"

"Just like a man! And I can't believe that a girl like Eva Ryan, only twenty-six and from an excellent family background back east, would cold-bloodedly assist in her husband's murder and then calmly take the time to pack up her clothes and her most precious possessions before making a getaway. It doesn't ring true. For one thing, how could she know that somebody in the building hadn't heard the shot and had called the police?"

"But wasn't that what did happen?" Malone looked bewildered.

"Fiddlesticks! At least an hour after the crime must have been committed, a man called the police and said he'd heard a shot in the apartment house, but hadn't reported it earlier because he'd been visiting a lady there who wasn't his wife. He wouldn't give his name, and hung up before they could trace the call." She sniffed. "He was the actual murderer, no doubt."

"Oh, his story could have been on the level," the little lawyer said judicially. "I remember certain occasions when even I—"

"Please, Malone—none of your smoking-room reminiscences." She looked at her watch. "I must be brief." Malone murmured something about that being the day,

84

and then poured himself another highball as the school-teacher went on. "There's more about this thing that you'll have to learn later, but our first visitor should be here any minute. In answer to my ad, you see."

"What ad?" demanded Malone reasonably.

She triumphantly produced a clipping from her capacious handbag. "I had this inserted in every paper in town:

$2,000 reward for return of or information about Army officer's luggage marked ASN 0922493, left or checked somewhere in Los Angeles area Friday or Saturday. Phone Arizona 70015.

"You see, there was no trace of Ryan's suitcases or duffle-bag in the apartment—just the dead man. His wife and her supposed paramour would hardly have burdened themselves with *his* baggage on their mad flight, so where is it?"

Malone was considerably more interested now, perhaps at the mention of the two thousand dollars. "You actually got answers to that ad? Sure it wasn't the police?"

"Quite sure. The police would never bother to memorize that serial number, even if they read the Personals. One of the two men who called me had a most unpleasant voice, oily and greedy. I'm sure he knows something."

"But why make a date with him here? Why not your place?"

"I had my reasons. One is that I happen to have a guest at my bungalow, who mustn't be disturbed. And I confess that I got cold feet about being able to cope

85

with a person who is presumably a member of the underworld. So, since I learned that you were in town, I took the liberty of giving him—and the other man too —this hotel and room number, since I figured that someone with a trained legal mind could perhaps handle it better."

"But he'll expect to meet a woman, not me!" Malone arose hopefully, brushing the cigar ashes off his lapel. "Suppose I just run down to the bar for a while, and you call me there if you need me."

Like the Ancient Mariner, she held him with her glittering eye. "John J. Malone, would you desert a lady in distress?" As he sank back weakly, she added, "Perhaps you could masquerade in women's clothes and a wig and *pretend* to be me?"

Malone almost bit a piece out of his glass. "No!" he cried.

"I was afraid of that," sighed the maiden schoolteacher. "But couldn't you be present at the interviews, lurking behind a closet door or something? This first man who called me—he said his name was Kyzer or something—had a most malignant voice, and I'd rather not be alone with him."

The little lawyer was of the personal opinion that Miss Withers could take care of herself with anything up to and including a saber-toothed tiger, but refrained from saying so. "Okay. You've got the two thousand dollars ready?"

Her eyebrows went up. "Good heavens, do I look like Hetty Green? On second thought I'd just as soon you didn't answer that. No, I have no intentions of paying that money even if Eva does—I mean, even if I had it handy. Not to a man who is hand-in-glove with thieves and murderers or worse. I thought we could worm the information out of him when he gets here—whichever of the two it is. But this Kyzer—"

"Of all your mad ideas . . ." Malone said. "If anybody does show up, which I doubt, he'll probably just turn out to be a bellboy at some hotel where Colonel Ryan checked in Friday night and left his bags."

"The first man I talked to was no bellboy. A distinct criminal type."

"Coming here expecting two thousand dollars—and me without a weapon in the place except a safety-razor blade!" the little lawyer moaned. "Suppose one of these guys is really a thug? Why, he might be outside in the hall right now, and when he finds out he's on a wild-goose chase—" The phone rang suddenly, and Malone dropped his glass.

"Let me," Miss Withers said quickly. "It must be our first visitor calling from the lobby to see if I'm really here." She picked up the phone, and after a moment put it down. "It's only the bartender downstairs," she said. "He told me to tell Mr. Malone that Sugar says she is leaving and that her bar checks are on your account. Well, thank heavens that's one minor obstacle out of the way. Now we can really put our heads together and figure out a way to save poor little Eva."

"Eva?" queried Malone weakly.

"Yes. Eva Ryan, the missing wife—I mean widow—the police are hunting for."

"Relax. They've probably found her by now," he said hopefully.

'The schoolteacher shook her head. "Not unless they've been looking in my spare bedroom, because that's where she's been for four days."

Malone made sounds like a small penguin choking on a large spiny fish. "Oh, it's perfectly all right," Miss

Withers assured him. "The girl phoned me at once when she heard over the radio that her husband was dead."

"When she heard it? But she was *there!*"

"No, she wasn't. She'd hastily packed and left before Ryan ever got to the apartment. She took off the second she knew he was in town, because for good and sufficient reasons she wanted no part of him. Eva stayed in a hotel that night and naturally when she found out what had happened she called me—I'm in the phone book and years ago she was one of my pupils at P.S. 38 back in New York and she'd heard of some of my other adventures in Lost Causes—"

"Harboring a fugitive from justice," Malone said ominously. "Accessory after the fact, obstructing justice, *et al.* For this they can throw the book at you—"

There was a knock at the door. "There's your man," Malone whispered. He moved swiftly toward the closet, taking the bottle with him—presumably as a potential weapon.

Miss Withers opened the door with her heart in her mouth—and looked upon a big man with the map of Ireland on his face—a palish, mutton-lard face, now wearing an apologetic smile. "Come in, Mr. Kyzer," she said.

He came in, but he wasn't Mr. Kyzer. "I'm Dan Tendler," he explained. "About this ad of yours—"

The schoolteacher motioned him to a chair. "Yes? You know about the luggage?"

"No, ma'am." The big man crossed his meaty legs, and then uncrossed them. "I don't guess I can qualify for your reward, but—well, you see, I run a bar and grill downtown, and Saturday night my bartender went and cashed a check for a customer, an Army officer in uniform. It was only twenty-five dollars—but the check bounced. And underneath the signature was that same Army serial number you have in your ad—we always require a phone number or address or something and that was all the guy had." He sighed.

Miss Withers brightened. "May I see the check?"

It was on a local bank, signed *W. J. Ryan*. "With business the way it is," said Dan Tendler, "I'd like my twenty-five bucks. If you know where I can get hold of this Ryan—"

"I believe you'll find him at the morgue," she said. "Don't you read the front pages of the papers?"

The pale face blanched paler still. "You—you mean *that's* the Ryan that got murdered?"

She nodded slowly. "And what can you tell me that would help to find his killer, for the sake of his innocent wife?"

But the man was standing up, sweating. "Lady, I know from nothing. In a business like mine, you lose your license for most anything. I want no part of it. The guy come into my place and had a few drinks and cashed a bum check; that's all I know. I'll kiss the twenty-five goodbye and gladly; I just wanta keep outa it." He edged hopefully toward the door.

"Wait!" said the schoolteacher. "Did Colonel Ryan have any luggage with him when he was in your place that night, a few hours before he was murdered?"

"No, ma'am. Not that I recall. Saturday night is a busy time on the street, people coming and people going alla time. I know from nothing—only I'm out twenty-five bucks. Now I gotta cut the drinks all next week."

"But whom was he with?"

Dan Tendler shrugged. "A coupla guys—no dames, anyway. I wasn't watching." He hesitated at the doorway. "Maybe you don't have to mention this to the police. I try to run a clean place, but the cops and the Liquor Board bear down on us guys. . . ." He smiled, nodded, and took off—leaving the check in Miss Withers' hand.

"A dry run," said Malone, emerging from the closet. "That's not the guy you want, he's just a saloonkeeper who got stuck with a check. Walter Ryan wasn't in too much of a hurry to get home to his wife, was he? I begin to think you have an angle."

He sat down, with bottle and glass. "What next?"

"I don't know," admitted the schoolteacher. "But things begin to fit into the pattern. Mr. Tendler may know more than he wants to say now, and it may take more authority than we have to make him speak. Perhaps the police—"

"The police are full of thumbs instead of fingers," pronounced John J. Malone as he settled himself in a chair. "Well, that's that. Nothing more tonight, so I can call Sugar—"

"No!" said the schoolteacher. "Mocambo can wait. Human lives are at stake."

"Speaking of steak—" cried Malone hopefully.

"We still have an appointment with Mr. Kyzer, the man I am most interested in. Sit tight."

Malone sat tight, getting slightly tighter by the moment. And then after perhaps half an hour there came a heavy knocking at the door. "Here we go again," said Malone softly. He picked up the bottle and was about to take off for the closet when a heavy, official voice called out: "Open up in there; this is the police!"

"Already!" gasped the indomitable little lawyer. "Remember, Hildegarde, I'm your attorney and you won't talk unless I'm there. I may be able to cop a plea and get

90

you off with three to five years." He moved toward the door. "Come in, officer. What's the beef?"

Not one but three officers came in as he opened the door, the foremost a weary, graying man in plain clothes who flashed a silver badge and then announced: "I'm Sanders, from Spring Street Homicide. You the Malone who has this room? We just want to know why there is a stiff down the hall with your room number scribbled on a piece of paper in his pocket."

Miss Withers opened her mouth to speak, but for once in her life she was beaten to it. Malone said. *"My* room number? There must be some mistake."

"No mistake, mister." The detective turned wearily toward one of the uniformed men. "Show it to him." It was a slip torn from a pocket memo book, and on it was scribbled: *Hotel Southmere, Suite 1014.* Sanders went on. "The guy was about 40, 5′8″, 170 pounds, wearing a checked tweed suit. He registered downstairs as William Ross—probably a phony—and asked for a room on the tenth floor, so they gave him 1055. You know anybody by that description?"

Malone hastily denied it. "Well," said the detective, "he knew you and your room number. Maybe you're the one that smashed his skull with a sap an hour ago?"

"Emphatically not," said the little lawyer firmly. "During the last two hours I've been sitting right here, talking with my friend Miss Withers."

"Talking—and working on a bottle, eh?" Detective Sanders looked toward the schoolteacher, plainly indicating that there was no accounting for tastes. "Well, Mr. Malone, suppose you come with us and see if you recognize the stiff."

They all moved out of the room, and Miss Withers— who hadn't actually been forbidden to come—followed them eagerly, trying to look as if she were not there at all.

It had happened in a small bedroom down the hall, a room now crowded with the usual wrecking crew of photographers and fingerprint men, picking up the pieces. By craning her neck the schoolteacher got a good look at the corpse on the rug—a stocky, unpleasant little man who had never had much forehead and now had none whatever. Then she turned her attention to the two pieces of luggage against the wall—an Army footlocker and a big canvas kit bag, both marked with the initials *W.R.* and with a certain serial number which she at least remembered.

Across the room Malone was gazing upon the remains with distaste, and announcing that he had never seen the man in his life. "Just a minute, officer!" cried Miss Withers. "There's something you ought to know—"

"Later, sister." A big blue uniform noticed her, and she found herself shunted none too gently toward the hall door.

"But Sergeant Saunders—"

"Lieutenant Sanders," he corrected, barely looking up. He waved her off with a gesture, then turned to the uniformed man beside him. "All right, Marvin. What d'you mean, this guy's no Army officer?"

"I mean I recognize him, sir. He's a private dick, or was before he lost his license after he was caught being a go-between for some second-story mobs that wanted to make deals with the insurance companies for the return of stolen property. Name of Barney Kyzer, that's it." The sergeant subsided, looking pleased with himself.

"A wronggo, eh? Small loss. Okay." Lieutenant Sanders came out into the hall, Malone beside him. "Well, mister, just how do you account for a shady character like Kyzer having your room number in his pocket?"

"Mr. Malone is a famous criminal lawyer," put in Miss Withers helpfully. "It's possible that Kyzer was a would-be client who was planning to retain him. And—"

"All *right,* sister!" said the detective wearily. "Button it, will you?"

Malone shrugged. "Officer, I wish I could help you, but—"

"I could help you considerably," murmured the schoolteacher under her breath. "But at the moment I wouldn't give you the correct time. *Button it,* indeed!" She moved away, obviously somewhat miffed.

"All right, Malone," the lieutenant was saying. "We've got nothing on you now. But stick around town until we get this cleared up, understand?" He turned back inside, temporarily washing his hands of them both.

"Malone, you'll live out the rest of your days in California if you wait until that man clears up anything more than his own unpleasant complexion," the schoolteacher remarked as she followed the lawyer back to his suite again. "He refuses to listen to anything. If you ever hope to get off to Honolulu, we've got to solve these murders ourselves!"

"Which calls for a solvent," Malone pointed out, and poured one.

"But it is obvious that Kyzer is our link to the murderer of Ryan, who must have followed Kyzer here to silence him, to prevent him from talking to us. Kyzer himself must have been a party to the first murder—"

"He damn well was a party to the second," Malone agreed. "*Ipso facto.*"

"So this proves anyway that we're on the right road!"

"Here's one for the road," said the little lawyer, and downed it.

"But what can we do? Think of something, Malone!"

He was already thinking of something; at the moment he was thinking of relaxing on a couch and calling up Sugar. A vacation was supposed to be a vacation; on second thought the little Irishman decided that San Quentin Prison was no place for a rest, and he could already hear the sniffing of bloodhounds at his heels. "I've got an idea," he cried suddenly, hoping that he really did have one. Yes, there it was, almost full-fledged. "We've got an errand, Hildegarde. Grab your muff and tippet, and let's go." He was already heading for the door, not forgetting to stuff the bottle in his pocket.

"I know what you're up to," she said. "That dead man down the hall—the ex-private eye. You think he must have an office somewhere, and if we could get there before the police and search it—"

She was following the little lawyer down the hall. "I mean nothing of the kind," said Malone. "Burglary is beneath me, and besides I never learned how to pick locks. But I was thinking that I ought to talk with Eva Ryan before some smart copper down at Spring Street connects that Army serial number with your phone number—"

"But I didn't give my name or address!"

Malone sighed. "The police have ways of finding those things out. Though the pretty little Ryan widow may not even still be there . . ."

"How do you know she's pretty?"

"I was only hoping," Malone said, brightening. "Beauty in distress." And he added under his breath, "Also the only person in this case I might ever hope to get a fee from."

As they came down into the lobby he started looking for a taxi, but Miss Withers indicated her own modest

94

coupé parked down the street. "Right," said Malone. "And don't spare the horsepower, both of it. If you get a ticket, I'll take care of it."

She looked at him. "You might have to take thirty days in Lincoln Heights Jail, that's what speeding nowadays usually means in this town." But she stepped it up to a reckless thirty-five. Even so it was a long drive, during which the little lawyer stole several cat naps and a couple of nips from his bottle, but they finally arrived at a little frame bungalow on a palm-shaded street. The windows were dark.

"Your bird has flew—I mean flowed," said Malone in deep disappointment.

"Not at all. Eva's probably asleep." Miss Withers used her key and they went inside. Malone, who had straightened his tie and slicked up his hair in preparation for meeting the beauteous widow, found himself suddenly set upon and almost knocked down by a large brown creature whose paws almost touched his shoulder. As he drew back in sudden alarm, the schoolteacher said, "Surely you remember Talley, my poodle? Talley, this is no time for antics. Get back to your stove."

"He—he cooks, too?" gasped John J. Malone.

"No, of course not. He just sleeps on the stove when the lid is down, because the pilot light keeps him warm and cozy—something he worked out all by himself. I only hope our Eva is as warm and safe." She raised her voice. "Eva—it's I."

There was a short pause, and then a girl came out of the bedroom, wearing red pajamas which did nothing to conceal the fact that she was very nicely arranged indeed. She had midnight hair, no lipstick whatever, and eyes dark-rimmed with worry—like two burned holes in a blanket, as the schoolteacher would have said. She was a surprised girl, and a tall girl—so tall that Malone looked up at her with wondering admiration as Miss Withers performed the introductions. "I never lost a client yet," he vouchsafed, encouragingly.

"A lawyer?" cried the girl in dismay. "Has it come to that, already?"

Malone bowed, swaying a little. "Shall we just say a knight in armor, devoted to a fair lady's cause?"

She smiled feebly. "Maybe then I better get dressed like a lady. Excuse me."

The little lawyer would have liked to suggest that she slip into a Bikini, but he refrained. The girl disappeared for a few moments, then came back in a terrycloth robe, still looking luscious. It was hard for Malone to believe that with a wife like this waiting at home any returning soldier would delay for thirty-six hours, or even thirty-six minutes, and he gallantly said so.

"I wasn't waiting," Eva explained. "You see, I'd learned months ago that we were never legally married —Walter's divorce from his first wife wasn't final and it was phony anyway. Some detective named Kyzer framed it. The girl got a rotten deal, and finally committed suicide. Of course, I didn't know any of that then; we married in Las Vegas on the spur of the moment, and were living in the apartment on Wilshire only a few weeks when he was recalled to active duty. As soon as I found out I stopped writing to him, and when he got home I was going to get an annulment."

"I wouldn't mention that to the police, dear," put in Miss Withers thoughtfully. "They'd consider it a possible motive."

Eva nodded, shivering a little. Then Malone spoke up. "Did you know he was finally coming home?"

"No. The first I knew about it was when he called me

that Saturday night. He must have been drunk—his voice was thick and fuzzy. He said he was in a bar downtown with a couple of friends, but that they were leaving and he wanted me to come there and celebrate our reunion over a few drinks. He also said he'd brought me something that would make my eyes sparkle and make me change my mind about the annulment."

"He didn't mention the name of the dive?" asked Miss Withers hopefully.

"Why—" Eva hesitated. "I didn't pay much attention because I had no intention of going, but I seem to remember something about Dante's *Inferno*."

"Aha!" said Miss Withers. "Malone, I smell a mouse." Then suddenly they were interrupted by a thin eerie howl from Talley the poodle, who up until now had been snoozing comfortably at the feet of his mistress.

The schoolteacher leaped up like a Jill-in-the-box. "Talley always does that when he hears a police siren— with a dog's hearing he can get it minutes before we can! And if they're coming here . . ." She seized Malone and the girl. "We can't take chances now! Out the back way, both of you. Wait in my car in the back parking lot, and if anybody comes around pretend to be necking or something."

Malone opened his mouth to say something gallant, but Miss Withers shoved him ruthlessly toward the door. "Wait!" she cried, and rushed into the bedroom, thrust Eva's more obvious belongings into the girl's weekend case, and then hurled the bag at the fear-paralyzed young woman. "Off with you, now!" Before Eva and Malone were through the back door the schoolteacher was out of her dress and slip and into her nightgown; all the lights in the house were off and the little bungalow was dark and silent as a tomb.

A few seconds later the silence was shattered by the wolf wail of sirens; a black sedan came tearing down the street and stopped outside with a screech of rubber. Miss Withers, peering through the venetian blinds, nodded grimly as officers piled out, one of them running back along the side of the house to cover the rear door. So, she thought, the police did read the Personal ads, after all. She hastily let down her hair, then rubbed her eyes to make them look red and sleepy. When the heavy pounding came on her front door she was as ready as she ever would be.

But she let it go on for a moment, while she donned a robe and slippers. "Just a minute, just a minute!" she cried, then crossed to the front door, put on the guard chain and peered out into the face of Lieutenant Sanders. "May I ask," she snapped, "why you are trying to break in my door at this hour of the night?"

"Police business. Open up."

She opened. As the officers crowded inside, Sanders' eyes bugged out. "It's *you* again," he moaned. "I mighta known!"

"And who else would be living in my house?" She clutched her robe in maidenly modesty.

"I don't know," Sanders snapped. "But I'll damn well find out." He came forward, menacing. "Now just what do you know about the Kyzer murder, and the Ryan shooting?"

"Do sit down," she said, politely offering an easy chair and pulling Talley the poodle away from his usual vociferous welcome of any guest. "And I'll tell you. I tried to tell you at the hotel a couple of hours ago, but you said to *button it*." And that's first round to me, she thought complacently. She went on to tell most, if not quite all.

"So you lured Kyzer to his death?" said Lieutenant Sanders.

"My dear man, it's been years if ever since I lured anybody, anywhere!"

"I mean with this Personal ad!" The man's temper was wearing thin. "You say the Ryan woman gave you this information about the serial number on the missing baggage over the phone? Where did she phone from?"

The schoolteacher shrugged. "Naturally, being a fugitive from justice, accused of a murder she never did, she didn't tell me. But I knew that the person who had Walter Ryan's luggage also had some guilty knowledge or could lead us to someone who did, so I put in an ad and got two answers—I also got Mr. Malone to help and we were waiting for Kyzer—only somebody else got there first. Kyzer checked into the hotel with the bags and took a room on the same floor so they'd be handy to turn over if he was sure we were on the level, obviously."

"You and this lawyer Malone, eh? Why didn't he come forward with the information, huh?"

"You'll have to ask *him*," the schoolteacher said sweetly.

"Don't think we won't." The lieutenant stood up suddenly. "Personally, I think you know where Malone is—and the widow too." He nodded to his men. "Shake down the dump." And as they moved in quick obedience, he whirled on the schoolteacher again. "So why do *you* have to play amateur detective in this thing, eh?"

"Amateur I may be," Miss Withers came back. "But I can think of some other things besides the missing bags that slipped your official attention. How about the autopsy? Have they analyzed Ryan's stomach?"

"There's not much need of an autopsy on a guy with a .38 slug in his brain!'

"And if Lieutenant-Colonel Ryan had been carrying a pistol it would have been the official .45," she countered. "I checked, and the Army doesn't use the .38. So there goes your neat theory about the man's being killed with his own gun."

Sanders scowled. "And," she continued, "I wish for your own sake you'd see if they did a stomach analysis, and if not, order it done at once."

"I'm giving the orders around here!" he snapped. He broke off as the two uniformed men came back into the room. "Well?"

"Nothing, Loot, only—" The man held up a pair of exotic red pajamas, and Miss Withers shivered in her slippers. "These surely ain't *yours,* lady?"

There was an icy pause, and then Miss Withers drew herself up haughtily. "Even maiden schoolteachers have their moments, if it's any of your business!" And she snatched the telltale garment to her bosom. "Is a lady to have no secrets at all?"

Lieutenant Sanders shook his head, but he was almost grinning. He nodded to his minions and they started toward the door. Then he paused, sniffing. His eyes turned toward a bowl holding the schoolteacher's precious African violets, on the rim of which she saw to her horror a fat, half-smoked perfecto. "You smoke cigars, *too?*" he said with heavy sarcasm.

"Some women prefer them—" she began, and then saw it wasn't going to work. "However, if you must know, Mr. Malone drove me home this evening and came in for a few moments' chat."

"Oh," he said flatly. "Malone again. I think we'll just have a nice talk with that little shyster, in the back room at headquarters. We'll take your statement later—you be at Spring Street Homicide at nine tomorrow or we'll

100

bring you there in the paddy wagon, understand?"

She beamed at him from the doorway. "I'll always be most happy to give you any advice I can at any time, officer." His snort was loud and rude, but he went off toward the police car. The car was hardly out of sight when Miss Withers was into her clothes again and hastily putting back her hair. Then she rushed out the back way to where the anxious—and widely separated—couple were waiting in her little coupé.

"Quick, Malone!" she cried. "They've gone off looking for you, and we'll have to work fast. You must go to the deputy-coroner's office and find out about the autopsy, and I must get down to that dive on Main Street called Dante's Inferno—more probably *Danny's!*"

"And what about me?" asked Eva plaintively. "Do I just walk the streets in a robe and slippers until somebody arrests me or I freeze to death?"

"You go back to bed, child," the schoolteacher said.

"But—"

"The police just searched the place and aren't likely to search it again. It's the safest spot in town for you. Run along now—and wish us luck." They roared away, with the girl and Talley looking wistfully after them.

Malone took a last sip from the upturned bottle and dropped it meticulously into a trash can as they came out of the alley. "I don't like this," he said.

"My driving?" She reared up.

"I don't like that much either. But I was going to say that you've got things all wrong. You can get more out of the deputy-coroner's office than I can—and I can certainly case a saloon better than you, being more familiar with the terrain."

"Again I advise abstinence," she told him. "But after all, there is something in what you say. So be it. When

101

I get through with my errand at City Hall I'll come down to the Inferno and drag you away from the bar and the B-girls."

"You wrong me, dear lady," Malone said. "If I do have to take a drink, it will only be to loosen the bartender's tongue."

She looked at him with a twelve-pound look.

Such was her haste that she dropped Malone off near a taxi stand on Park Place, turning north toward City Hall. Miss Withers spent twenty minutes in finding the right office—the one lighted office in a long dusky corridor—and another half hour in getting the information she sought from sleepy incumbents, during which she had to swear to all sorts of imaginary kinship with the murdered man. "But then," she told her conscience, "all humans are cousins, under Adam or the apes."

Anyway, she had found that her hunch was true. It had not been only alcohol which had made Lieutenant-Colonel Walter Ryan's voice sound thick and fuzzy over the phone to his estranged wife—the wife who was so frightened of his coming that she had packed and got out of the apartment posthaste. There had, it seemed, been a routine test made of the dead man's stomach, and while alcohol had shown up in abundance, there had also been traces of chloral hydrate.

"Knockout drops!" said Miss Withers as she wheeled down Main Street, the Skid Row of Los Angeles, past honky-tonks and burlesque houses and all-night movies, past tattoo palaces and a hundred evil-looking bars which advertised "girly" shows. The place called Danny's Inferno would, she felt, bear some looking into, since that was where Ryan had cashed his check and no doubt

102

been drugged. She felt certain qualms about Malone's being there at all, and wished she had warned him to abstain completely from drinking anything. Not that it would have done any good, she said to herself.

She nearly missed the place when she came to it, for the big electric sign was dark. Hastily parking in a yellow zone—and resolving to make Malone pay for the inevitable ticket—she rushed up to the front doors, which bore a handprinted sign: SORRY. CLOSED.

The curtains were drawn tight, but she fancied she could see a faint crack of light. She hammered firmly on the door, but nothing happened. Then, placing her ear against the panel, she heard male voices raised in song; it was a duet in which the more prominent voice was one she knew only too well. "Malone rides again!" the schoolteacher said with a sigh, and went on hammering.

The duet continued unabated—they were doing "The Rose of Tralee" with flourishes. In exasperation Miss Withers kicked the door.

"Step aside, sister," said a hoarse male voice behind her. "We'll gladly smash it in for you." She turned, to look again into the not especially pleasant face of Lieutenant Sanders. "Oh, *no!*" he cried. "Not three times in one night! How do you get around, on a broomstick?"

"I'd prefer a broomstick to a nightstick any time," she snapped. "But go ahead and see if you can get inside the place. Malone is in there, and I fear the worst."

"Him too?" Sanders took a pistol from his pocket and tapped the glass of the front window, almost but not quite hard enough to crack it. "Malone I want to see," said the lieutenant grimly. "And when I do, he's going to sing out of the other side of his mouth." He rapped again, harder, and this time the glass did crack. The singing inside stopped abruptly, and a moment later the door was jerked open.

"What the bloody hell—?" roared Dan Tendler. "Can't you see I'm closed?" His voice trailed away as he caught a flash of the badge cupped in Sanders' hand, and his pudgy pale face grew paler still. Silently he stepped back, and they entered a dimly lit, longish barroom, smelling of stale alcohol and staler tobacco, and with murals on the walls which Miss Withers glanced at once and then kept her maidenly eyes well away from.

Malone was leaning at the far end of the bar, a glass of beer in his hand, a bottle of rye before him. He looked up with innocent pleasure. "Why, if it ishn't the Loot and my pal Mish Wizzersh! Join the party, folks. Have a drink on my good friend Danny—'

"Shut up, shyster," snapped Sanders. "Your turn comes later." He whirled on the owner of the place. "Listen, you. Did a bum known as Hoppy work here?"

The big man nodded. "Sweeps out the place, cleans up tables, washes glasses. Or he did. Hoppy didn't show up Sunday."

"You know why?"

"Somebody said he was took sick."

"He was took dead," Sanders rasped. "About an hour ago in County Hospital—from something he drank in this dump!" The policeman edged closer. "You know what that means?"

Tendler looked from one to the other, with tears in his eyes. "Honest, I know from nothing. Hoppy had a habit of finishing any drinks left on the tables, and maybe—"

"No maybe. You know what he got."

The big man nodded slowly. "It musta been a Mickey.

I phoned the hospital, and that's what they said. He had a weak heart—"

"That's why you're closed up, at only midnight?"

Tendler nodded again. "Outa sympathy for poor Hoppy. And—and because—" The man smiled sheepishly. "You know when somebody gets a Mickey in a bar, the place is padlocked. I was just having a sort of wake about it with Mr. Malone here."

"No friend like a new friend!" sang out Malone happily, and then at the lieutenant's look buried his face hastily in his glass.

Sanders stuck a pugnacious chin into the bigger man's face. "All right, Tendler. Why'd you do it?"

"*Me,* Lieutenant? By my sainted mother in heaven, I never slipped anybody a Mickey in me life!" The man was shaking like jelly.

"Just a minute, please," spoke up Miss Withers. "I think I know who really did it." As Sanders turned on her, she continued sweetly, "I happen to know that Walter Ryan phoned his wife from here that night, and his voice was thick and fuzzy—one of the first symptoms of chloral hydrate. And I also happened to check with the deputy-coroner's office a few minutes ago, and Ryan was undoubtedly unconscious from the drug when he was shot. He must have got the knockout drops here —given him, presumably, by one Barney Kyzer."

"*What?*" Sanders ripped a photograph from his pocket and shoved it before the big man's eyes. "You know this fellow? Was he here that night?"

Tendler took a hopeful breath. "Sure I do, sure," he said, wincing a little at the dead, bloodied face. "He came in quite often—yes, I seem to remember he was here that night."

"With this guy?" Sanders produced another morgue

photo, this time of a handsome youngish man with an Army crew cut.

"I—I think so. Yes, they was sitting in that rear booth, and they stopped talking whenever I brought over another round of drinks. The good-looking guy cashed a bum check, and once he staggered over to the bar to get change for the phone. He was definitely feeling no pain."

"You see, Lieutenant?" Miss Withers' voice was sweet.

But he ignored her. "There were just the two of them, then?"

"Yes—I mean no." Tendler's eyes narrowed in concentration. "First the two, then three."

"And the third man?"

Tendler was thinking hard, evidently most anxious to please. "I seen him once or twice before, I guess. Not a regular. He was a lean, gnarly little guy with a nose too big for him, dressed sorta zoot-suit style, with a high squeaky voice."

The lieutenant was making notes. "And that," put in Miss Hildegarde Withers, "is the man who killed Kyzer in the hotel tonight—to keep him from giving the whole show away by turning their victim's luggage over to me, in the hope of making an extra two thousand dollars. Don't you see. Lieutenant? They must have doped Ryan's drink, of which he drank only a part. He still had strength enough to phone his wife and get out to the apartment in a taxi before he dropped. They followed him there, found him unconscious and shot him."

"Speaking of drinks—" began Malone.

But Sanders faced Miss Withers. "Lady, what motive would anybody have to kill a man who'd been out of the country for years?" The policeman was weary.

106

"What motive indeed—unless Ryan was in possession of something very valuable that he'd brought home from overseas? According to Eva Ryan, her husband's job with the army of occupation was with JAG, which was charged with the impounded assets of the National Bank of Tokyo. There must have been jewels—if so, that would explain Ryan's remark to his wife over the phone that he'd show her something to make her eyes glitter!"

"I always have found," Malone put in reminiscently from his distance, "that breaking a hundred-dollar bill in a bar does the same thing."

"Go on!" Sanders ordered grimly. "I mean *you*, lady."

"I'll try. It's all deduction, with a smattering of guesswork. But if Ryan pocketed a fistful of precious stones at the time of the fall of Japan—"

"You mean to tell me that a guy like that would sit there for that many years waiting to cash in?"

"Of course he would! He was smart, smarter than the Army officer who pulled the same trick in Germany and came home only to get caught when he tried to trade an emerald for a new automobile—you read about that. That's why Ryan didn't ask for leave or discharge for so long; he wanted the missing loot to be forgotten and he wanted to wangle some Korean duty so he could come back from a combat area as a hero. I understand there's little or no customs inspection for such people."

Sanders nodded slowly. "Some sense in that. But why would a guy that smart hunt up Kyzer and another thug and get drunk and tell them all about it in a bar?"

"He didn't, Lieutenant. He must have hunted up Kyzer—who had once worked for him on a framed divorce case and who he knew had lost his license for deal-

107

ing with the underworld—because he thought that for a fee the man would introduce him to a professional receiver of stolen property."

"A fence, we say." In spite of himself, Sanders was growing interested.

"Evidently Kyzer pretended to fall in with it, and introduced him to the third man. But the two thugs put their heads together, having correctly figured that Ryan must have hidden the loot in a railroad station locker or in a hotel. They drugged Ryan, followed him home, found the locker key in his pocket and then shot him to silence him forever—figuring the murder would be blamed on his wife, as it was."

"Beautiful wife," put in Malone helpfully. "Never shushpected her a minute."

Sanders waved at him, "Go on, lady. It's mostly maybes, but go on."

"Well," continued Miss Withers, "even for a fence, jewels take time to handle. Kyzer was greedy, and he fell for my trap and the offer of the reward for the now valueless luggage—which of course by this time they'd found and stripped. But the third man also read the ad, watched Kyzer, followed him to the hotel and bashed out his brains before Kyzer could spill anything, thus leaving himself in full possession of the loot. Simple, isn't it?" she added.

Lieutenant Sanders' mouth was tight. "The third man! Well, we gotta good description. We'll round up every fence in the area first thing tomorrow morning and have a line-up." He turned to Dan Tendler. "You be at my office at nine sharp, Fatso. If you can identify this guy for us maybe I'll see that you don't get padlocked after all."

The big man's face lit up with hope. "Sure, and I'll be there," he cried, shaking Sanders' hand until the detective winced.

The lieutenant started to go, then whirled on Malone. "As for you, shyster—"

"Mr. Malone didn't offer any information at the hotel because he thought he was protecting his client's interests," Miss Withers put in quickly. "Or the girl he thought might become his client. Besides, he's in no condition to be questioned now."

"None whatever, ash you can plainly she," agreed Malone amiably.

The detective hesitated. "All of you at my office, then," he capitulated. "Or else!" He went out without farewells, slamming the door so that the cracked window cracked a little more.

The barroom was silent for a long moment. "Come, Malone," said the schoolteacher firmly. "Time to go beddy-bye."

"No!" he protested, clutching his bottle. "The wake's not over. I'll have 'nother drink and 'nother singsong with my pal Danny-boy." He draped his arm lovingly over the big man's shoulders. "You know 'Mother Machree?'"

Tendler was apologetic. "Sure do, Mr. Malone. But I guess I better close the place up. I'm not feeling so good. Some other time, huh?" He went over to the cash register, hit a key and scooped out every last dime. Then he reached into the back row of bottles which lined the rear of the bar, choosing a bottle of rum. He stripped off his apron and lovingly stuffed the bottle in his coat pocket. "Nothing like a hot rum toddy to make a man sleep after a hard day—and believe me, folks, this was plenty hard. Murder in my own place—probably lose my license—a bum check . . ." He sighed, and moved toward the light switch. "Okay, folks."

Malone finished his drink somewhat reluctantly, while Miss Withers tapped an impatient foot. "Look," the little Irishman cried, suddenly inspired. "We can't just let my pal Danny go home alone, and him in his cups and not feeling himself at all."

"Aw, I'm okay!" Tendler protested.

"No. My pal Mish Wizzersh here gotta car outside—we'll drive you." The big man protested, but Malone would not take no for an answer—though the school-teacher, thinking wistfully of bed and also of the anxious girl waiting for her at home, glared at him. They came out to her car—which had its ticket, as she had expected—and wheeled off, Malone and his lifelong friend of one evening together in the back seat, singing, "In Dublin's fair city, Where the girls are so pretty. . . ."

Luckily for her eardrums and for her temper, it was a relatively short ride to a modest apartment in the Ambassador section. Dan Tendler climbed out hastily, said a mumbled word of thanks and went a bit unsteadily inside, evidently deaf to Malone's suggestion that they had just time to come in for one last drink. The doors closed behind the man, and Miss Withers put the car into gear.

"Hold it," said Malone when they were halfway down the block.

She looked at him askance. "Isn't it time for all the bars to be closed?"

"No bars indicated," he said, in a different voice.

"Malone, you're cold sober!" she gasped.

"Only relatively, ma'am. I spent a lot of time, and

had to have a lot of drinks, trying to get next to Mr. Tendler."

"Yes, I know. But *why?*"

"Turn the car around and park over there in the shadows, and I'll show you."

Bewildered, she obeyed, and they sat there for a few minutes. "I've made a bet with myself," Malone explained. "And I think I'll win it. Watch."

They watched for nearly half an hour. Then a taxicab came up before Tendler's apartment house and beeped its horn three times. The man came out a moment later, wearing a hat and topcoat and carrying a small suitcase. He entered the cab, which made a U-turn and roared off south.

"Here we go," said John J. Malone. "Hildegarde, will you for *once* see if you can get this heap out of second gear?"

It was a lost cause. Miss Withers almost caught up with the taxicab at one red light, but traffic at this late hour was light and, once on the boulevard, the cab drew steadily away. Finally it was gone. "What do we do now?" she demanded.

"Keep going," said Malone sensibly, gesturing toward a sign at the intersection which read: LOS ANGELES INT AIRPORT—5 MILES. "That's where he's headed, and if there's a plane leaving for anywhere in the next few minutes we're ruined! Can't you go any faster?"

"I suppose I could get out and push," snapped the schoolteacher. "But I still don't understand—"

"Tendler is the third man," explained the little lawyer. "I thought you were getting suspicious too when Tendler remembered Ryan and Kyzer after so long a time and could even describe the third man down to his clothes and voice—the voice he wasn't supposed to've

111

heard because they stopped talking whenever he came near. And the description of the third man was just the exact opposite of his own—he overdid it there! He wasn't calling on you in the hotel because of the check —I'd guess he wrote it himself as an excuse to butt in and find out what was going on; he found out enough to make him see he had to get rid of Kyzer then and there, which he did. But it puts him in the hotel at the moment of the murder. I wasn't really sure, however, until he took home a bottle of rum—after him drinking good Irish whisky with me for two hours! A whisky man doesn't drink rum, not with him having the choice of the bar."

The schoolteacher gasped. "And he's going to get away with it? Not on your life. I have one shot left in my locker, so hang onto your hat." She shot it; coming to an intersection where a motorcycle officer was lurking, she crossed the street against a red light with her horn blaring. There was the howl of a siren and she was flagged down. "Thank heavens," she said fervently as the very young, pink-cheeked officer came forward.

"Just where is the fire, lady?"

"It'll be under your pants," Malone told him, "unless you use your little radio and get a cruise car out to the airport in time to stop a big fat man who's probably getting out of a taxi right now and climbing aboard a Mexico City plane. We're on the trail of a double murderer, my man. Working with Lieutenant Sanders."

"I've heard 'em all, but that's a new one. You say you know Sanders. Describe him."

"He's a rude, impolite character who throws his weight around," put in Miss Withers. "He has a potbelly, an unpleasant complexion and a most unpleasant manner."

The officer froze, and then his face broke into a reluctant grin. "You know Lieutenant Sanders all right; I worked under him before I got transferred. Just for the hell of it, I'll make that call."

Miss Withers and Malone sat with crossed fingers while he spoke briefly into his walkie-talkie. Then something he heard galvanized the youthful cop into action. He leaped aboard his motorcycle and dashed away.

"It's a shame," said the schoolteacher thoughtfully, "that he didn't give us a chance to tell him to look for the jewels in the bottle of rum which your bosom pal Danny Tendler is intending to smuggle *into* Mexico."

"They'll find it," Malone assured her. "We gave them enough and they can figure out the rest. My pal Danny is going nowhere but to the gas chamber."

She turned the little coupé around. "And now, Malone, you can go back to your hotel and nurse your hangover—which I'll admit you acquired in a good cause. I'll go home and take the good news to little Eva. And tomorrow night you can take Sugar to Mocambo."

John J. Malone hesitated. "Hildegarde, have you ever been to Mocambo?"

"Me? No, of course not. My tastes and my wardrobe are more fitted for Barney's Beanery, with its $1.25 dinners. But if you insist—"

"I think I insist," said the little lawyer gallantly. "But do you know, Maggie will *never* believe this!"

*

Rift in the Loot

ͲͲͲͲͲͲͲͲͲͲͲͲͲͲͲͲͲͲͲͲͲͲͲͲͲͲͲͲͲͲͲͲͲͲͲͲͲͲ

"I AM IN NO MOOD to face it now, whatever it is," said John J. Malone firmly as he came into his office shortly after eleven that morning. "Maggie, have we any aspirin in the place, and if not will you be a good girl and run down to the drug store?"

"No, *twice*," said his long-suffering secretary. "You can sweat out your hangover the hard way. I've got to stay here by the phone; it's been buzzing all morning. First, Joe the Angel called and said that just after you left his bar last night a man came in asking for you. Joe said he could always smell a *wronggo* a block away and maybe you ought to watch yourself."

Malone watched himself in the little wall mirror, wincing slightly. He adjusted his lush Countess Mara tie, already well-dusted with cigar ashes. "So what? In the legal profession one meets all kinds of people."

"Joe the Angel seemed to think that this was one you wouldn't want to meet in a dark alley. And, boss, it *may* be coincidence, but it says here in the *Tribune* that

Eddie Vance busted his way out of Joliet yesterday."

The little lawyer's face brightened. "Eddie the Actor is loose? This may be good news—maybe he'll get to where he stashed that bank loot and finally pay me my fee!"

"Maybe he'll cut your throat, too," Maggie said darkly from behind her typewriter.

"But *why?* I saved him from the chair, didn't I? Never lost a client yet."

"Yes, you saved him. But he still got a hundred years at hard labor, remember? And before he went to the penitentiary he is reported to have squawked very loud that you double-crossed him and must have made some deal with the D.A.'s office."

Malone grinned. Harbin Hamilton, deputy district attorney for Cook County, had for years been trying to nail Malone's hide to the barn door, and the little lawyer wouldn't give him the correct time. But Malone's grin was feeble. "Yes," he admitted thoughtfully, "Vance may have got stir-happy. I suppose I could leave town until they pick him up."

"I have just seven dollars between me and a life of shame, which they say is nice work if you can get it. You couldn't get to Evanston on seven bucks." Maggie looked at her desk pad. "Also Miss Hildegarde Withers is in town, stopping off en route to New York on a holiday, and she wants to have lunch with you."

"Not that—not *today!*" Malone had three times been involved in murder cases with the irrepressible schoolma'am, always with considerable risk to life and limb and with no appreciable fee; but he still had an inexplicable fondness for her. "Okay, call her back and tell her I'll meet her at Henrici's at one."

116

"Since *I* have to put up the money," said Maggie sensibly, "we'll make it Thompson's cafeteria." She reluctantly produced five dollars out of the remainder of her week-before-last's pay check. "And watch yourself, Malone. Eddie the Actor is a very nasty character, and I wouldn't be at all surprised if he's the man with the oily voice who's been calling all morning and trying to find out when you'll be in and refusing to give his name. *Why* we ever took that case—"

"I was appointed by the court as a public defender," Malone reminded her. "Eddie was supposedly broke, though we all knew that he had some $50,000 of the bank's money hidden somewhere—only he never could get to it and wouldn't or couldn't tell me or anybody just where it was. If he'd talked and turned back the loot, I could maybe have got him off with only fifty years."

"Which still is a long time to hang by your thumbs or sit on a red-hot stove, any way you look at it," Maggie said with a certain tone of veiled sarcasm.

"Not so long when you consider that a bank guard got killed during the caper. We were lucky."

"*We?*" Maggie echoed.

But she relented and went out for the aspirin.

"Exactly why," demanded Miss Hildegarde Withers over their luncheon coffee at Thompson's, "are you looking over your shoulder so often, Malone? Guilty conscience?"

"Maggie believes that I am a marked man," the little lawyer admitted hollowly.

"Another murder case?" cried the schoolteacher, brightening. She wore a hat which could have been put

117

on top of a Dutch chimney for storks to nest in, but her gray-blue eyes were keener than ever. "I could stop over a day or so and help solve it."

He blinked. "This one was solved three years ago—no mystery about it at all."

"Then why are you as jittery as a Mexican jumping bean?"

"Well—I'll fill you in on the story. Eddie Vance, known in underworld circles as Eddie the Actor because he has a wardrobe of uniforms and always manages to look like somebody else when he pulls a bank job, knocked over the Irving Trust, dressed as a window cleaner, with the help of three masked confederates. During the fracas one of them, a cheap hood named Jack Shaw, lost his head and killed a guard. The other two accomplices were shot down by police outside the bank, but Eddie Vance and Shaw escaped in different directions. Eddie himself has never been known to carry a gun, but of course technically he was accessory in a murder. He got away with the loot, some $50,000 in small bills; he was free for just one day but during that time he managed to hide it somewhere. Shaw is still being sought by the police, but since he had no previous criminal record and they have no photographs or finger-prints to work on, it's a tough job. I was appointed to defend Eddie the Actor, and got him off with a hundred years, a minor victory."

"A hundred years is a rather long time," said Miss Withers.

"You took the words right out of Maggie's mouth. But there's still the matter of that cache of dough. Eddie promised me ten grand of it if I saved him from the chair—which I did, with a neat bit of legal sleight of hand, even if I say it myself—but I never saw a red cent

118

of it. Now he's suddenly busted loose and Maggie thinks that maybe he has a grudge because I wasn't able to get him off with a lighter sentence. Maybe she's right, too. Eddie the Actor is a guy who could fight a rattlesnake and give it the first two bites."

"Dear me!" gasped the schoolteacher. "The company you criminal lawyers keep! Malone, it's obvious that you must get out of town for the next few weeks, until the police succeed in re-arresting this unlovely character. You can come along with me to New York; my car is having something done to its remission or whatever they call it, but they promised at the garage that it would be ready tomorrow."

Remembering her driving, Malone almost thought that he would rather face Eddie the Actor, but with his usual gallantry he refrained from saying so. "Maybe—"

"Maybe me no maybes. You're coming. I just got a nice bonus on that movie cartoon case I told you about, and I can afford to finance you if necessary, as I presume from past experience that it is. The first thing is to get you packed and out of your hotel before this Eddie character tracks you down. Come on, time is of the essence."

The little lawyer obediently followed her out of the restaurant and they took a taxicab to his hotel. "Maybe you should wait in the lobby?" Malone suggested.

She bridled. "Certainly! Do you think I'm in the habit of going to men's hotel rooms? Besides, the place is probably a shambles."

It was—not to the surprise of John J. Malone when he entered the room, since he had left it so. The only surprise was that a bellboy sat in the one easy chair, reading early editions of the *Herald-American*. On second look he was a rather mature bellboy with a very short haircut and the face of an intelligent weasel. The

119

little lawyer did a double take. "Eddie Vance!" he cried. He took a deep breath. "Now, Eddie-boy, there's no need to get tough about this."

Vance smiled. "You got me entirely wrong, shyster." His hand hovered near his lapel, and it was fairly obvious that if Eddie the Actor had once had an allergy to firearms he had conquered it while in prison. "Siddown, shyster, and listen. I busted out of the pen, see? I came out in a can on the garbage truck—"

"Type casting," murmured Malone under his breath.

"—and I'm going to stay out, understand? I'm going away, to South America or Cuba maybe, but first I've got to get to that dough of mine. You help me get it and I'll see you're taken care of." He made an unpleasant gesture. "If you *don't*—"

Malone sat down very, very carefully on the unmade bed and tried to relight a cigar that was already glowing. "Er—an interesting idea, Eddie. Somewhat startling, and a little out of my line. Where is the stuff?"

"It's safe, in spite of that punk Shaw, the hophead who blew up and blasted the bank guard. He's been trying through the grapevine to get me to spill where I stashed the loot so he can dig it up and get his cut—or more likely, if I know him, to take it all and scram. I figure he's got nothing coming." Malone could see that point of view, and nodded. "Anyway," continued Eddie the Actor, "the place where I hid the stuff I can't go near it, see? On account of right now I'm hotter than a three-dollar pistol and there's always a chance that the law has a stake-out there. So you're going to pick it up for me."

"Have you ever considered that my face is as well-known to the police as yours, if for somewhat different reasons?"

Obviously Eddie hadn't. He thought. "Then you've got to get somebody else to go, somebody you can trust, if you want your fee—and you want to stay alive." The man, Malone thought, was obviously as tense as an E-string. "How about your secretary?" Vance suggested hopefully.

Malone shook his head. "Maggie is strictly on the up and up—she'd have none of it."

"Well then, somebody else—or *else!*" The man was desperate.

At that auspicious moment there came a sharp knock at the door. Malone started to rise, but a pistol popped into Eddie's hand, waving him back. The knock came again, and then a voice from the hallway. "Malone? I know you're there, so open up!"

"It's only—only a client I'm expecting," the little lawyer improvised hastily. "And I've just got the idea that she might be the answer to our problem." He rose and went to the door, to admit Miss Hildegarde Withers.

"Malone, I waited—" she began, and stopped, seeing the ersatz bellboy.

But Malone shook his head at her warningly. "Cut it, Tillie. You don't have to go into your act here. Toledo Tillie, this is Eddie the Actor, a former client of mine, and he wants something done that I think you can do better than anybody—for a reasonable cut, of course. Nothing rough, it just involves picking up some merchandise, and picking up maybe a grand for yourself."

Miss Withers sniffed, sighed resignedly and sat down on a hard chair. "So what's the caper?" she inquired, in her best approximation of a voice likely to be Toledo Tillie's.

Eddie Vance was staring at her, almost incredulously. Malone said hastily, "I'm defending Tillie when her case comes up next month, charged with conning department stores. She's out on bail now."

"Hiya, Tillie," said Eddie, extending a hand. "You certainly got the front—you look *too* respectable, almost." He turned to Malone. "Can we trust her?"

"I'd trust her as I would my sainted mother," swore the little lawyer shamelessly; his sainted mother had abandoned him on the steps of an orphanage when he was a few days old. "As you can see for yourself, Eddie, she could walk right past any police stake-out without the cops giving her a second look. She could go right into your girl friend's house, maybe peddling books or something—"

"Wait a minute!" cried Eddie the Actor. "How'd you know . . . ?"

"I didn't, until you just told me," Malone admitted. "Though it seemed only natural that you'd have stashed the loot at Ethel Megrim's house somewhere, just as it seems natural the cops would be looking for you to show up there now. Even if they searched the place at the time of your arrest and found nothing. They know how close it was with you and Ethel. Miss—I mean Tillie here can walk into the place and get Ethel to hand over the money. Well, what do you say?"

Eddie Vance scowled, looking at the schoolteacher rather as if she were a used car that he contemplated purchasing. *"Maybe,"* he conceded. "Say something with uptown class in it."

"I *beg* your pardon!" Miss Withers sniffed again. " 'Beauty is truth, truth beauty; that is all ye know . . . and all ye need to know.' Keats."

She's got the lingo," admitted Eddie the Actor grudgingly. "I'm not one to trust dames much. I didn't even trust Ethel when the thing happened; I sent her out for a jug that night and stashed the loot while she was gone. She has no idea of where it is, so she can't just hand it over to this old dame or anybody, see? And"—he continued as Miss Withers seethed inside—"I don't want Ethel to know about it now, or she'd insist on tagging along with me to Cuba or somewhere and help spend the dough. I'll pick me a señorita down there."

"Very sensible," observed Malone coolly, avoiding Miss Withers' glare.

Eddie the Actor threw away his cigarette and nervously lighted another. "Only how do I know Tillie here doesn't just grab the loot and lam?"

"She wouldn't think of that—" began Malone.

But the schoolteacher interrupted. "Nobody can say that Toledo Tillie is a double crosser—there are ethics in my profession, Mr. Vance. I only steal from marks. Anyway, I don't need your dough, only I could use a small cut because of this con rap I'm in at the moment."

Vance nodded. "Okay. But remember, even if I'm hot I got connections, and if you did try to get out of town with my money you wouldn't get farther than Gary, Indiana, before you'd feel a shiv in your back. Understand?" He said it almost pleasantly. "Well, then —here's the dope." And he told them where the bank loot was hidden—under the rosebush in Ethel Megrim's back yard.

"How clever!" Miss Withers said admiringly. "It should be a cinch."

"Not unless we get Ethel out of the house while you do the job," Vance insisted. "She's sharp, and she'd catch on if you showed a sudden interest in the garden or anything. There's only one way to work the pickup." And he told them the address and the phone number and the plan—and a rather ingenious plan it was, too.

123

"Take it from there," said Eddie the Actor. "I'll meet you—no, I'll phone Malone here sometime tonight or tomorrow. And no tricks. Understand?"

He went quickly out the door.

"It's much too tricky for me," said Miss Withers to Malone after she had got her breath. "I played along because you obviously wanted me to, but this isn't honest. We should call the police at once. Malone, I'm disappointed in you."

"We haven't much choice," pointed out the little lawyer wryly. "Go ahead, and don't ask too many questions." He picked up a bottle. "I don't suppose you'd care to join me in a highball?"

"There wouldn't be room enough," snapped the schoolteacher, and huffily departed. She had always known that the little lawyer cut corners now and then, but this—even under duress—was violating all sorts of laws about receiving stolen property and harboring a fugitive from justice and heaven knew what else. Well, she had given her word—or Toledo Tillie's word—and was morally or immorally bound to go through with it.

So she sought out a big bookstore on Michigan Boulevard and provided herself with the first volume of an expensive set of encyclopedias; thus armed she set forth for Rogers Park. Argyle Street was mostly lined with apartment houses and stores, but here and there were sandwiched brick bungalows of which Ethel Megrim's was one.

The block in question seemed to be deserted except for a woman with a baby carriage filled with groceries and baby, an empty taxicab and two small boys who were manfully trying to wreck each other's tricycles. Yet she took no chances, working her way along the street

124

from door to door, peddling her wares. Few people were home at this hour; most of the apartment houses had *No Peddlers or Agents* signs, or locked entry doors, but somewhat to her surprise she got orders for two sets of the encyclopedia before she finally came to the apartment building across the street from Ethel Megrim's home. It had been too good to last. There was a burly, pink-faced man in the lobby, leaning against the wall and reading a newspaper somewhat too elaborately; from where he stood he had an excellent view of Ethel's doorway. "Oh, my prophetic soul!" murmured Miss Withers. "The law is already here." But, as she knew from experience, a frontal approach is often the best. So she came boldly up to him. "Excuse me, but do you have the time?"

He looked at her. "Three-thirty," he said, unsmiling.

"Oh, dear, only that? And two more hours I've got to spend canvassing for this old encyclopedia before I can take my shoes off and relax." She sighed, and then smiled hopefully. "It's an excellent set—if you don't have one at home would you like to look at the sample volume?" She extended it. "Real buckram."

"No, lady," the man said, with considerable finality. The schoolteacher paid a token call at two apartments in the building, and then went across the street feeling that the man was watching her over his newspaper. Prudently she first tried the house next door to Ethel Megrim's—and walked into an open-armed reception from a wrinkled old lady with incredible, henna-flaming hair, who was obviously dying for someone to talk to. The schoolteacher's pitch for the encyclopedia was almost drowned out by a spate of words; she had to accept a cup of tea and listen to the bright sayings of Mrs.

Gardner's grandchildren, admire their snapshots, lend an ear to all the neighborhood gossip, and be regaled by a play-by-play account of a morning soap opera.

Finally in desperation Miss Withers rose to go. "And I'll think about the encyclopedia," Mrs. Gardner conceded. "You drop back tomorrow, and we'll have another chat and another nice cup of tea."

The schoolteacher nodded vaguely. "I must get back to work now, though. How about your neighbor; do you think she might be interested?"

"That Ethel Megrim? I shouldn't think she reads much—she's too busy hanging on that TV set of hers when she isn't carrying on with her boy friend. He's a taxi driver and if you ask me . . ."

Finally Miss Withers tore herself away and rang the bell next door. Luckily Ethel Megrim was at home. She turned out to be a rather prettyish woman in her late thirties, carrying a bit of extra weight and somewhat long in the tooth. She was wearing a housecoat that had seen better days; the television set was blaring and she had evidently been enjoying a can or more of beer. She did not feel any desperate desire for a set of encyclopedias, which was no surprise to the schoolteacher; while polite, Ethel was evidently anxious to get back to her beer and her TV program. But as Miss Withers took her departure she managed to distract the younger woman's attention just long enough to press the button which disengaged the Yale-type lock of the front door. Hurdle one was over, anyway. She took the El back downtown and found John J. Malone in his hotel room, alone except for half a bottle of Canadian rye.

"I'm giving you a case of Antabuse for Christmas," she said tartly. But she condescended to report on the recent exploits of Toledo Tillie. Malone sobered up instantly.

"Then all we've got to do now," he announced, "is to figure out a way to lure Ethel out of the house."

"That shouldn't be difficult. Have your precious Eddie Vance call her up and ask her to meet him under the statue in Lincoln Park or somewhere."

"Fine. Only we don't have the faintest idea of where to reach him."

"Too true." Miss Withers tapped her somewhat prominent front teeth with a fingernail. "Wait—I have an inspiration! Ethel Megrim is *mad* for television. Suppose you phone her and pretend to be representing some TV program and if she'll be in the lobby of the Tribune Building at eight tonight she'll be paged and taken up to the broadcasting studios to appear on a new secret giveaway program with a chance at a truckload of prizes if she can pick the right tune or something?"

Malone stared at her, then raised his glass. "To a brilliant suggestion!"

"And to a brilliant hangover tomorrow morning, if you keep trying to climb into that nasty bottle." But she smiled proudly. "Well, Malone, get on the phone."

It was no sooner said than done, or almost. Ethel Megrim was incredulous at first, but when Malone in his most histrionic manner assured her that her name had been chosen by lot out of the phone book she swallowed the thing hook, line and sinker. Malone turned to Miss Withers. "We have time for dinner," he said. "Except that the only place I have credit is Joe the Angel's City Hall Bar. . . ." He ruefully surveyed the remains of Maggie's five-dollar bill.

"I insist on treating," the schoolteacher announced.

127

"We'll go to the Empire Room at the Palmer House and fortify ourselves with succulent viands for the nefarious enterprise on which we are embarking."

"You have twisted my arm," Malone told her. "I always like to do my housebreaking on a full stomach."

A couple of hours later they came down Argyle Street in the misty rain, huddled under Miss Withers' umbrella and with Malone's Borsalino pulled well down over his eyes. But there was no sign of the man in the doorway. "Natch," said the little lawyer. "Ethel went out on our fake setup, and the cop tailed her hoping she'd lead him to Eddie the Actor." They went across the street to the narrow brick bungalow. The front door opened easily and they were inside the dark living room, which smelled of cheap perfume, beer and dust.

"No lights," Malone warned Hildegarde quickly. He cupped his hand over the bulb of his flashlight and they walked through the deserted house which made up in depth for what it lacked in width; it had been built like a New York railroad flat. There was a bedroom and a bath, a dining room, and a long narrow old-fashioned kitchen which Miss Withers thought smelled faintly of mice. They went through a service porch and at last came out into the back yard.

"Holy St. Vitus!" gasped John J. Malone. There were at least *twenty* rosebushes in the narrow place, completely enclosed by a six-foot fence topped with barbed wire. And the only tools available seemed to be a rusty hoe and a trowel. "Where to begin?"

" 'Begin at the beginning; go on until you come to the end and then stop,' " quoted Miss Withers. And so they set to work in the feeble glow of Chicago's moonlight, filtered through the scattering rain clouds, their labors only slightly lightened by the blare of radios

128

from the open windows of the apartment house next door. One was playing a Crime Doesn't Pay program, which the schoolteacher thought especially appropriate under the circumstances. Gloves and fingers were torn on the savage thorns; stubborn roots clung tightly to the sticky clay. They dug and they dug and they still dug, and they still failed to come up with the money.

Suddenly Miss Withers dropped her trowel. "What was that, Malone? Wasn't it a scream?"

"Sure. On the radio programs they always scream. Or maybe a tomcat on one of the fences. Back to work, we've got seventeen more bushes to disinter."

She bent down, and then straightened up again. "Malone, we're wasting time."

"You mean Ethel found the dough? Believe me if she had she'd be halfway across the world by now."

"Not that. But remember, Vance said the money was buried under *the* rosebush, which he then replanted. Wouldn't that indicate—?"

"That when he stashed it she had only one, and later she planted others?"

"You know nothing of roses, except perhaps Four Roses, which I believe is a brand of whisky. We have only to look for the *oldest* rose—the bush with the thickest stem."

Which they did, and it was there under a foot of muddy earth: a bundle of bills big enough to choke a horse, or at least a pony, wrapped tight and dry in one of the plastic bags ordinarily used to keep vegetables fresh in the refrigerator. Malone reached out his hand, but Miss Withers dusted off the package and placed it firmly in her capacious handbag. "Not so fast," she said firmly. "The disposition of this blood money has to be discussed, and I intend to make one last appeal to your conscience. It isn't rightfully yours, or Eddie Vance's, and—" She stopped short.

From where they were standing, in one corner of the garden, they could see part of the side of the long narrow house. A light had suddenly come on in the windows of the front room!

"She's come home ahead of time!" the little lawyer gulped. They were trapped, just at the moment of victory. He glanced at the fence. "Do you suppose—"

"No, Malone. I couldn't climb that fence in my prime, which I am definitely not in. Nor could you. We've got to go out as we came in, if at all."

He nodded ruefully. "But *why* would she come back now?"

"I can guess. Suppose that on her way down to the studio Ethel just happened to remember that she had a *private* phone number, known to Eddie Vance but unlisted? So the TV people couldn't have picked her name out of the phone book for their program. She smelled a rat and came home. Now we're in for it."

"Maybe she'll get tired and go beddy-bye?" Malone suggested hopefully.

"You forget there's no second floor to the place. We have to go through her bedroom, and there's every chance that she'd wake up and grab a pistol and shoot us both for burglars—which in a sense we are." The schoolteacher shook her head. "I don't like any part of this, and besides I think I'm coming down with double pneumonia."

For an eternity of minutes the two conspirators huddled together in the chilly dark. Malone was shivering too, in spite of occasional nips at the trusty fifth in his topcoat pocket. "I'd rather dodge bullets," he whispered through chattering teeth, "than freeze to death. I'm going to reconnoiter. You wait here."

He tiptoed toward the back steps, but Miss Withers tiptoed right behind him.

"Where you go, I go," she told him firmly. "Up to a point, that is." They moved silently across the service porch into the kitchen, which was as dark as the bottom shaft of a coal mine, though somewhat warmer. Malone felt his way forward and into the dining room, with Miss Withers sticking closer than a sand burr. His cupped flashlight cast a faint glow ahead.

Through the bedroom they crept, toward the faint crack of light under the door. Malone waved Hildegarde back, and cautiously squatted in front of the keyhole.

"What do you see?" the schoolteacher whispered.

"Nothing but a piece of wall," he muttered. "Hildegarde, it's *too* silent in there!"

"Maybe she's gone out again?" Miss Withers suggested hopefully.

He turned the knob, a fraction of an inch at a time, and then softly pulled the door toward him. As it swung open, the bright lights of the living room half blinded them—and then they saw it. Miss Withers bit her knuckles to keep from crying out.

Ethel Megrim lay sprawled in the center of the rug, her limbs every which way—like a puppet loosed of its strings. There was red seeping through the bleached honey color of her hair, and blood on her face. As the two intruders bent over her, she raised herself a little and moaned something through bruised and battered lips. Then they heard her say, "He—he hurt me— I didn't *know*, I *didn't*—" Her body gave a convulsive shiver, and she fell back again.

131

"Do something, Malone! Get an ambulance!"

He shook his head, and surreptitiously crossed himself. "There's nothing for us to do now but make tracks out of here—and quick!"

Malone was mistaken about that. They weren't going anywhere, according to a pink-faced, burly man who stood in the door of the front hallway, hands in the pockets of his gray topcoat. To Miss Withers he looked at least half again as tall and as broad as he had looked that afternoon, pretending to read his newspaper in the lobby across the street.

"Officer, we can explain *everything!*" she cried quickly. "We were out in the back yard, and we heard a scream. . . ."

He came slowly forward, tense and frightening. "I heard a scream too," he said. His hand went into his pocket, and they caught the flash of metal. "Kelleher, Fourth Precinct. Get back against the wall, both of you." He looked down at the dead woman, almost incuriously. "Pistol-whipped her, eh?"

"But we don't even have a gun!" Malone put in. "You can search us! The person who did this must have got out through the front door—"

"And if you were watching the house from across the street you must have seen him go out!" finished the schoolteacher triumphantly. "You did, didn't you?"

"I'll ask the questions," the big man said. "First, who are you and what in hell were you doing in the back yard at this time of night?" He looked at them. "Making mud pies?"

"See my lawyer," said Miss Withers, nodding at Malone.

Malone gulped. "Look, officer—I'm John J. Malone,

132

the attorney. Call Captain Daniel von Flanagan at Twelfth Street; he'll vouch for me. I hope!" the little lawyer added under his breath.

"Shut up. So you're Malone, eh? The criminal attorney who defended Eddie Vance—and now you're caught red-handed over the corpse of his former girl friend! This is bigger than I thought. What did you come here for, Malone? And where is it?" The big man took a .45 automatic out of his pocket. "I said, *where is it?*"

He had backed Malone against the wall and was deftly frisking him. Then he stood back. "Okay, take off your clothes and throw 'em over here to me!"

"Please!" gasped Miss Hildegarde Withers in horror, stumbling swiftly into the bedroom and closing the door firmly behind her. There were sounds of fervent protestations from Malone, which suddenly ended. There was no arguing with a detective who packed a .45, Miss Withers conceded. Again she thought longingly of that back fence—if somehow she could hoist herself over it. . . . And then a better idea came to her.

But ten minutes later, when the door was flung open, she was standing in the bedroom, looking as innocent as a newborn babe is supposed to look—by anyone who has never seen a newborn babe.

"*Your* turn, sister!" announced Kelleher.

"Over my dead body!" the schoolteacher snapped. "You have no right even to suggest such a thing! When you call headquarters to report this you can ask them to send a matron, but until then—" She raised her omnipresent umbrella menacingly.

"That's the law," put in Malone, "as you know very well, officer."

The man hesitated uncertainly, and then compromised by patting her exterior somewhat gingerly. Next he reached for her handbag. "Give, sister."

"Has a lady no privacy?"

"Not when it's homicide, she hasn't." He snatched the bag from her fingers and unceremoniously dumped the contents on the floor. It was Malone's turn to gasp—there was everything in that magpie's nest *except* Eddie the Actor's loot! The little lawyer stared at her in wonder.

"Blast it!" their captor swore, with trimmings. He hesitated for a moment, then made up his mind. He snatched the tie which Malone was at the moment replacing around his neck and tossed it to Miss Withers. "Tie his hands behind him—behind the back of that chair!" The gun waved menacingly, and the school-teacher obeyed. The belt was whipped from Malone's waist, and she had to strap it around his ankles. Then, horror of horrors, she was herself tied up in the same fashion with curtains ripped from the windows. "There, I guess *you'll* stay put," said the man with the gun. And he disappeared into the back of the house, whence echoed sounds of a frantic search.

Miss Withers looked from Malone to the stiffening corpse on the floor and back again. "For a policeman, he has very unorthodox methods," she said calmly.

"He's no cop," Malone agreed. "He didn't phone in, and cops in Chicago carry .38 pistols, not .45 automatics. He's obviously after that dough. Where'd you hide it?"

"Never you mind! We've got to get out of here, now!"

"Now, *how?*" the little lawyer asked reasonably.

"I tied you with a granny knot, naturally. It'll slip if you work at it."

"No!" But she had and it finally did, and they went

into what was undoubtedly the fastest disappearing act in recent history. It was not until they were half a dozen blocks away that Malone slackened his pace and entered a drug store to telephone, emerging almost immediately. "That was quick," the schoolteacher remarked. "What did von Flanagan say?"

"I didn't talk to him. I just told the cop at the switchboard that I was a neighbor of Ethel Megrim's and that I'd heard a scream there . . ."

"But we ought to go back and be around when the police arrive!"

"You mean be around when that thug comes out shooting! And, Hildegarde, he's a cinch to have found that money by now, wherever you hid it."

She shook her head, smiling a Mona Lisa smile. "No, Malone."

"Well, where is it?"

Another shake. "No, Malone."

"You don't trust me," the little lawyer said sadly.

"Of course I do—just the way I'd trust my poodle with a piece of T-bone. And now, if you don't mind, it's late and I'm wet and muddy and I've just had about all an old-maid schoolteacher can take for one day. Good night, Malone—phone me in the morning." And she popped into a waiting taxi and was off and away. Malone stared after her with some bitterness, and then noticed the lights of a bar and grill across the street, gleaming a welcome through the mist.

"With my luck it'll be a mirage," he muttered gloomily. "But at this point even the mirage of a saloon would be better than nothing."

In the cold gray light of the early morning, something awakened John J. Malone. He sat up in his own bed and gingerly shook his head to see if it would fall off, which it almost did but not quite. It was amazing that a man could get a hangover like this on one bottle and two bucks to spend in a bar; somebody must have liked the way he sang "By Killarney's Lakes and Dells" and set up the rest of the drinks.

Then the knock at the door came again, more insistently. He fumbled his way into a robe and shot the bolt. "Come in, Eddie," he said.

But it wasn't Eddie Vance; it was six feet of policeman in the shape of his ancient adversary, Captain Daniel von Flanagan, who almost trod on Malone's toes as he pushed his way into the room. He was smiling, but you could have refrigerated Death Valley in July with that smile. He folded his arms. "I should have known better," said that worthy if thumb-fingered policeman with some bitterness, "than to trust a lawyer any time, anywhere."

"Wha-a—huh?" muttered Malone brilliantly. "Look, Captain, I haven't even had breakfast—"

"Well, pour yourself three fingers of breakfast and then talk. See if you can talk yourself out of having your meals behind bars for the next dozen or so years. Let's start with Ethel Megrim, huh?" He plumped himself down in a chair.

"Oh, *her*." Malone drank, choked, and drank again.

"Yes, her. She up and got herself murdered last night, as if you didn't know."

The raw whisky hit Malone's stomach with a comforting warm thud, and rose slowly to dispel some of the fog in his brain. "And just *why* should I know?"

Von Flanagan snorted. "Because you yourself called Twelfth Street before the poor woman was cold, and reported it without giving your name. Only the man at the

136

switchboard happened to recognize your golden tenor voice." Malone said nothing, and the other pressed on. "There's them downtown that think you yourself killed her."

"Me? Why?"

"Maybe because she came home unexpectedly and found you burglarizing her place, looking for that loot of Eddie Vance's. Maybe it was you who was digging up her back yard?"

Malone's mind was dashing about like a bird dog in a thicket. "How can you say such a thing, Captain?" Von Flanagan made no answer, but he was staring significantly at the heap of muddy clothing flung on the radiator last night. The little lawyer winced, and decided to retire to previously prepared positions. "All right," he said resignedly, "I'll tell you. It was the fake cop who did it. When Miss Withers and I—"

"Not *her* again?" cried von Flanagan. "This is too much!"

"I was saying that when Miss Withers and I came in out of the back yard we took him for a cop attracted by the scream—he was in the doorway, only he must have been just *leaving* instead of just coming *in*. Only he hadn't got what he came for, and went along with the gag when he saw us, thinking that maybe we had it . . ."

"The dough—Vance's loot! And you did have it? Where is it, Malone? Did he get it?" The questions came thick and fast.

Malone shrugged. "I'll swear by all the saints in heaven, I'll swear by the memory of my blessed mother, God rest her soul, that I have no idea of where on earth that loot is, unless it's still somewhere in Ethel's house."

"Phooey! My men tore up every inch of the back

137

yard, they ripped up floors and knocked out walls, and I'll swear that there isn't even so much as a postage stamp that they missed! But go on talking."

Malone talked as he dressed. He told the whole story, with some cautious emendations—all about the talkative woman next door who had told Miss Withers about Ethel's new boy friend who was a chauffeur or taxi driver or something, about the fake summons from the TV studio that was supposed to keep Ethel safely out of the way, about the cop who wasn't a cop at all and who had tied them up while he went on searching the house. . . . He told everything except about the money; at the moment that wasn't his secret anyway. "So there's your murder case, Captain," he concluded, "tied up in a bag. With Eddie Vance safe in prison, this guy started to cultivate the ex-girl friend, because he must have figured that she knew where the money was. Eddie's prison break forced his hand—he watched the house figuring Eddie might come there to pick up the cash. When Ethel left the house last night he tailed her, figuring maybe she was going to meet Eddie somewhere. She got wise, turned around and came home, and he followed her in and tried to beat her into telling him where the loot was. But she couldn't tell him because she didn't know, and he lost his head and hit her too hard—just like he blew his top and killed that bank guard three years ago."

"*Shaw!*" cried von Flanagan triumphantly, as if it had been his own discovery.

"Who else? All you have to do is pick him up—"

"Phooey! If we couldn't pick up Shaw for that other killing after three years of trying, how do you expect us to pick him up for this one?" The policeman shook his head. "Get the rest of your clothes on; we're going down

138

and see the D.A. This is one time you've overreached yourself, Malone."

The little lawyer thought fast. "And just what do you think Deputy District Attorney Harbin Hamilton will say when he finds out about a certain phone conversation we had yesterday?"

It didn't stop von Flanagan, but it slowed him down a little, and Malone worked fast on his temporary advantage. "I've got an idea," he said. "We're all in this pretty deep, but I see a way out. You want Eddie the Actor for prison break, you want the loot, and you want Shaw for two killings, right?" He went back to the selection of a tie, almost too casually. "What do you think of this one with the hand-painted flamingoes?"

"I wouldn't wear it to a dog fight. Yes, we want Vance and Shaw and the dough. But you've fixed it so all three slipped through our fingers . . ."

"Well, then," said Malone—and in a few well-chosen words he stuck his neck out farther than ever before in his checkered existence. It took some fast talking, but he was used to bedazzling twelve jurors and a judge, and von Flanagan was only one man and not too bright at that.

"It better work, before seven o'clock tonight when I go off duty!" warned the detective from the doorway. "Or I know somebody who'll get disbarred but fast." He went out, slamming the door. Malone sighed, and knotted the tie with the pink flamingoes, but his heart wasn't in it. And what to tell Hildegarde when he called her? He decided to fortify himself first with another drop, but had barely lifted the bottle when there came a knock at the door.

"Western Union for Mr. Malone."

Wearily he opened the door. "Come in, Eddie." This

139

time it *was* Eddie Vance, shaking the drops from his uniform cap. He kicked the door shut behind him.

"Well, shyster? What luck?"

"Plenty," Malone said quickly. "Sit down and have a drink. I have every reason to believe that Miss— I mean Toledo Tillie—was successful, but it's a ticklish situation and I haven't got in contact with her yet. You see, Ethel Megrim got killed last night—"

"I heard," Eddie said. "Poor Ethel. But what about my dough?"

"Tillie is under wraps because of the murder, but she'll find a way to get in touch with me. Only we've got to be careful—von Flanagan was just here."

"I saw him in the lobby," said Eddie the Actor. "And if you're thinking of making a deal with him—" He patted his pocket with an evil grin. "I want my dough and I want it today, see?"

"You name the place and we'll be there, or at least she will. How about Field's basement at closing time, or the I.C. station at Randolph when the commuters are all going home? Or the south lion in front of the Art Institute?"

Eddie hesitated. "I like to work in the open. I guess the Art Institute is best. Six o'clock, okay?"

"Okay. You can take the dough, hand over my fee and Tillie's cut, and lose yourself in the crowd."

"Check. But tell her to be there on the dot. And don't foul this up, Malone, or you'll both be using a marble slab for a mattress, see?" He went out, slamming the door. Malone took a deep breath and a deeper drink, then called up Miss Withers. The schoolteacher was in a somewhat better mood than last night, and agreed to buy him a cup of coffee in fifteen minutes. He went out of the hotel through the rear service entrance, just in

140

case von Flanagan wasn't trusting him, and shortly thereafter he was seated in the Palmer House coffee shop opposite his partner in crime. Her guilty conscience was not preventing her from attacking a copious repast of oatmeal and bacon and eggs, all of which made Malone feel slightly green.

They were both slightly green when he told her what he had promised von Flanagan in order to get rid of him. Miss Withers dropped her spoon. "No!" she cried.

"Yes," he said. "Look, you know where the dough is, so that takes care of Point One. We can deliver Eddie Vance, who's so crazy-mad for his loot that he'll walk into the trap. . . . I'll phone von Flanagan to have his men at the Art Institute at six. Then all we've got to do is to get ourselves off the murder rap by locating Jack Shaw—unless he found where you stashed the money and is far away by now."

She shook her head. "I'm positive he didn't, or the police either. Let me think, Malone. We know Shaw is a cab driver. If we checked all the taxi companies—"

"It would take days, and undoubtedly he's using a phony name. It isn't as if we had a picture of him," the little lawyer objected. They sat for a while in glum silence. Then the schoolteacher's long and faintly equine face lighted up like a lamp.

"But I *have* a picture of him, indelibly imprinted on my mind! Don't you see? The man has gone scot-free so far because he had no police record, no photos or fingerprints on file, and he wore a mask on the bank job. But now it's different. Now two people know what he looks like! Malone, do you know any friendly newspaper reporters?"

"I know all of them," he said with some pride. "And they're all friendly."

141

"Well, one of them is going to have a story for the early afternoon editions. Because it will help if while we're looking for Mr. Shaw *he* is looking for *us!* We'll spill the news that there are two eye-witnesses to the Megrim murder who can positively identify him!"

"A trap—with you and me as the cheese? Look, Hildegarde, isn't it enough to have Vance and the police on our tail without bringing Shaw into the act too? I'm too young and too wicked to die just yet." But Miss Withers prevailed, as she had a way of doing, and Malone went ahead and phoned one Ned McKeon at the *Herald-American.* "He says he'll squeeze it on page one somehow," the little lawyer reported. " 'Two unidentified witnesses, names withheld, at scene of the Megrim murder . . .' Only Shaw can identify *us* all right."

"And so perhaps can your friend Captain von Flanagan?"

Malone said that he wasn't sure von Flanagan could read, and that if he could, and did see the story, he'd probably keep his promise to hold off long enough to give them rope to hang themselves. They could only wait, and hope. The waiting, they decided, should be in or around Malone's office; his name and address were in the book and if Shaw came sniffing after the bait he would presumably come there first.

It was Miss Withers who brought up the moot question of what, if anything, they could do with or to Mr. Shaw if he did come. Malone thought. *"Maggie!"* he said.

"I have the greatest admiration for your secretary, but—"

"Maggie has a brother, and the brother has friends," Malone explained.

So it was that some hours later—about the time the

Herald-American hit the stands—Miss Withers found herself staked out in the vacant suite across the hall from Malone's office, in the company of the little lawyer and two very tough-looking characters indeed, who had mumbled, "Pleasetameecha," and then settled down to a fast game of pinochle.

"Gangsters?" she whispered.

"Worse," Malone came back. "From the circulation department of the *Gazette*—to them murder and mayhem are jolly pastimes."

"Are they armed?—I hope?"

"Tire irons and a length of heavy chain."

So they waited and waited—and still waited. The hands of the old-fashioned watch pinned to the schoolteacher's old-fashioned blouse crawled around and around. There was no sound anywhere but the snap of the cards and the occasional tinkle of small change. Nothing happened, and nothing kept on happening. " 'The watched pot—' " quoted Miss Withers.

And then the phone rang suddenly in Malone's office across the hall, whose door had been left invitingly open. Malone leaped eagerly to answer it, since Maggie for obvious reasons had been given the afternoon off and sent out of the combat area. "Hello?" he cried breathlessly, Miss Withers leaning over his shoulder. "Hello? John J. Malone's office—hello?" He put down the phone in disgust. "They hung up on me!"

"You mean *Shaw* hung up on you! Obviously he was making sure you were here. Malone, it's working!" She almost did a little dance.

"It had better work, before seven o'clock!" he came back grimly. "Von Flanagan is a man of his word and if we don't make that deadline . . ." He shuddered, and they went back across the hall, eyes glued to the crack in the door, ears keyed to the sound of approaching foot-steps. . . .

Five o'clock—then five-fifteen. "I can almost hear the clang of that cell door right now," Malone murmured sadly.

"Well," the schoolteacher said sensibly, "why not get out of town? My car ought to be fixed by now—we could be halfway to New York by morning."

"And von Flanagan could have Wanted flyers out for us before that. We'd be hauled back in handcuffs." They waited some more. It became five-thirty, then five forty-five. "That's that," said Malone. "We've just got time to get to the Art Institute and keep the date with Eddie Vance. Let's go." He borrowed a ten from Miss Withers and slipped it to their troops, who departed in some dis-appointment.

"Von Flanagan should certainly settle for two-thirds of what you promised," the schoolteacher said. "Getting Eddie the Actor—and the money—"

"Maybe," said Malone, without much hope. "He is a reasonable man, but not very." They hurried out of the building. There was a taxi at the head of the line, the driver a shortish stocky man deep in a racing form, a battered uniform cap over his eyes.

They hustled inside. "The Art Institute, and hurry," Malone ordered. He leaned back in the seat, and re-freshed himself from the remains of his bottle. It was the hour of densest traffic, and Miss Withers felt that they could have made better time by walking. Once or twice their driver cut through alleys with the dexterity of long practice, but always sooner or later they found themselves hemmed in with traffic again.

"Malone, isn't the Art Institute east of us, on the lake front?"

He barely opened his eyes. "Yes, Hildegarde."

"Well, our driver is going west."

"Probably making a circle to avoid the jam at the Loop."

She was silent for a block or so. "Malone!" she whispered. "Notice the door handles?"

He looked, then gaped—there weren't any! "Driver!" cried Malone, and tapped on the glass partition. The driver half turned, suddenly sitting up straight so that his bulk showed. He also showed an automatic pistol in his left hand, and his face was the face they had seen last in Ethel Megrim's living room over her dead body.

"*Shaw!*" gulped Malone.

Miss Withers was frantically pounding on the door window with her umbrella handle, and waving pleadingly at passers-by. One or two of them waved back at her, but that was all. She tried to scream. . . .

Shaw rolled down the partition and waved the gun in their general direction. "Cut it out," he spat at them. "Or you'll get it here and now."

They cut it out. The man was driving like a madman, but evidently that was the way taxi drivers were expected to drive. They beat red lights and raced past boulevard stops, heading west and south, with the driver keeping one eye on the rear-view mirror. Miss Withers moved a little closer to Malone, as if for comfort, but he caught her lips moving almost soundlessly. "Next stop—the one, two, three." He nodded a quarter of an inch. . . .

There was a moving van at the next light, waiting for a left turn, and the taxi had to screech to a stop. Miss Withers kicked Malone sharply on the shin, and then her trusty umbrella came up like a striking snake, the crook of its handle around Shaw's neck, and she jerked with all her strength. The gun went off through the top of the cab and John J. Malone lovingly brought down his whisky bottle on the man's head to finish the job. "Bull's-eye," said Miss Withers placidly.

It took only seconds for the little lawyer to climb over into the front seat, shove the unconscious Mr. Shaw to one side, and take the wheel. It had all happened so fast that they had rounded the corner and were a block or so north again before he remembered to pick up the uniform cap and put it on his own head.

"It's only ten after six!" announced the schoolteacher. "Perhaps we can still make the Art Institute in time!"

Malone's only answer was to put his foot on the accelerator and his hand on the horn. A traffic cop or two whistled shrilly after them, but as luck would have it they met no minions of the law on wheels, and soon they were rocketing up the Boul Mich, now heading north. They roared up before the Art Institute at last, to find the area practically deserted. There was no sign of Eddie Vance, no sign of von Flanagan and his men. Two husky street cleaners were sweeping the gutters nearby and putting refuse into a Department of Sanitation truck—but both were too tall and brawny to be Eddie Vance. The only other figure in the vicinity was an art student with owlish glasses and a smock who was painting a portrait of one of the benign stone lions against a background of lighted skyscrapers. He was obviously not Vance either.

"You'd better get out and look around and let yourself be seen," advised Malone. "I'll stay here and sit on Shaw—maybe you'd better give me your scarf so I can tie him up."

Hildegarde left the cab, strolled up the sidewalk for

half a block, and then back again. It was almost six-thirty, and she had a deep presentiment that they had missed the boat. Back at the steps of the Institute again, she paused to pat the north lion, paused again to admire the painting of the solitary artist. . . .

There were two sharp beeps from a cab which had just pulled up in front of Malone's. "Taxi, Tillie?" It was a voice she recognized, though it now wore a mustache.

She leaped a foot in the air, and then started down the steps, her knees trembling like Jello. Her eyes flashed this way and that in a desperate appeal for help—but there seemed no help in sight. Malone was either bent over his bottle or his prisoner, or both. There was nothing to do but to get into that second taxi—and what Eddie the Actor would say and do when he found she had double-crossed him . . .

Eddie leaned back to open the door for her and she stumbled inside. The taxi moved ahead.

And then suddenly the truck from the Department of Sanitation pulled out squarely in their way. One of the street cleaners produced a riot gun, the other a pistol. Wonder of wonders, the artist on the Art Institute portico ripped off his glasses, kicked aside his easel, picture and all, and turned out to be Captain von Flanagan. Miss Hildegarde Withers flung herself to the floor of the cab, both hands over her ears—and then it was all over, without a shot being fired. Eddie the Actor came out into the street, both hands held as high as he possibly could. When frisked, his pockets produced only a water pistol.

"Take him away," said Captain von Flanagan to the two street cleaners, who turned out to be crack detectives from Fifty-fifth Street. "And him too," he ordered, when Malone opened the other cab door and Jack Shaw rolled out into the gutter.

Miss Withers took Malone's arm, and they stood there, waiting for von Flanagan's applause. But the Captain squirmed out of his smock, hurled it to the ground and faced them belligerently.

"I'll never hear the last of this down at Twelfth Street," he growled. "And say, you—where's that loot you were supposed to deliver?"

Malone shrugged, and looked at Miss Withers. "I could tell you," she said, "but I'd rather show you—if you don't mind a trip to Ethel Megrim's house."

"We searched that place with a fine-tooth comb!" von Flanagan roared. "I'll eat my hat—or your hat or *anybody's* hat—if there's so much as a dime there!"

"Did you ever read *The Purloined Letter* by the late Edgar Allan Poe?" she inquired sweetly. Von Flanagan snorted, but it was nothing to the snort he snorted when, after a fast ride uptown in a squad car, she led them to Ethel's refrigerator and took from the vegetable compartment a plastic bag containing lettuce. Inside the lettuce was a wad of currency large enough to choke a horse, or a small pony. "The loot, Captain," she beamed. "As Poe definitely would not have said, 'Look for the lettuce in the lettuce.' I put it there while Shaw was searching Malone's clothing for it, since at the time I trusted neither Shaw nor Malone."

There was a long silence. "Hildegarde, you wrong me," said the little lawyer sadly. "I was always going to turn it in, wasn't I, Captain? Didn't I phone you when all this started and promise to deliver it if you'd keep hands off for a day or so?"

The policeman nodded.

"Well, then," said Miss Withers. "I owe you an apology, Malone. I thought you were after the money, or a large slice of it. But virtue, this time, is its own reward."

Malone smiled. "There are *other* rewards. This is bank loot, remember—and banks have surety companies. We should not do too badly. Now let's get out of here before Captain von Flanagan keeps his promise and eats your hat!"

*

People vs. Withers & Malone

ⲦⲦⲦⲦⲦⲦⲦⲦⲦⲦⲦⲦⲦⲦⲦⲦⲦⲦⲦⲦⲦⲦⲦⲦⲦⲦⲦⲦⲦⲦⲦⲦⲦⲦⲦⲦⲦⲦ

"Don't look at me so *askance!*" said John J. Malone as he crept into his office at two P.M. "I can't stand much more."

"You could stand a bromo," said the faithful Maggie. Then she saw his eyes turn hopefully toward the Emergency file. "You took the bottle with you when you left last night. That was just after you borrowed my last ten dollars."

The little lawyer winced at the noise of the fizz, but he raised the glass, squaring his shoulders under the nearly new, somewhat rumpled, dove-gray Finchley suit. "To the memory of my once illustrious career," he toasted hollowly.

"I gather you had no luck last night."

"You gather correctly. I hit every saloon from here to the boondocks, but never a trace of the missing Mr. Taras. They've got him hid, all right." Malone sighed. "The latter part of the evening is a blur—in fact, I seem to have had a blackout. However, I just might have

151

stumbled on something; I found a string tied around my finger when I woke up in a Turkish bath, I find I wrote a check without filling in the stub and I seem to remember the name Little Helga, but that's all."

"I hope the check was for under $3.65," Maggie told him. "Because that's the current bank balance."

The little lawyer searched his pockets, fished out a lone cigar with a greenstick fracture which he tried vainly to light. "Maggie dear, you can put this down in your diary as Black Wednesday."

"Only it's Thursday," she corrected. "Which means that our client dies in less than a week, and then it's *your* turn to go before the grand jury, as if we both didn't know."

They were silent for a long minute—which was more than could be said for the apparition in raincoat and umbrella which suddenly swooped in on them like a large raven looking for a bust of Pallas Athene on which to perch. But this bird did not croak, "Nevermore"; it only cried, "Malone! Maggie! Here I am!" Miss Hildegarde Withers, whom they had thought safely busy with her own pursuits in faraway California, now warmly embraced them both. "I came as soon as I heard how bad it was," she told them.

"Welcome to the wake," Malone told her.

"Fiddlesticks! You can't win 'em all—this Coleman case was lost even before you got hold of it."

"Yes? Well, Junior Coleman only got life at the first trial, when he was defended by his rich father's stuffy old law firm. I won him a new trial and what did *I* get him? A death sentence!"

"I'm more worried about this subornation charge against you."

"Leaving ethics out of it, when did I ever have a thou-

152

sand dollars at one time—for bribery or any other purpose?"

"A good point. What steps are you taking, Malone?"

"Looking for clues," said Maggie. "And in the usual place—at the bottom of a bottle."

"I was trying to locate that witness, Taras, who said in court that I'd tried to bribe him. He disappeared right after the trial. And just maybe I did get a lead on him last night." He told about the string on his finger, the missing check and the name "Little Helga."

"Probably a tip on a horse," said Miss Withers. "Well, I know it's always been your proudest boast that you never lost a client, but you must accept what you cannot change. You did your best."

"There isn't even a chance that the Governor will intervene," Maggie put in. "Our client as good as confessed to a reporter who got to him in the death cell yesterday. Said he can't remember having done it, and he must have been crazy to do a terrible thing like that —but he's resigned to his fate."

"*He's* resigned!" yelped Malone. "Junior can't do this to me—he's stir-crazy, that's what he is!"

"It's too late for an insanity plea," Hildegarde moaned, "but something *must* be done. Mary Margaret O'Leary, don't just stand there. Coffee is indicated— black and piping." She shooed the secretary on her way, then firmly sat herself down on the edge of a hard chair. "I've been too occupied to follow the case closely. Fill me in, Malone."

"You mean who did what and with which and to whom, as in the old limerick?" The criminal lawyer grinned feebly. "Well, at three A.M. one foggy morning more than a year ago a canary billed only as 'Jeanine' came out of Le Jazz Hot, a joint on Sixty-third Street, said good night to the doorman and cut across the street toward her apartment. A dark, open sports car came out of nowhere, without any lights, and—curtains for the canary. The girl always finished her last turn and left at just about that time, and she always wore a distinctive pastel mink coat—so all the killer had to do was to wait up the street with his motor idling until she stepped off the curb. At least, that was the theory of Captain von Flanagan."

Miss Withers remembered that worthy Homicide officer from many previous cases, and nodded. "Thumb-fingered, but a bulldog."

"That's von F. At first the police had no clues worth a darn. The girl was supposed to have had a secret lover around the club, but she kept to herself, and it was always 'hands off with the customers.' But she had more jewels and furs than her two-hundred-dollar-a-week salary from the club would justify."

"But wasn't there a husband in the picture? I seem to remember—"

"An ex-husband—a Navy man she'd divorced in Mexico a couple of years ago while he was still at sea. Name of CPO Johann Zimmer, recently assigned to Great Lakes Naval Training Station up the shore. But that was all over; after the divorce he never tried to look her up or showed any further interest."

"Which seems odd. And of course he had a perfect alibi?"

"Fair. He'd been on shore leave, but half a dozen of his mates swore they were together at a dive in Cicero whooping it up that night. As a matter of fact, the police would have never known he existed if the guy hadn't come forward to try to see if he couldn't inherit Jeanine's fur coats and jewelry, on the ground the Mexican divorce was invalid. But he had no access to a car—and certainly not to a late-model Jaguar, which is what the doorman decided the murder car was, after he'd been shown a lot of photos by the police. And there was no trace of Zimmer having hired a car—the police checked thoroughly.

"Well, von Flanagan got a list from Motor Vehicles of all registered Jag owners in Cook County. Finally he came to the name of Walter A. Coleman, Jr., playboy socialite and heir to several million bucks when and if his invalid father up in Evanston ever kicks the bucket. At first Junior seemed in the clear. His dark green Jaguar showed no signs of having been in a crash, or in a body shop either. Junior's name had never been linked with Jeanine's in the gossip columns, and no credible witnesses ever came forward to swear they'd seen the couple together.

"Junior denied they'd had an affair. He claimed his car had been safe in the basement garage of his apartment building that night, and that from about one P.M. on he'd been cuddling with a female guest whose name he gallantly refused to divulge. But he was just the type to fit the role of the guy everybody was sure Jeanine was carrying on with. . . ."

"But surely they'd have been seen at least once—at his place or hers."

"She lived in a walk-up, and the elevator man and garage attendant at his apartment left at midnight. There are motels, and lots of bars and night spots where there's only candlelight; also, Jeanine had several costume wigs, those fancy things made of real human hair, so she was never recognized except when she wanted to be. Anyway, that was the picture the authorities were painting. Junior had reasons for secrecy; he was mixed

155

up in a divorce that wasn't final, and his father had threatened to disown him if he didn't quit helling around."

"Circumstantial evidence—every bit of it—and no real motive," the spinster schoolteacher objected.

"Listen, Hildy. Max Taras, the doorman, was an eye-witness. He finally remembered that the driver of the car had been wearing a beret and smoking a pipe, both of which fitted Junior. That identification—"

"The man saw a lot on a dark and foggy night and in only a few seconds," Miss Withers remarked witheringly. "So Junior was arrested?"

"He was. And he came up with his alibi, which was confirmed by the lady who admitted spending the night with him. It turned out to be his ex-wife Frances, bluest blood in North Shore Chicago. She'd been out in Santa Barbara for a year, watching the boys play polo and getting herself a California decree. Now she was back, and she claimed that on that fateful day she'd got senti-mental and phoned Junior because it would have been their wedding anniversary. One thing had led to an-other, and they'd had dinner at the Beachcomber's and then done the town, coming back to his apartment a little after one. That was her story, though she indig-nantly refused the polygraph test when it was suggested."

Hildegarde sniffed. "Even *I* wouldn't call staying out until one o'clock 'doing the town'! But a lady would hardly make up the story—it must have been embar-rassing."

"The divorce wouldn't have been final for months yet. Frances made a good defense witness. She ridiculed the D.A.'s insinuation that Junior could have slipped out and come back without waking her. She said they hadn't even used the Jaguar that night, because they were going to take the champagne route and Junior already had a couple of drunk-driving charges."

"I don't see where his car comes into it anyway, since you say there were no marks on it. I have always understood that modern scientific methods—"

"Yes, but the police came up with a lap robe, torn and bloody, shoved into a refuse can a block from where Junior lived. Von Flanagan figured it had been draped over the hood of Junior's Jaguar as a sort of buffer."

"The man gets cleverer as the years go on!"

"You haven't heard the worst. The value of Frances' testimony was completely negated when the authorities turned up a surprise witness—a private eye named Finch who swore that Frances Coleman, while still out on the coast, had retained him to shadow Junior! She couldn't deny it, so she tried to explain it away by saying she just wanted to find out if he was pining for her or had found comfort somewhere else. Only the snooper, Finch, admitted he'd been stringing his client along and taking her money for nothing—he swore he hadn't always been able to tail his quarry because the Jag could outrun his old Ford."

Miss Withers was busily making notes. "I already smell a dozen rats. Tell me more about the victim, Malone."

"Lovely and cold," said the little lawyer. "She sang naughty French songs in a teasing bedroom voice, and she was stacked like—"

"Spare me the vital statistics. Do you speak only from hearsay?"

"Well, I might have caught her act once or twice, and sent her an orchid or two in tribute to a lovely artiste.

But I never got to first base—she wouldn't even take a drink with me." He sighed. "One thing more. The D.A.'s men found an autographed photo of Jeanine, wearing nothing but Chanel Number Five, as the saying goes, under a blotter on Junior's desk. It was warmly inscribed—and how."

"That would link them together beyond a doubt."

"So the jury thought. But those photos were widely circulated. I myself might have one somewhere in my hotel room. She signed 'em for everybody—and all of 'em with love and kisses. I managed to bring out at the second trial that the photo hadn't been found by the police when they first searched the place—it was the D.A.'s men who later 'discovered' it. The way they discovered pipe tobacco exactly like Junior's brand in Jeanine's wastepaper basket."

"Well, Malone! You as his attorney must know—*were* they lovers?"

"A privileged communication, but—frankly, yes. But he denied absolutely that she'd been putting the heat on him and demanding marriage; she was perfectly satisfied with things as they were."

"A likely story! No woman is ever satisfied with things as they are. But go on."

"Anyway, I had to go and stick my finger in the electric fan. I'd followed the first trial, and I'd seen Deputy D.A. Hamilton make fools out of the defense, which was mostly handled by young Gerald Adams, not too long out of Harvard Law School and no criminal attorney at all—though he seems to have ambitions in that direction. He got his big chance only because old man Coleman trusted Gittel and Adams, who'd always handled his legal affairs. After the first verdict I got word to Junior in his cell that I believed I could get him a new trial on the grounds of prejudice and judicial error, so he dumped his lawyers and retained me."

"You seem to have been borrowing trouble."

"Borrowing? I won permanent possession. But I'd found out that when the doorman, Taras, was first questioned by the police, he said all he saw was an open sports car with no lights come roaring out of nowhere. The stuff about the pipe and the beret and the similarity to Junior's boyish face came after Taras had been locked up for weeks and practically brainwashed by the D.A.'s men—and after they'd showed him a lot of composite photos of Junior in his car, wearing a beret and smoking a pipe! I got to this Taras and found him plenty sore at the way he'd been shoved around; he opened up and promised to tell the truth at the second trial—and without any inducement from me, though maybe he expected the Coleman estate would take care of him later. So comes the trial, and he corrects his testimony just as he promised, and just as I think he's making a big impression on the jury, he wilts under re-cross-examination, reverts to his original testimony, and swears that I'd come to him and offered him a thousand dollars to change his story! That took the wind out of my sails, and the jury brought in a verdict of guilty *without* a recommendation. That was that."

"And a pretty kettle of fish it is!"

"You haven't heard the half of it. Right after Junior was sentenced to die, his father finally kicked the bucket, leaving nobody to inherit . . ."

"You mean he'd changed his will, and cut his son off?"

"No—but a man under sentence of death is *not legally alive,* and can't inherit a dime. Look it up, it's the law. I had no claim against the estate, because Junior had retained me against his father's wishes. Not only did I get no fee, but I'm stuck with the cost of the appeals!"

"A pity. But you have more than money at stake now, Malone."

"You can say that again. The only reason I'm not under indictment already is that a man under sentence of death is entitled to his attorney's services right up to the end. When my client dies, next Wednesday at dawn, the ax falls on me. Sometimes I'd like to change places with him."

"What a depressing thought! But the question is— what can we *do?*"

"I don't know about you, but I'm going out and get plastered!"

Miss Withers was shocked. "Malone, what utter madness—and at a time like this!"

"There is madness in my method, or do I mean vice versa? But seriously, Hildy, I have a hunch that I ran into an important clue last night. Otherwise, why would I have written a check? There's only one thing for me to do—get into the same condition I was in last night, retrace my steps and hope my memory will come back to me if I go through the same motions."

Despite Miss Withers' protests and Maggie's disapproval, Malone bowed, sprinkling cigar ashes all over his pea-green Sulka tie, and departed. "That *man!*" said Maggie.

"*Men!*" said Miss Withers. "Well, we must sit down and put our heads together. Let's start over. Malone wouldn't try to bribe that witness—but it would appear that somebody else did get to him. That somebody could be the real killer. Malone is no fool, and he believes his client completely innocent, doesn't he?"

"He *always* believes them innocent!" Maggie admitted.

"But the police do make mistakes sometimes, especially when they have a too ready-made, too obvious suspect at hand. We must act on the presumption that the murder was committed by somebody else. Take that ex-husband of Jeanine's, for instance. Suppose he brooded over being discarded? His shipmates would have gladly lied for him to give him an alibi. He could have stolen Junior's car out of the garage, and if the key wasn't in it he could have hot-rodded the ignition—"

"You mean 'hot-wired,' " corrected Maggie.

"And what about this Mrs. Frances Coleman? She could have decided to eliminate the only person standing in the way of a reconciliation with her husband."

"But she didn't even know Jeanine existed. Finch swore—"

"I wouldn't believe a private eye under oath—*any* private eye. Most of them are blackmailers at heart. Suppose he had been shaking down Junior or Jeanine, or both, and they had threatened him with the loss of his license or with jail? His story about *never* getting the goods on Junior sounds weak to me." The schoolteacher looked considerably brighter. "So we have Frances, Zimmer, and Finch—three possible suspects. I'm going to circulate among them and act as a sort of catalytic agent, while Malone is out treading—rather, retreading—the primrose path. My first call will be on Mr. Gerald Adams."

"You mean he's on your list of suspects too?" Maggie asked in surprise.

"At this point everyone is. But, Maggie, you've given me an idea. Suppose Gerald Adams himself has playboy tendencies, and has been financing his fun by dipping into the Coleman funds; and suppose Jeanine came to find out about it, and—"

161

"Take it easy!" cried Maggie. "When Mr. Coleman, Senior, died the estate naturally went into probate and everything was in good order. I know because Malone had the same idea at one time, and we checked."

"Too bad—it was a nice thought. But since Adams handled the defense at one time, and knows Junior well, he may have some ideas."

"He did phone Malone asking if there was anything he could do, but I think he felt he had to make the gesture. He didn't like being dropped from the case in favor of Malone. He sounded very conservative—sort of stuffy."

"I can deal with him then—some of my best friends are Republicans."

The spinster schoolteacher picked up her handbag and umbrella, and metaphorically girding her loins for action, galloped off in all directions.

Meanwhile back at the ranch (Texas Slim's Ranch Bar and Grill, on Twenty-second Street), John J. Malone was vainly trying to re-create last night's roseate glow. He had started out as usual at the City Hall Bar, where Joe the Angel had let himself be fast-talked into a "quick fifty" for the evening's expenses. After that there had been Soapy Sullivan's Place, and Mike's Beer and Pizza Parlor, and the Grotto and—it all blended into a sort of photo-montage.

Now and then he got a clue as to his course the previous night from a bartender or a friendly taxi driver, but it was rough going. He knew he must be loaded to the Plimsoll mark and beyond, but the important part of last night's adventures was still shrouded in impenetrable fog. He really should eat something. "Bartender, will you put an olive in my next drink? Oh, make that a hardboiled egg, if you've got any."

"Specialty of the house. You got through half a dozen last night."

Malone took a big bite of egg, shell and all. "I really *was* in here? You're sure?"

"Don't you remember our five-man quartet and how good we got going on 'The Rose of Tralee'?"

"Was I with anybody? Who were my friends?"

"Just about everybody in the place. But one of the guys singing with us was Luke Swenson who runs the bowling alley down the street."

"Did I leave here with him?"

"No, not exactly. A big blonde dame come in to meet Luke, and you got talking to her and then I saw the two of you cut out . . ."

"Blondes I have always with me," confessed Malone. He slapped himself smartly on the side of the head. "If I could only remember—" He turned suddenly to the barman. "Mind joining me in a bar or two of a song— just to help me think?"

The customer, at Texas Slim's, is always right. The bartender took a deep breath and then came out with a baritone blast, above which Malone's tenor rose like a soaring bird. "The pale moon was rising above the green mountain, The sun was declinin' beneath the blue sea . . ."

"Blue sea!" cried Malone. "I told her her eyes were as blue as the sea! That was Luke Swenson's *sister*, Little Helga, a queen-size Viking goddess! I am in love with her, practically!"

It all came back to him in a rush. The little lawyer was already at the phone, dialing with fingers suddenly steady again. "Hello, Maggie? You still there?"

163

"I figured somebody better be minding the store . . ."

"Maggie, it *worked!* I remember everything! Say, did I get any phone calls?"

"Yes, boss. Your *horse* called."

"That's Little Helga, my Norse goddess! Look, Maggie, she isn't a horse; she happens to be a teller in the South Side Bank where Max Taras has his account! She recognized my name as the attorney of record in the Coleman trial, and one thing led to another—"

"How much did you write that check for, Malone?" she said ominously.

"I *didn't!* I tore the check out because it has my phone number on it and I was out of business cards. She promised to look up something in the bank files for me and call me back."

"Well, she did. So you needn't have gone out and wasted all this time and money and got yourself in whatever condition you're in. Miss Swenson left her home number and said to call her."

"Fine, fine! Maggie, this is going to blow wide open. Taras actually *was* bribed! Because he deposited one thousand dollars in his account the day after he crossed me up at the trial. And get this—it was a *thousand-dollar bill!* That's just the sort of bait that would work with a simple jerk like him. But thousand-dollar bills can be traced—banks keep records. I'll make that guy squirm!"

"Remember, he used to be a wrestler, so watch yourself."

"I will. Is Hildegarde still hanging around?"

"She phoned and said to tell you she'd had a very busy afternoon and that she'd checked into the Y.W.C.A."

"Well, it looks as if we won't need her help after all. You go home and get some sleep now—I've got another call to make." It *was* his night, after all. He dialed, and Little Helga, with a voice like hot buttered rum, answered the phone.

"Sure, sweetie, I got everyt'ing," she told him proudly. "Mr. Taras' address and phone number right outta the files, like I promise. You gung *keep* your promise, hah?" Malone could only gulp. "You promise to take me to dinner and dancing Saturday night, remember?"

"Wild horses couldn't keep me away! But first, where is Taras hiding out?"

She told him, and he memorized the address and phone number. But when she started on the serial number of the thousand-dollar bill, he interrupted. "That's too long and complicated to get straight over the phone. Suppose I drop by and take you out for a nightcap?"

"I'm not dressed, I mean for *out*. But beer I got here . . ."

"*Meeerow!*" said Malone. "I mean, okay, I'll be there."

He paused to straighten his tie, purchased a pint of Canadian because he only considered beer fit for chasers, and started toward a taxi. Then he got another idea. The situation called for psychological warfare. If he could make Max Taras sweat for an hour or two, the man would be ripe for cracking.

Malone phoned the number Helga had given him and when a guttural voice answered, he snapped, "Max, this is Malone, the attorney. I'm coming down to see you in a little while and you better be there!"

"I got nuttin' to say to you! I don' vant—"

"Shut up. You're going to tell me the name of the crook who gave you that grand note to double-cross me in court! And don't try to run—that would only be a confession!" There was a gobble of profanity, presumably in Czech, and Malone hung up, very pleased with himself.

Luckily he still had money enough for a taxi, because he was now on cloud nine and the El would have been beneath him. It was well worth it when Helga answered the door, wreathed in smiles and a frothy negligee. That blackout of his must have been the worst in medical history! To think that he could have forgotten, even for a few hours, a gorgeous female like this! Even without make-up, and with lashes and eyebrows as pale as her wheat-colored hair, she was a vision suited to the wide screen.

"Come in, sweetie. But be quiet—mustn't wake Brunnehilde!"

Into each life some rain must fall, as the poetess said. Malone tiptoed in—the last thing in the world he wanted to do was to wake a roommate named Brunnehilde! It meant working under wraps, because his greatest asset had always been his golden voice, and it is hard to do justice to a fine Irish brogue in a whisper.

Far uptown, Miss Hildegarde Withers was engaged in giving her hair its requisite hundred strokes before turning out the light. She found it conducive to sleep, and tonight she wanted to sleep—and to dream. Her dreams were always sensible, and sometimes enlightening. She was also thinking of Junior Coleman, who would be lying now in his cell in the death row at Stateside, staring up at the ever-burning light in the ceiling. . . .

Some time later, give or take half an hour, Malone found himself being kissed a warm good night at the door. It had not been an entirely wasted visit; he was full of coffee and smorgasbord, was comparatively sober, and he now had another firm ally. Helga had even become so caught up in the spirit of it all that she insisted on lending him the pistol she sometimes had to carry on bank errands. It might come in handy in a heart-to-heart talk with an ex-wrestler.

Speaking of wrestling, Malone had tried one last hold in the doorway, and in the scuffle they had finally awakened Brunnehilde. She came literally flying out of the bedroom, screaming protests, and startled Malone out of a year's growth. Then she perched on Helga's shoulder, twittering suspiciously.

Lovebirds were certainly misnamed, said the little lawyer as he went down the stairs. But he was all the more in the mood to face Taras. He managed to catch an owl trolley south and finally came to an old brownstone apartment not far enough away from the stockyards. It looked empty and next on the list for condemnation, but this was the right number. There were no names on the mailboxes in the lobby.

Of course, by now Taras would be in a state of extreme jitters, and his apartment would be the one with the light under the door. Malone rapped at 2-B, rapped harder and then tried the knob. The door swung slowly open, and he stepped belligerently into a tawdry living room.

Suddenly the taste of the imported perfecto in his mouth became bitter as ashes—for there was Max Taras' body lying on the twisted rug, eyes staring sightlessly at the ceiling.

Malone swore softly. While he had been dallying with the fair *svensk flicka,* somebody else had beaten him to the all-important witness. Then all speculations as to who, when, and why were suddenly interrupted by a feeble moan from the corpse.

Taras wasn't dead! The little lawyer's first thought was to reach for the pint in his pocket, and then he remembered that liquor should never be forced on an unconscious man. He himself was not unconscious, though. The logical thing was to call an ambulance. Only he *had* to talk to Taras before anyone else did. Perhaps water. . . . In two strides he was in the kitchen.

Then the roof fell in.

Eventually Malone came back to consciousness, and immediately wished he hadn't. There were no words to describe his headache. He managed to stand up, brushed automatically at his clothing and then realized that perhaps he had missed an exit cue. He looked into the other room; Taras still lay there on the twisted rug.

But something new had been added. Now the ex-wrestler stared up at the ceiling with an extra eye in the middle of his forehead.

The little lawyer knew without even looking that the disaster would be complete. Yes, the little pistol was in his pocket, and it stank of raw cordite. He could hear voices on the stairs, and the distant wolf-wail of sirens coming closer. He ran back through the kitchen, caroming off table and stove, and threw open a back window. There had to be a fire escape! There was, but the upraised ladder was rusted tight.

He could think of only one thing to do—hang by his hands and drop into the dark—so drop he did. He landed heavily, and one leg turned beneath him with a white-hot stab of pain; then he blacked out. It was just as well—the ensuing formalities were such that he would have preferred to miss them anyway.

Meanwhile Miss Hildegarde Withers was also having her setbacks. First, she had barged into the law offices of Gittel and Adams, noting that the place appeared not to have been redecorated since the Big Fire, if then. The plumply pretty redhead at the reception desk was doing her face over at the moment of Hildegarde's arrival. She was sorry but Mr. Gerald Adams was busy; wouldn't Mr. Gittel or the elder Mr. Adams do?

The schoolteacher said she would wait. Then, one girl to another: "That lip rouge is *just* your shade. I've always wished *I* had red hair."

"You could, the same way I got mine." The name was Gertrude, and she had been here for years but was now looking for a more interesting job. No, the firm didn't do much trial work and rarely handled criminal cases. "Oh, there was one," Gertie added. "Mr. Gerald got Kirsch, the big-shot bookie, off on an assault charge last year; but the state's witnesses all disappeared, so we don't brag about that one."

"And there was the murder trial, of course. Were you in court?"

"We don't even talk about *that* one! Mr. Gerald tried so hard, too! Wasn't the verdict a shame?"

"A shame indeed, for others as well as Junior Coleman. By the way, one thing I came here to get is the address of Mrs. Frances Coleman."

"You're not another of those reporters?"

"Just an *amicus curiae*. The case is being reopened, which is why I want a talk with the lady."

Gertie hesitated, then grinned. "Funny your asking. Want to know where she is right this minute? In *there*, taking dictation from Mr. Gerald! Believe it or not, she's his new private secretary, which is one of the reasons I'm reading Help Wanted ads. When she came in I got demoted."

"Oh, dear! No wonder you are somewhat put out."

"Huh? Oh, I didn't have any crush on him, if that's what you mean. Mr. Gerald is strictly business. I think he gave her the job because she needs it real bad. She doesn't get alimony any more, and all Junior ever had was the allowance his father had us pay him every week. I guess Mr. Gerald has a soft heart after all, or else he gets a kick out of having a former Junior Leaguer on the payroll and I'm sorry but we haven't any record of that—" Gertie's eyes flashed quick warning.

The door had opened and a tall, willowy, jet-haired girl was coming out, hands adjusting her striking hairdo. The eyes were blue-green with darkish shadows, the chin small but arrogant. "Coffee break, Gert," she said in passing.

"That means Frances is having a quick one at the bar downstairs," Gertie translated. "Can you blame her, under the circumstances? I'll find out if Mr. Gerald is free now."

Gerald Adams, rising politely from behind an over-size, immaculate desk, was a youngish man, medium Brooks Brothers in dress, medium handsome, with a medium voice, medium traces of Russian Leather lotion, and a rather tight mouth. Nevertheless, he could smile, and did. "Though I don't see what I can do," he said, after Miss Withers had introduced herself as a special representative of an imaginary Committee on Miscarriages of Justice. "It would be highly unethical for us to intervene when Walter Coleman, Junior, has seen fit to retain other counsel."

"For which decision the young man is undoubtedly

sorry. But I need your help. You *do* believe he's innocent, don't you?"

"What I personally believe is of no moment. Two juries—"

"As a trial lawyer you must know that juries do make mistakes."

Gerald Adams rose and stalked up and down the room. "I admit that Hamilton, the Deputy D.A., outfought me in court. Though at that I did better than my successor. But the circumstantial case against Junior was very strong. Still, this fellow Malone might have got him off scot-free if his trying to tamper with a witness hadn't backfired."

"Malone claims he didn't bribe Taras, that someone else did."

"Who else would have a reason? *Cui bono,* as we lawyers say."

" 'Who benefits.' And my question is, who really benefits here?"

"You mean by the death of Jeanine? Who but Junior Coleman, it would appear. He had become entangled with the girl, she was making excessive demands and he wanted to end the affair."

"You are stating the prosecution's side. But couldn't someone else have wanted to end that love affair, even by drastic means?"

"If you are trying to involve Frances Coleman, the very idea is preposterous. I felt it my duty, while I was defense counsel, to look into the possibility of casting a reasonable doubt, and of directing suspicion at someone other than our client. But Frances is obviously in the clear. She was hoping to re-establish the marriage, and had hired that private detective just to see if Junior

171

was telling the truth about having given up his wild ways. But remember, she didn't even know the identity of the girl, or if such a person existed!"

"But Junior did contemplate marrying Jeanine, didn't he?" It was a wild shot, but it hit home. Mr. Gerald sat down suddenly.

"Who told you that?" he demanded. "If there has been a leak in this office—"

"Please, this is no time to be stuffy—not when the man is to die in less than a week!"

Mr. Gerald frowned. "Well, it is a matter of record. Walter, Junior, tried to sound us out in an interview about ten days before the murder, as to what we thought his father's reaction would be to his getting married as soon as his divorce from Frances was final. No names were mentioned, but we gathered that the lady was some-one not *quite* a lady—definitely someone of whom the elder Mr. Coleman would not approve."

"Junior asked you that, in so many words?"

"As a matter of fact, he spoke to my father."

"Why? Didn't you and Junior get on?"

Mr. Gerald sighed deeply. "Madam, it has been my unfortunate duty for some years to put the brakes on Junior Coleman, to thwart him when he wanted extra money for useless extravagances such as a new foreign sports car every year, and to get him eternally out of scrapes. I'm afraid he looks on me as a sort of combined governess and truant officer."

Miss Withers felt herself suddenly more in sympathy with this earnest young man. "If Junior's thoughts of matrimony had come out in court, it would have bol-stered the prosecution's case, would it not? On the other hand, it might have made it look worse for the former

172

Mrs. Coleman, who wanted to get him back and would have perhaps gone to considerable lengths to do so—"

"I do *not* agree! Both parties swore that they became reconciled that night, which of course invalidated the interlocutory decree. Why would she feel it necessary to leave her newly returned husband and go out intent on murder? Besides, I have heard that when a person turns to murder, he uses the weapon with which he is most familiar. Women murderers lean toward the subtle way of poison, while murder by auto is, according to most authorities, a man's method."

"Or it could be chosen by a woman simply because it *is* a man's method. A smokescreen, a red herring—like the pipe and the beret."

Mr. Adams was amused. "I know Mrs. Coleman well enough to feel that she is utterly incapable of violence. And granted that she even knew of Jeanine's existence, why would Frances of all people try to put the blame on Junior, using his car, and so on? She would only be defeating her own ends."

"Too true." Miss Withers was nettled. "I've been grasping at straws. But in this case there are so few suspects to clutch at."

"You're telling me! I must confess I liked CPO Zimmer for a time. But he showed no evidence of being still in love with the girl, and how could he have got hold of Junior's car?"

"And what about that shady private detective, Mr. Finch?"

"A nasty type, but hardly courageous enough in my opinion to commit murder. Unless he is deeper than he seems—"

"Aren't we all? You yourself, Mr. Adams—aren't you

whitewashing Frances because she is a very attractive woman? Haven't you even taken her in and given her a job?"

The man picked up a heavy ash tray, and for a moment Miss Withers thought he was going to brain her with it. But he only surveyed its contents thoughtfully and then emptied it into the wastebasket. "That must not get out to the newspapers," he said, "or the sob sisters will start making her life miserable again. We'll absolutely deny it."

"Not to me. I just saw her here."

Mr. Gerald managed to look both belligerent and sheepish. "I—we had our reasons. Even though she has no claim against the estate, it wouldn't look well to have her slinging hash or working as a saleslady."

"Speaking of the estate, which I understand Junior cannot inherit while he is under sentence of death, who *does* come into the money now?"

Mr. Gerald seemed much happier with the change of subject. "I cannot be sure. There are supposed to be some distant cousins in East Germany, but it will probably take years before they can be located and their claims validated." His expression indicated that any claim would take a great deal of proving before Gittel and Adams relinquished a red cent.

"If by some miracle Junior got a commutation of sentence and could then inherit, would your firm continue to handle the estate for him?"

"I should think so. I doubt if he could manage it from a prison cell. The administration of an estate like that is a vast responsibility. Of course, he could choose some other firm . . ."

He was looking at his watch, and Miss Withers hastily rose, thanking him and promising to get in touch if

174

there was anything at all he could do—which bit of one-upmanship left the gentleman looking just a little bewildered. As she left the suite, not without a smile and a nod to Gertrude—a very useful contact—the schoolteacher had much to contemplate. It was late in the day to come up with anything new on the case. But most murders, she knew, were attempted for gain. And so far nobody seemed to be thinking about the Coleman money.

As she went out through the lower hall she turned on impulse into a dim and aromatic cave, under a sign reading *"Cocktails."* Customers were few, but Frances Coleman was perched on a bar stool. Her dark head was keeping time to the beat of a juke box, which was playing something soft and miserable as a wet kitten.

Miss Withers ordered lemonade, then slid over beside her quarry. "Excuse me—they said I'd find you here. I've just been talking to Gerald Adams," she whispered meaningfully. Frances turned slowly, like a mechanical doll, her face blank. But at least she didn't jump up and leave. "I'm a sort of citizen's committee of one, trying to work with Mr. Malone to save your ex-husband's life."

"Why?" said the dark girl.

"I've been called a champion of lost causes, a tilter at windmills and a meddlesome old snoop. But I do need your help."

"There's nothing to be done." The enunciation was painful.

"But surely you of all people know he's innocent! Why aren't you down at Springfield, hammering on the Governor's door? If Junior never left your side that night—?"

Frances stared into her glass. "Yes," she said slowly.

"I testified to that, didn't I? But Walter had had years of practice in deceiving me. We'd had a good deal to drink that night—I guess he *could* have waited until I was asleep and sneaked out and— She was after money, of course, whatever he had or would get. Not that that's any excuse. Now, if you don't mind—"

"But I do mind! Even Gerald Adams is giving me more cooperation than you are. *He* hasn't washed his hands of the case."

"Is that what you think?" Frances walked over to the juke box, balancing very carefully, to put in more coins. "Love that number," she explained on her return. "Dave Brubeck's 'Gloomy Sunday'—it's my mood music."

"But you were saying?"

"I don't remember what I was saying. I don't want to talk about it." Frances shoved her empty glass toward the bartender.

"Mr. Adams seems to agree with me that there are reasons for suspecting this Finch, who may be deeper than he seems."

"*That* nasty little man? I hired him long distance, and have seen him only once. He'd do anything for money —anything."

"But he could have found out more than he reported to you, and tried to use the information for his own purposes?"

"You really are tilting at windmills! I'm surprised you don't try to make out a case against *me*—or are you?"

Miss Withers let that one go by. "When are you going down to see Junior for the last time, Mrs. Coleman?"

"I'm not. I don't owe him any more favors. It's none of your damn business, but Walter sent word he didn't want to see me. It would just break us both up, and for what? I can't help him—nobody can. Not any more."

176

"But you realize that if we found new evidence, there might be a commutation of his sentence?"

"And Walter, even in prison, would inherit the family money and I'd be a wealthy woman! Is that what you're thinking? But I'm talking too much, and I wish you'd go away. I'm going to get stoned and stay stoned until it's all over."

"That's a *defeatist* attitude! If you love Junior and really want to save him, would you consent to take the lie detector test you refused?"

That struck deep. "You want to know why I couldn't? Because if you must know, I *wasn't* with him that night, not after midnight! We had dinner and we also had a row because I can't stand him when he gets a weeping jag on. He called me a couple of days later and begged me to give him an alibi, but for all I know he *did* kill that girl!"

She turned and ran unsteadily out of the bar.

"Sometimes I should let well enough alone," said Miss Withers as she found she was stuck for the check.

"Lie still, Malone, and smell the pretty flowers!" came an all-too-familiar voice. The little lawyer blinked the one bleary eye that showed through the bandages; he knew vaguely that he was in a private room in Cook County Hospital with one leg raised high in traction, that he had no interest in any flowers except perhaps Four Roses, and—hadn't that been a stiff-starched nurse who just tiptoed across his line of vision?

"Friend or enema?" he demanded cautiously.

"Be serious," said Miss Hildegarde Withers. "And keep your voice down—there's a policeman stationed outside the door. I had to talk to you, though you're not allowed visitors, so I borrowed the plumage from a friend of Maggie's and am to all intents and purposes a head nurse. Now for heaven's sake what happened to you last night?"

"It's not as bad as it looks," he confessed. "It's worse." Then he told her all. "Taras must have panicked when I phoned him, and called somebody for instructions. Only this somebody didn't bother to bribe him again, but decided to drop by and silence him for good. I intruded in the midst of it, and got set up as the patsy. The gun is easily traceable to me, and from the official point of view I had plenty of motive. If I were acting as my own attorney, I'd advise me to cop a plea!"

"Nonsense! *We* know you didn't kill Taras. There *must* be a connection between the two murders. Somebody killed Jeanine and framed Junior for it, and the same somebody must have killed Taras and framed you for it. If we can only prove it—"

"Yes, and if we had some tonic we'd have some gin and tonic if we had some gin," he said morosely.

"But, Malone, I *am* getting somewhere even if I don't know just where!"

She told him about her visit to the offices of Gittel and Adams, and of the admission she had got from Frances Coleman.

"But there goes the last shred of my client's alibi!" Malone complained. "You're doing fine, just fine—running toward the wrong goalposts!"

"The truth must out. This development doesn't make Junior look any worse than he did—nothing could. He didn't ask Frances for the alibi until days after the murder. And you can't tell me that an inebriated man would think of putting a lap robe over the front of his car. I have a lot of unanswered questions, Malone."

"Such as, why didn't you stay home with your African violets?"

"No. For example, why does she say she'd be a rich woman if Junior got a commutation to life imprisonment?"

"I can answer that. If they both swear they spent the night together, the interlocutory divorce is null and void and they are husband and wife. It doesn't matter to the law if they actually did, or not."

"Interesting, but not immediately pertinent. Right now my feminine intuition tells me—" She broke off as she saw his face. "Don't sneer. Intuition means being able to come to the right conclusion without going through all the steps between. Malone, I let it drop in several places that the case is being reopened. That should make the murderer nervous, to say the least. Whoever it is, I am going to put the fear of God into Finch, into that sailor at Great Lakes who was once Jeanine's husband if I can get in there—"

" 'And although she's barred from the Navee Yard . . .' " sang Malone softly. "Hildegarde, what good do you think all this is going to do?"

She surveyed him coldly. "You know, Malone, I think there was a mirror over the sink in the Taras kitchen, and you caught a glimpse of the person who slugged you. Or you caught a whiff of something—strong tobacco or shaving lotion or expensive perfume—"

"There wasn't, and I didn't. And it was no lady who whammed me!"

"You can't be sure—a sandbag is a sandbag. And I didn't mean all this actually *happened*. You could just hint at it and it *might* flush the killer out of hiding. Say, a press release?"

179

"So that Mr. X will sneak in here and eliminate me while I'm a sitting duck on a pond! No, I'm putting my faith in something more sensible. If I could only get to my clothes, I've got the serial number of that thousand-dollar bill Taras was bribed with. That can be traced."

"Maggie and I have already been in touch with Miss Swenson, and we have the number. Maggie has been checking with local banks all morning, but no luck so far. Unfortunately, everyone agrees that it will take weeks."

"And meanwhile my client gets executed and I get indicted—not just for subornation, but for the murder of Taras! Please go away."

"You concentrate on getting well. Leave everything to me and Maggie and Miss Swenson, who I think has honorable intentions. I must be off—I hear the rattle of lunch trays in the hall."

"Wait! As head nurse, you could maybe find where they keep the *spiritus frumenti?* Or maybe just a tot of pure alcohol for what ails me?"

"As far as I am concerned, you are on a cold turkey diet," the schoolteacher said firmly, and was gone.

It turned out to be just in the nick of time, for on the way down the corridor she passed Captain von Flanagan and his two aides, who looked very grim but who luckily did not look at her. They were headed for Malone's room, and she would dearly have loved to listen at the door. But for once she decided that discretion was the better part of valor.

Back at the office Maggie greeted her with a barrage of questions. "He'll live," the schoolma'am told her. "Just suffering acutely from withdrawal symptoms."

"The poor man! He'll only be needing a small pint to quiet his nerves, and believe it or not he always thinks more clearly when he has a wee drop in him."

"Now don't go soft on him—or on me!" said Miss Withers. "That man is just aching to be reformed. Any phone calls?"

"Just the reporters, who've caught on that something is up."

"That gives me an idea. Are any of them friendly?"

"Most of 'em. You should see our Christmas list!"

"Well, see if they will run the number of that thousand-dollar bill. *Alerting all bank personnel*—that sort of thing. It would be far quicker than phoning one bank after another."

"Okay. Oh, yes, there was one other call. It was Mr. Finch—did you know his first name is Boris?—and he insisted that he had to get in touch with Malone."

"Aha! My plot is working. Where's his office?"

The sign on the door read FINCH AND ASSOCIATES, but the moment Miss Withers entered she realized it was strictly a one-man operation. Mr. Boris Finch himself was busy on the phone in the inner office; she could hear enough of the one-sided conversation by putting her ear to the door panel to gather that he was stalling somebody about money.

The schoolteacher was just getting interested in a last month's copy of *Time* when Finch poked his head out and said cautiously, "Yes?" He was a small man somewhat gone to fat, somewhere in his fifties and past whatever prime he might have had. If he had shaved that morning it had been with a dull blade.

She introduced herself as "Miss Withers, Mr. Malone's associate," and went on. "Poor Malone happens to be incommunicado in County Hospital, but if anything important is on your mind I thought you could talk to me, as his partner."

Finch blinked. "John J. Malone has a lady partner? Well, I'll be—"

"I don't practice in this state," she said truthfully. "But sometimes I'm called in as a consultant on complicated cases, such as this Coleman affair seems to be. It's reopened, you know."

The man nodded, then led her into his private office, which was furnished with a minimum of battered essentials plus a couch with the appearance of having been slept in often and recently, a hot plate, and a large bookcase filled with old *Holiday* and *National Geographic* magazines and worn paperback whodunits. He saw her glance at the latter. "Oh, them. You know, I get a lot of ideas outta them—to use in my work."

"I can imagine," said Miss Withers as she sat down gingerly on the couch.

"You say you're *really* in Malone's confidence?" the man demanded. "You got the power to speak for him?"

"Absolutely. Check with his secretary, Miss Maggie O'Leary, and she'll tell you that I've been associated with him on several very successful cases in the past."

Finch immediately took her at her word, picked up the phone, and dialed. Whatever Maggie said, he seemed to be satisfied. But he went out and locked the front door, very carefully.

"Now I'll get down to cases," he said. "You and I know Malone is in the biggest jam of his life. He's got two charges against him and he's gonna lose a client and get no fee. So wouldn't it be worth five grand to him to get out of it, free and clear? Has he got that kind of money, or could he get it from the Coleman estate or anywhere?"

Miss Withers hesitated, thinking of her own modest savings, and of how much she could borrow on her cottage in Santa Monica. "Possibly," she conceded. "But I'm not buying any pig in a poke. What's it all about?"

"Let me take a look in your handbag," he said slyly.

"What? Surely you don't think I have that much with me?"

"I just wanta make sure you haven't got a tape recorder going," he told her. "Because while I don't mind saying certain things to you, I might wanta deny 'em later."

The schoolteacher, somewhat amused, proved to his satisfaction that she was not wired for sound, and he relaxed.

"Okay, lady, here's the deal. It takes Malone off the hook three ways. Now on payment to me of five thousand bucks, in tens and twenties, I make a deposition, see? I swear that while I was shadowing Junior Coleman I *did* succeed in getting the goods on him and the Jeanine girl, and I *did* report it to my client, Mrs. Frances Coleman."

"Then you lied to the police, and under oath in court?"

"I was just protecting the interests of my client. She paid me some, and she was going to pay me more. But that ain't the point. I offer to make a deposition that I was still shadowing Junior the night of the murder, working on my own because I had a hunch. I was staked out near his apartment, and I saw Frances Coleman come in with him about one and I saw her go out about two-thirty *in his car!*"

"*Mr.* Finch!" gasped the schoolteacher. "You kept silent—?"

"I had reasons. Maybe I was thinking that when she got her hands on some of the Coleman fortune she'd like to take care of me. After I told her the favor I'd done her. But I've thought it over, and my conscience is bothering me, see? So now I can't keep silent while an innocent man is going to be executed, can I? It makes sense, lady. She's testified that Junior was sleeping beside her at the time of the murder, and the D.A. suggested that he could have got up and gone out and done the killing without her knowing. But it could have worked out just as well *the other way around!*"

Miss Withers did not bat an eyelash. "Do you think your word, or even your deposition, would carry any weight under the circumstances?"

"Try it and see! The newspapers will do plenty with it. Frances Coleman had an even better motive to kill Jeanine than Junior did. As for the Taras murder, the man used to be a wrestler, and he was on his guard. Who else but a luscious dame could get close enough to sap him? She must have bribed Taras originally for fear he would tell the truth about his phony identification of Junior as driver of the death car, which might have won Junior an acquittal and put the heat on her as the next likely suspect! Digging up the money to bribe Taras must have taken her last thousand bucks, which is why she's now broke and working as a secretary—"

"My goodness gracious!" whispered Miss Withers. "Why, this is the answer to everything, all neatly tied up in a parcel."

"Is it worth five grand, or isn't it? I want just enough to get me down to one of the banana republics, where there's no extradition and where I'll be out of this whole mess."

"But your deposition wouldn't stand up, if you're away . . ."

"Who said it would have to stand up in court? It would be enough to hit all the papers, and force the Governor's hand so he'll *have* to grant a stay of execution. This would take the heat of Junior and off Malone, because it would cast the finger of suspicion at somebody else. Is it a deal?"

For almost the first time in her long and stormy career Miss Hildegarde Withers was at a loss for words. All this —after what Frances had let slip? Of course she could have been lying, or this man could be lying, or *everybody* could be lying!

As Hildegarde hesitated, Finch threw in the clincher. "Tell you what I'm gonna do! In my deposition I'll add just one more thing. Taras fell for a bribe of a thousand-dollar bill, right? Malone is having it traced through the banks, because bills of that denomination are used only in transactions between Federal Reserve banks. With one exception—that's the underworld, the Syndicate boys and such. Okay, I'll swear that I got that grand note for Frances from one of the surviving members of the Hook gang out in Cicero! You can get anything in Cicero if you got connections. Same place I'll swear I got the chloral hydrate for her, the Mickey Finn she slipped Junior that night so he wouldn't wake up while she was out on a murder romp in his car! How's about it, sister?"

"I'm thinking," she said. The trouble was, she wasn't at all sure that Malone wouldn't be tempted to go for it, hook, line and sinker. "Just how much truth is there in the story?" she asked quietly.

"Never mind. But it'll serve its purpose. We got a deal?"

"I—I'll have to speak to Malone," she parried. "When he regains consciousness, of course." And she made a hasty exit.

She stopped off in her room at the Y.W.C.A. to soak for a few minutes in a hot tub with plenty of soap, and then went on to Malone's office where she unburdened herself to the faithful Maggie.

"Sure it would work," said Maggie. "It would make Frances Coleman sweat for a while, but I doubt if it would really stick—and even if it did, with her looks she'd probably get off. Malone says that people always believe a man when he slings mud that also gets all over himself. People like to believe the worst."

"You think I should tempt Malone with the offer?"

"Huh? Oh, you're afraid he'll want to go for it. You don't know the man like I do. But he ought to know what's up. The story fits the known facts so well, it's a shame that nasty man made it all up!"

"Did he? I mean, is it? Maggie, a lot of things in this crazy, mixed-up world are a shame. 'O cursed spite, That ever I was born to set it right!'—*Hamlet.*"

"You'd better have a nice cup of coffee."

"No time, Maggie. You know, it occurs to me that the name of Cicero has been cropping up in this case a good deal."

"It's a real tough suburb, out southwest. You're not *going* there?"

"Not yet. I've been thinking in other directions, Maggie. I have one more interview coming up. In the first ones, Frances managed to implicate Junior even deeper, and Finch offered to pin the whole thing on Frances— I wonder what's next? How does one go about getting

186

into the Navy Yard—I mean the Great Lakes Naval Training Station? Or at least getting in touch with a sailor there?"

"Ten years ago I could have found out easy," sighed Maggie. "But the bluejackets haven't been whistling at me lately."

"Well, be glad you have memories! Let's try the telephone."

They managed to leave a message for CPO Zimmer to call back, and call back he did. He even consented to an interview that very evening, since he had shore leave, and would meet the schoolteacher in any convenient bar and grill if she would pick up the check.

"And where else but Joe the Angel's?" suggested Maggie from the sidelines. "You can sign the tab."

CPO Zimmer was, at the beginning, something of a disappointment. He turned out to be a solid, earthy, red-faced man in civilian clothes. Somehow Miss Withers had expected a real salty Jack Tar with a multitude of hash marks and a tattoo on his wrist. Nor was he overly cooperative, even after she had bought him three beers and a T-bone steak.

"I thought when you said it had to do with Jeanine it was something about that jewelry and clothes and furniture of hers," he said.

"But if you were divorced, how could you expect to inherit?"

"Who else has a better right? She just mentioned a Mexican divorce in one of her post cards, but I never got served with any papers. And she went right on drawing my allotment, even for a year after that."

"Which all added up to making you naturally resentful, yes?"

He drew back. "Oh, it was just one of those things.

187

Dames are dames. That Jeanine could spend more than five men could earn. Always said she was going to marry a millionaire, and poor kid, I guess she pretty near made it."

"When you were transferred to duty near here you never even wrote to Jeanine, or went to see her act at the Le Jazz Hot Club?"

"Naw. She'd quit writing me. And those night clubs are all clip joints. She didn't want to see me, she'da had the bouncer throw me out."

"But the night she was killed you were supposed to be raising the roof with a group of your shipmates out in darkest Cicero?"

He blushed. "Lady, that was no night club. It—it was Jenny's Place. Jenny would alibi me."

"I see," said Miss Withers coldly. "But you do have contacts out in Cicero, then. I've heard it's a place where you can pick up anything—such as a thousand-dollar bill that can't be traced through the banks, or even a neat little packet of knockout drops? If I were to ask you, you'd know right where to lay your hands on something like that, wouldn't you?"

Zimmer rose suddenly to his feet, grabbed his hat and backed away. "Lady, you're *really* SICK!" he cried, and rushed off.

"Well, you can't win 'em all," Maggie comforted Hildegarde over the phone.

"As I said to Malone yesterday—or was it only yesterday? My immediate worry is about what I'm going to say to him tomorrow, poor man."

"You'll think of something," Maggie told her. "Sleep on it."

Which was easier said than done. The schoolteacher gave her hair its requisite hundred strokes with a brush,

188

tried vainly to seek what she would have called the Arms of Morpheus, and finally turned on the light and tried to work a Double-Crostic puzzle in the current *Saturday Review,* coming out second best. Finally she must have slept, though all she could remember of her dreams was that they were nightmares. . . .

With mixed emotions Miss Withers again assumed the costume of a head nurse the next morning—and found when she reached the hospital it hadn't been exactly necessary. There was no uniformed officer outside Malone's door.

"But the heat is still on," the little lawyer told her "I guess the police just figured out finally that a man with a leg raised in traction isn't going anywhere. Did you maybe bring me a pint or anything?"

"I brought you something much more interesting," she said. And she told him of the surprising offer from Mr. Finch. Malone's one good eye brightened through the bandages.

"Holy St. Paul and Minneapolis! If it was only *true!* Of course we wouldn't go for it even if I had the dough, but he might make a deal with the newspapers if he thinks of peddling his information there."

"I imagine they'd be afraid of the laws of libel."

"You could be right. Nothing new on that thousand-dollar bill?"

"No. And it's Saturday, so the banks will be closed today and tomorrow. We have so little time! The only real hope we have is that the murderer will believe you are actually unconscious here in the hospital, and that he will make a desperate attempt to silence you before you miraculously regain your wits and can talk—"

"Now *wait—a—minute!*"

189

"We should have the cooperation of the hospital authorities, and of the police, of course. You could be removed to some other room, if you're nervous. We could have a dummy, or a policeman, in your bed."

"Is there a difference?" He grinned. "No, I wouldn't miss it for the world. Hildegarde, I have a confession to make. This traction thing is a phony. The doctor on the ambulance was a fellow for whom I'd once done a favor; he brought me here and fixed me up this way so I wouldn't have to go to the jail hospital. All I got is a bad sprain." He swung his legs over the side of the bed, and tottered to his feet.

"Malone! When I think of all the sympathy I've wasted!"

"You would have given the gag away if you'd been in on it."

Her sniff was devastating. "Well then, you are mobile and even ambulatory, so that makes it easier. I suggest that you carry on as usual today, and then tonight we'll set the trap. This hospital is so big and overcrowded that practically anybody can come and go as he pleases, and the killer won't have the slightest difficulty—"

"It is my private opinion that you are nuttier than a fruit cake."

She bridled. "That is the *second* time in the last few hours I've been accused of mental aberration, and I don't like it. My plan is perfectly sound—it worked perfectly some years ago when dear Inspector Piper got knocked on the head in the Blackboard murders. I'm sure that under the circumstances Captain von Flanagan will cooperate—"

"He will, will he?" roared that irate policeman, bursting in at precisely the wrong moment. He looked at

Malone, who was now hastily burrowing back under the covers. He looked at Miss Withers in her borrowed white uniform. "So *both* of you are as phony as three-dollar bills. I should of knowed it! Okay, counselor, you're going over to the jail hospital—"

"Wouldn't tomorrow do just as well?" put in Miss Withers hopefully. "Malone can explain everything."

"Well, lady, *you* better explain this supposed leak from my office that went to the newspapers—about how when he recovers from surgery John J. Malone is expected to be able to put the finger on his assailant and break the Coleman case. One of the city editors checked back on it—and I got a good idea where it started. There's a law against impersonatin' an officer!"

"Which you've been doing for years," said Malone irreverently.

The Homicide Captain's face got redder than ever, but Miss Withers stepped quickly between them. "Captain, I didn't actually take your name in vain. And if you'll listen I can explain—"

"That's just dandy! You'll do all your explainin' downtown." He gripped her elbow and propelled her toward the door.

"Plead the Fifth Amendment!" Malone shouted helpfully after her.

But she soon found herself in a small interrogation room in the Detective Bureau, facing von Flanagan and a policeman with a stenotype. She was on a hard chair under a bright light, but was relieved to see that no rubber hoses were in evidence. "Now talk!" barked von Flanagan.

Which was his first mistake. It was the opportunity of a lifetime for the spinster schoolma'am, and she made the most of it. Now and again he tried to interrupt and get it in the form of questions and answers, but Miss Withers had a way of answering her own questions and questioning her own answers. Both von Flanagan and the stenographer were worn out before Hildegarde showed any signs of running down.

". . . and the main trouble is that both you and the District Attorney's office were so sure from the beginning you had the right man that you never looked anywhere else! Everybody mixed up in this case is lying—including Junior Coleman, but he shouldn't be executed for that, or for being a useless parasite on society either. The Taras murder proves that the killer is still at large. Even you, Captain, cannot believe that Malone would shoot anybody in cold blood."

"Well, he had motive and he came there with a gun! Taras was going to be a witness against him at the subornation hearing—" He broke off. "Hey, I'm supposed to be *asking* the questions!"

"You do have a conscience! You'll be asking yourself one question for the rest of your life, if you stand by and permit this miscarriage of justice. Sooner or later that thousand-dollar bill *will* be traced. If Malone had used it to tempt Taras, would he now be moving heaven and earth to prove it on himself? The D.A. has had it in for Malone these many years, but surely you yourself—"

"Harbin Hamilton don't like nobody. He outranks me. The case is outta my hands."

Miss Withers explained at some length how he could get it back into his hands. "Just consent to leave Malone where he is until tomorrow, and have a couple of your men hidden nearby."

"I can't. I been told to lay off. The moment I start

assigning men the word gets around to Hamilton's office."

"Then can't you further the cause of justice by simply not interfering? The killer is as jittery now as a cat on a hot tin roof."

Von Flanagan gave her an odd look. "You got an idea who it is?"

"Of course I have an idea! But I'm tired of having it suggested that I have lost all my marbles. The criminal has to expose himself! It came to me this morning, when I picked up a magazine puzzle that stumped me last night."

"I got puzzles enough here on the job." Von Flanagan forgot why they were originally here—at least, to the point of sending out for coffee.

"Your bark is worse than your bite. Captain, I'm only in this case because I hate injustice. I hate to think of a murderer going around laughing at us!"

"What d'you mean 'us'?"

"Everybody who's on the side of law and order. You can't tell me you're really satisfied with the Coleman case? So please don't move Malone, and please phone the papers to use that story."

Von Flanagan chewed on his unlighted cigar. "Okay," he said. "I can't put guards in the hospital, because I'd be criticized for making a stake-out that might endanger other patients with possibly some wild shooting and all. But the story can run, only I'll put a tail on every single suspect in this case tonight, so that if one of them even heads in the direction of County Hospital with a bomb or a gat or a shiv on him, we'll nab him *before* it can happen!"

"Thank you," said Miss Withers, grateful for all

193

favors. In spite of what von Flanagan had said, she herself was going to be hidden in that hospital room. She knew from experience how easily a suspect could slip a tail, especially if he knew he was being followed—as easy as it would be for anyone to walk unnoticed into the hospital at any hour of the day or night, if he simply walked straight ahead and seemed to be there on legitimate business.

And megalomania—the delusion of being smarter and more powerful than anybody else—was at the core of every murderer's psyche.

"Of course you'll come along with me tonight," the schoolteacher told Maggie as the two of them lingered over dinner at Joe the Angel's, each of them fortified by a small glass of sherry. "Two heads are better than one, I always say."

"To be shot at, maybe," said Maggie, and ordered another sherry.

"If I can masquerade as a head nurse, you can be a nurse's aide. The hospital is so overcrowded and so busy that anything goes."

"The things I do for eighty dollars a week—when I get it!" said Maggie.

So it was that late in the evening the two devoted admirers and co-conspirators converged on the hospital room of John J. Malone, well after visiting hours were over. They waited until they had seen the floor nurses finish their midnight rounds and then came up the back stairs. Luckily Malone's room was not in direct view of the main desk.

He greeted them tenderly, too tenderly. In fact, he was mellow. "Malone, how *could* you, at a time like this?" cried Miss Withers.

194

"How?—as the Indian chief said to the mermaid. Well, if you must know, there's a disreputable old bum allowed to come through with his cart, selling newspapers and candy. He seems to have a side line, so I traded him my gold-plated cigar lighter for a much needed pint."

"Where have you hidden the nasty stuff?" demanded Hildegarde.

But Malone refused to answer on the grounds that it might tend to incriminate him. So the two women searched—in the bed, under the mattress, everywhere. While they were looking in the closet and bathroom, Malone yawned copiously, reached over to the vase on the bedside table, lifted out the flowers, and took a purely medicinal dose—which would have been better without the weedy taste of the plant stems, but you can't have everything.

Maggie finally found the empty bottle in the waste basket, and they gave up.

"And this is one time I wanted you to be on your toes," Miss Withers said.

"Name's Malone, not Nijinsky! But don't worry. I'll rise magnificently to the occasion, if there is one. Wish I knew who we're supposed to be expecting."

"Whom," corrected the schoolteacher automatically. "I think I know, but you'll only accuse me again of having lost my wits. The answer, if it is an answer, came to me while I was working a Double-Crostic in the current *Saturday Review.*"

"Crossword puzzle stuff?" Malone yawned again.

"Infinitely more complicated. There's a list of definitions, and you have to guess the right word or phrase —such as that 'Jam today' is the one thing Alice in Wonderland couldn't have. The individual letters go on the proper squares, and after you have made a dozen guesses or so on the definitions, you've got bits and pieces of the main puzzle, which is supposed to be an author's name and a quote. But at this point it seems to be hopeless, and you drop it."

"A good idea. Let's recite classic limericks. I have to do something to keep awake; the sleeping pill the nurse gave me is taking effect."

"Listen, this is fascinating. Sometimes when you come back to the puzzle and take a fresh look at it, you suddenly see the whole pattern; the missing letters fall into place and make words, and the words make phrases. That happened this morning. And then I realized that the same technique applies in solving a mystery. I realized that the key word in our present puzzle is M-O-N-E-Y . . ."

"Money's root . . . all evil," said Malone helpfully.

"The correct quotation is '*The love* of money,' and so forth. But come, we have preparations to make."

In a matter of minutes the trap was set. Malone was under the bed on a blanket, with sheets arranged down the sides of the bed to hide him. Extra bedding and Miss Withers' raincoat suggested a sleeping form in the bed. The room was dark, except for what glow came through the hall door, slightly ajar.

Maggie was stationed in the bathroom, and Miss Withers in the closet. The schoolteacher was very hopeful. Somewhat unjustifiably hopeful, because—as she was soon to realize—she had failed to remember Murphy's First Law, which is "If Anything Can Possibly Go Wrong, It Will!"

The minutes passed, and the hours. Apart from the lawyer's snores from his lair beneath the bed, the vast hospital was silent as a tomb. It had other attributes of a tomb, too—including a pervading chill.

"The watched pot never boils," said Miss Withers to herself. "They also serve who only stand and wait. But they get cramps doing it."

There was the hint of gray dawn in the sky when they gave it up as a bad job. Miss Withers found Maggie asleep on the seat with her head and arms in the washbasin. *"Don't* say 'I told you so,'" warned the schoolteacher. "Leave that for Malone."

But the little man had nothing to say when the two women got him semi-awake and back up into his bed again; his snoring hardly missed a beat.

"He's passed out and happy," said Maggie. "Let's go!"

"Good night, Malone," said Miss Withers to the recumbent form. "Relax, nobody walked into the trap."

She started out, then stopped. *"But somebody did!"* she wailed.

A wave of terror engulfed her—because there was no single pint ever distilled that would make John J. Malone pass out!

In a second the lights were on, and she was forcing his eyes open, staring at the pupils.

"Maggie, go get the nurse. A doctor! He's been poisoned!"

Maggie didn't go, but she stood still and screamed like a banshee, which served. All hell broke loose.

"Well," said a philosophic young resident, after the stomach pump had done its job, "if he had to take Seconal enough to kill a horse, he picked a handy place. Barbiturates mixed with alcohol are triple deadly, but if we can keep him awake and walking and full of coffee he's got a fifty-fifty chance."

197

Von Flanagan had shouldered his way into the picture by this time, and was very disgusted. This never had made any sense to him.

"Oh, be *quiet!*" cried Miss Withers, beside herself. "I'm thinking! Malone said he got the whisky from the old man who comes through the halls selling candy and newspapers."

Which was all very well, only it turned out that there *wasn't* anybody of that description peddling papers and candy through the hospital—not last night or any other time. Except perhaps in this one room. . . .

"If you ask me—" began von Flanagan.

"*Shut up*, please!" blazed the furious schoolma'am. "Captain, I feel a streak of homicidal mania coming on. Lend me your gun, I want to go out and kill somebody. Or if you'll come along, perhaps you can prevent actual bloodshed!" She whispered something in his ear.

"But—but I can't do that without a warrant!"

"Can't you get one, if I swear out a complaint? Only, of course, all the evidence will be destroyed by then. Captain, we *must* act now!"

There was something compelling, something hypnotic in her intensity.

"We'll skip the warrant," he decided. "I'm only going along to keep you from committing felonious assault, anyways."

So it was that Miss Withers and the Captain went tearing across the sleeping city with sirens screeching. Never before in Chicago's history had so many thousands of irate citizens been rudely awakened at that ungodly hour of a Sabbath dawn. But the most surprised and indignant of all was their quarry, who finally came down, half dressed, to answer the doorbell.

"This is a citizen's arrest," said Miss Withers very formally. "Gerald Adams, I arrest you for the murder of John J. Malone."

The man only stared at them blankly. "I guess it's the law," began von Flanagan apologetically. "Under certain circumstances . . ."

But the bright young attorney wasn't pleading the law, which both visitors knew was technically on his side. He was trying to slam the door in their faces, which from von Flanagan's point of view was an error. Mr. Gerald was collared before he could lock himself in the bathroom.

The search that followed was unsuccessful—there were no traces of a false beard, stage make-up or spirit gum, or a bum's clothes. All that evidence had been disposed of.

But none of it was needed—for Gerald Adams had John J. Malone's gold-plated cigar lighter in his pocket.

"He just couldn't bring himself ever to let go of anything valuable!" pointed out Miss Withers in weary triumph.

It was sometime later, and the two oddly assorted partners-in-crime-and-detection were having dinner at Henrici's. Malone, still looking pale and wan, had even refused to look at the wine card, being very much on the wagon—for the time being at least. But he, and Miss Withers too, were making up for it with the vichyssoise and pheasant under glass and fresh asparagus hollandaise.

"It is rather a shame you missed the final scene," she told him.

"I was damn near having a final scene, all alone," he reminded her. "Anyway, you did fine. I can still boast

199

that I've never lost a client yet, and this time I have a client who can and will pay."

"It was the money, of course," Miss Withers was saying. "A sort of love story—the love of Gerald Adams for the five-million-dollar estate."

"I stopped suspecting him for the same reasons you did—when I found that nobody had been dipping into the till . . ." Malone sighed.

"But neither of us realized that just the *management* of that much money would bring in $35,000 or more a year to the firm of Gittel and Adams! Gerald couldn't stand to have the firm lose that revenue, which it was bound to do if Junior inherited. More than that, he couldn't stand to think of Junior wasting all that money on women and liquor!"

"I wouldn't call it exactly *wasting*," said Malone with a touch of his old fire.

"Gerald knew that the old man was about to die, so he killed Jeanine and effectively pinned the crime on Junior. Junior was his intended victim from the beginning, but he could be taken care of this safe way—who would suspect Gerald Adams of the murder of a girl he had never even met, and who would suspect the lawyer for the accused, the apparent murderer's own attorney? But the net result was that the estate would be in the firm's hands forever!"

"Sure," said Malone. "It's all clear now. Gerald knew where the car was kept, and since he handled the purchase of such major extravagances he could easily get a key. All he wanted was Junior safe in prison and the precious estate in his own hands. When it looked as if I would expose Taras as having been overpressured into the identification of Junior, Gerald first bribed the man to double-cross me at the trial, and then, when I got wind of the bribe, killed him. Adams undoubtedly got that thousand-dollar bill from the big-shot bookie he once defended. What I don't understand is why he took Frances Coleman into his office."

Hildegarde shrugged. "Probably so he could keep tabs on her, and possibly to set her up as the next logical suspect if by some miracle you got Junior off. I wouldn't be at all surprised if the private detective, Finch, approached Gerald with his wild proposition before he came to us. But you must admit now that we'd never have pinned anything on Gerald if he hadn't been forced out into the open and hadn't tried to kill you with that bottle spiked with Seconal."

"I should have recognized him, but the room was dark. I just got the impression of a kindly old guy with whiskers and dark glasses," Malone admitted. "My eyes were on the bottle."

"If it had been an anonymous gift in the mail, it would have aroused suspicion," she pointed out. "But that was sheer talent—the man offering to trade the bottle for your lighter when you had no money. But he should have disposed of the lighter in spite of the fact that once he had his hands on anything—even the Coleman estate—he wouldn't let go!"

"The lighter is evidence; I'll probably never get it back," complained Malone. "Von Flanagan will keep it. Say, he let you down on one thing, though. He promised to have *all* the suspects tailed that night."

"The slip was mine," confessed Miss Withers. "By that time I was suspecting Adams, and plenty! But I hadn't communicated my suspicions to poor von Flanagan, or even to you. So his men watched only Finch and Frances Coleman and Zimmer—leaving Gerald Adams free. Von Flanagan never even considered Gerald as a suspect. And the man simply walked in and did his dirty work before the trap was even set! Yes, I goofed, Malone. In the words of the greatest detective of them all, if it should ever strike you that I am getting over-confident of my powers, kindly whisper 'Norbury'—I mean 'County Hospital'—in my ear."

"Well, everybody's satisfied, except Gerald Adams. Junior is out of prison, and I hear he and Frances are going on a second honeymoon."

"And what about you yourself and the lovely Helga Swenson?" Miss Withers was beaming with approval.

"She wanted to reform me," he said, a little sadly. Just then the waiter came closer, to ask if there would be anything else—a brandy or a liqueur perhaps?

"That will be *all*," said Miss Withers firmly.

And it was.

*

Withers and Malone,
Brain-Stormers

ттттттттттттттттттттттттттттттттттт

"THEY'RE AFTER ME!" gasped John J. Malone as he stumbled into Miss Hildegarde Withers' cottage. He set down his tinkling briefcase and sank wearily into her easiest chair.

"Who? The men with the strait jacket?" queried the surprised schoolteacher. She had heard nothing of the handsome, irrepressible little lawyer for more than two years, but now here he was—and obviously beside himself. She sensibly shot the night bolt, then peered out through the venetian blinds, but the side street in Santa Monica-by-the-Sea seemed as quiet as usual. "I don't see anyone," she reassured him. "But it is said that the guilty flee when no man pursueth . . ."

"Well," protested Malone, who was at the moment trying to regain his breath and also to fend off the overfriendly advances of Talley the standard French poodle, "I may be guilty and I may not—that's for the jury. But somebody did pursueth me most of the way from the airport. I had to jump out of my taxi a couple of blocks from here and do a sprint across lots and through alleys. It was two men in a black sedan, and boding me no good, believe me!"

"But *who?* Surely you must have some idea."

He shrugged. "Anybody! I am *persona non grata* with Harbin Hamilton, deputy D.A. for Cook County. And with Captain von Flanagan, detective bureau of the Chicago police. *And* with Filthy Phil Pappke the bail bondsman, *and* with a wealthy bastrich named Bedford, *and* even with Joe the Angel at the City Hall Bar. To say nothing of Maggie."

"Then it must be bad! You're welcome here, even if I haven't done my breakfast dishes. But go on—tell me what brings you all the way out to California."

"Murder," Malone admitted dismally. "Maybe two murders, and one of 'em my own."

The Withers eyebrows shot up. "I don't quite understand."

"So do I! We've got to prevent a murder, only—" He sighed. "It's a *long* story. Any refreshments in the house?"

"I can offer you some coffee and cookies," she said firmly, and disappeared into the kitchen. Life had been rather dull of late for the retired schoolteacher, but now she was perking up. Whenever she had crossed paths—and sometimes swords—with John J. Malone in the past the adventures had always been memorable. She even had the scars to prove it. In a moment she was plying her unexpected guest with dull refreshments and sharp questions. Malone spiked the coffee from a bottle stashed in his topcoat pocket, and fed the cookies to the eager poodle whenever he thought Hildegarde's back was turned.

"I'm really out here looking for a girl," he confessed.

"Quite out of my line," Miss Withers told him. "I'm a Miss, not a Madam. Have you tried breaking a hundred-dollar bill in a hotel bar? I thought that was your sure-fire method of making friends."

"Listen, Hildegarde! I mean one special girl—name of Nancy Jorgens. A lovely, very impetuous and very unpredictable girl, age 24, size 38-24-36 . . ."

"Spare me the vital statistics."

"Nancy is supposed to be out here—somewhere in the Los Angeles area anyway. But it's like looking for a needle in a haystack."

"Which is not such a difficult task, if you have a big enough magnet!" Miss Withers was brightening. "In this case, the magnet being whoever or whatever brought her out here—"

"That would be Paul Bedford." The little lawyer spoke the name as if it had a bad taste. Then he added hopefully, lifting his cup, "Do you mind if I sweeten this?"

"You've already *sweetened* it three times, but who's counting?" The schoolteacher sniffed disapprovingly. "Anyway, get on with your story."

"You'll remember that it's always been my proudest boast that I never lost a client yet? Well, that's been true —up to now."

"An execution? But I thought the murder hadn't happened yet."

Malone shook his head, spilling cigar ashes over his new Finchley suit and flamboyant Countess Mara tie. "I mean lost, literally. Nancy flew the coop yesterday. She's a fugitive from justice and because of her I'm a fugitive, period! You see, it was because of that paternity suit I lost—then the forgery indictment, the conspiracy charges, and—" The little lawyer sighed. "But I'll tell you about it on the way downtown."

"The way downtown *where?*"

"L.A. police headquarters. There's so little time— we've got to have official help. Surely, with your connections—"

"This is not Manhattan—there's no friendly Inspector Oscar Piper out here. I am known downtown at Headquarters, yes—but I'm afraid I'm known as anathema. We can expect no help from that quarter."

"But we've *got* to find Bedford before Nancy finds him! She disappeared yesterday, just after I got her out on bail, taking with her only some summer-weight clothes and a pistol that was a prop in the show she'd been playing in when she got arrested. But there was a note in last Sunday's *Trib* society section saying that Paul Bedford, of the Winnetka Bedfords, had left town to spend a few weeks in the Sunny Southland of California. Nancy must have seen that item. She didn't even phone me to say goodbye—probably afraid I'd try to talk her out of it."

"Does she know where Bedford is?"

"They were pretty close at one time, so maybe she does. But *we* don't."

"Hmmm," mused Miss Withers. "Is Bedford a prominent person?"

"And how. Even before the trial and all that publicity, he was front-page or society-page stuff. Football star in some Ivy League college, also crew and track. Flew a desk in the Pentagon during the war, but got a decoration. And his collection of rare autographs is famous—he has a complete set of the signers of the Declaration of Independence, including a disputed Button Gwinnett that a book got written about. He and his sister Doris inherited over four million bucks when their mother died a few years ago—"

"Enough, Malone. The gilded rich have predictable habits, like migratory wildfowl. He'll almost certainly be in Palm Springs, Santa Barbara, La Jolla, Malibu Beach, or Balboa Island. And never underestimate the power of a long-distance phone call. Who could put through a person-to-person call from Chicago to any of those places? How about Maggie?"

"Maggie takes a dim view of all this. But you could ask her."

Hildegarde proceeded to do just that. "Miss Withers!" finally came Maggie's voice across the miles. "I might have known that you'd get dragged into it! So Malone got as far as your place. Is he—?"

"Medium so. I am about to make some more coffee."

"Good! But try to keep him away from *that woman!*"

The schoolteacher never batted an eye. "Yes, but it's Bedford we've got to locate." She explained her plan, in detail. "And hurry, Maggie!" Hanging up, Miss Withers turned to Malone. "She'll try. But just why does Maggie refer to Nancy Jorgens as 'that woman' and advise me to keep you away from her?"

Malone fidgeted. "Maggie's prejudiced. You see, Nancy came into my office one day about a year ago—and a visitor of loveliness she was. Hair like spun honey, eyes blue as the Lakes of Killarney, a figure that—"

"Skip it. She's an actress, you said?"

"Model, singer, actress—she was just another pretty girl trying to break into show business. But what I was going to say about her figure—when she came into my office, *her slip showed.*"

"I beg your pardon?" And then Miss Withers read between the lines. "Oh!"

Malone nodded. "She was 'in trouble.' Said the man was Paul Bedford, of the canned-beef Bedfords. According to Nancy it was the old, old story, right out of *East Lynne*. She'd appealed to him when she discovered her indelicate condition, but—"

"He just sneered?"

"No, he told her to go see a shady doctor. When she refused to do that, he had her thrown out and the door slammed in her face."

"The skunk! Only I apologize to the entire genus mephitis."

"So I brought suit against Bedford on bastardy charges. I thought sure he'd settle out of court for maybe a cool hundred grand—but no dice. I think that vinegary-Vassary sister of his, Doris, put him up to fighting it. Anyway, they yelled 'legal blackmail,' and got Walt Hamilton to stand for the defense—he's the younger brother of Deputy D.A. Harbin Hamilton, who's been trying to nail my hide to the barn door for years. So my client and I had to go to court. . . ."

"Let me put a little more coffee in your whisky," Miss Withers offered sympathetically.

"Thanks. In court I had a regular field day—at first. I was never more eloquent, if I do say so myself. By the time the case came to trial Nancy had had her baby and got her figure back—she made a very appealing witness. It was an all-male jury, and when I rested our case, with Nancy sitting there in the courtroom with little Johnny in her arms, there wasn't a dry eye in the house."

"I can imagine—" She did a double take. "Little *Johnny?*"

"Yes," sighed Malone. "She named the little tyke

after me, out of gratitude. You see, I'd paid the doctor and the hospital—any attorney would have done the same for a client. I'd even found a nice foster home for the kid—with some relatives of Maggie's out in Berwyn."

"Hmm-mm," murmured Miss Withers. "Go on."

"And then the defense pulled a knife on me—right in my back. They produced a parade of witnesses, gentlemen—and I use the word in quotes—who swore on their sacred oath that they had bounced in the—pardon me, I mean swore they had enjoyed the favors of my fair client."

"Oh, no!"

"Oh, yes! Some of them were probably just hired from a casting office—it must have cost Bedford plenty. Anyway, we were snowed under. There was no time and no money to finance an overnight investigation of those lying witnesses. A couple of them had actually had dates with Nancy, and there were notes and autographed photos to prove it. She had accepted trinkets from some of them—nothing big like mink or emeralds—but you know how girls in the profession are."

"I hope," murmured the schoolteacher, "that we're speaking of the *same* profession?"

"Objection!" said the little lawyer, reddening. "Nancy Jorgens isn't—"

"Go on, Malone."

"Well, unfortunately she didn't have any letters of Bedford's written during their brief but flaming affair. That in itself proves she wasn't mercenary!"

"Or that he was too cautious to write any! So you lost the case?"

"Not quite. I got a mistrial—a hung jury. Of course I was going to move for a new trial when either Nancy or I could dig up the costs. But meanwhile she has to eat, and she's supporting the baby, a cute little shaver. So she gets a part in a melodrama some shoestring theater group is putting on, mostly on the strength of her cheesecake publicity at the time of the trial. And she proves she really can act!"

"I have no doubt of it," admitted Miss Withers. "Particularly when she has a sympathetic male audience. How long have you been in love with her, Malone?"

"Me in love? Don't be silly! Anyway, Nancy gets good reviews in the play and the show moves into a downtown Loop theater and everything is going swell—then blooie! She gets herself arrested on the charge of forging Paul Bedford's name to a $25,000 check!"

"Dear, dear!"

" 'Dear-dear' isn't the word for it. It comes as a complete surprise to me. You see, she received the check in the mail, she says—"

"She *says!*"

"—and she rushes jubilantly over to me with it. I endorse it and then Joe the Angel, my old pal who runs the City Hall Bar, puts it through his bank for her. Do we celebrate *that* night!"

"I can imagine. But the check bounces—I mean bounced?"

"Higher than the Wrigley Building. Before I know it, my client is in jail, and I'm up to my ears in trouble. Harbin Hamilton in the D.A.'s office throws the book at Nancy. He's out to get me for conspiracy, accessory before the fact—or at the least disbarred!"

"Was the signature such an obvious forgery, then?"

"No, it was almost perfect. You can see yourself—I've got the enlarged photocopies in my briefcase here, along with the transcript of the preliminary examination. But

210

every single handwriting expert said it was traced—they can tell by the variations in pressure used on the pen or something." Malone rose suddenly, tripped over the poodle, apologized, and then began to stalk up and down. "According to Nancy, the check simply arrived in the mail. The envelope and all the rest of it were typed, including an 'In Release of All Claims' just above where the endorsement would go. Naturally she thought Bedford had had a change of heart, and so did I." Malone was now peering out the window. "Say, that black sedan has gone by twice!"

"Relax, Malone. You're safe here. But this whole thing doesn't make sense! How could anybody in his right mind believe that a girl would forge a check like that, knowing that it would immediately come to light —or just as soon as the man got his bank statement?"

"The D.A.'s office had an answer for that. You see, Paul Bedford was supposed to be going off on a world cruise about that time—according to another of those squibs in the society column; but at the last minute the trip had been canceled because of his sister's health— she probably needed a transfusion of ice water. The authorities thought that *Nancy thought* that he wouldn't find out about the check until she had got the money and disappeared with it!"

"And of course such an idea would never occur to her?"

"Of course not. Unfortunately, however—on the same day I got the check cashed for her—she went to a travel agency and made a reservation to fly to Mexico City. Perfectly innocently, of course."

"Of course. She came into money, so she was going to leave her career—and leave you—"

"I was going along," Malone confessed sheepishly.

211

"Just for a week or so. I haven't had a real vacation in years and I needed one."

"You needed to have your head examined! But never mind that. I still don't see that the prosecution has much of a case against your client. How could a girl like that prepare an almost perfect forgery?"

"Hamilton didn't say that—he thinks I took care of that angle. You see, I got Harry the Penman acquitted only a few months ago, and others in the profession owe me favors. Not that I'd ever stoop to a thing like that."

"I'm sure you wouldn't. I wish I were as sure about Nancy. Because it all boils down to *cui bono,* Malone. Who stood to benefit? Who stood to pocket the $25,000, except the person to whom the check was made out? Riddle me that!"

"I know," admitted Malone, still eying the window. "Oh-oh, there goes that black sedan again. Hildegarde, we've gotta get out of here! Why oh *why* doesn't Maggie call?"

"Possess your soul in patience, Malone. Be calm— whoops!" The phone had barely started to ring when the schoolteacher pounced on it. "Hello? Yes—yes, this is she! Put her on, and hurry! Hello, Maggie?"

It really was Maggie, being the perfect secretary again. And the plot had worked; Paul Bedford had been located, up at Malibu. ". . . so he's sitting by that phone, waiting for the call to be completed," came Maggie's excited voice. "And I don't dare answer the office phone because I don't have anything to say to him; I don't even dare use it—I'm calling from a phone booth and I'm out of quarters—"

"Bless you!" cried Miss Withers. "Goodbye!"

"Wait!" Maggie screamed. "Tell Malone I just got a tip that Harbin Hamilton is on a plane headed for

California, with a bench warrant in his pocket! It's not for the Jorgens girl, it's for—" And just then the operator cut them off.

"Good for Maggie," said Malone. "It's nice to be warned about Hamilton, but it'll all be over before he gets here. So Bedford is at Malibu. No address?"

"Just the phone number—Grove 2-2533. But we'll find it."

"What are we waiting for?" the little lawyer demanded.

"For my hat." She rushed out, and Malone took advantage of the opportunity to replace the empty pint with a full one from his briefcase; there might be snakes at Malibu. The schoolteacher's hat, he decided immediately upon her return, was something that could only have been inspired by a Rorschach ink blot test, but he followed her in silence as she led the way out through the back door. "We'll take Talley with us," Miss Withers decided, as she quietly raised the garage door. "Since we're headed up Snob Hill, the presence of a French poodle may give us a certain *cachet* . . ."

Malone climbed into the ancient coupé, with some mental reservations. But the schoolteacher eventually got it going, and then they were headed down the alley, bouncing along a short street, then down more alleys, winding and twisting. "Just to throw anybody off," she explained.

"You just about threw *me* off at that last corner!" the little lawyer said through clenched teeth. He hung on tight as she whirled the little coupé onto Wilshire, down the ramp, and onto the Coast Highway heading north. The dog now had his head resting on the back of the seat between them, whining,

"Maybe he wants to drive," Malone suggested. "I wish

somebody would—you missed that gravel truck by half an inch." They rolled on, at a dizzy fifty miles per hour. Then it was fifty-five, then sixty. "Will you please slow down?" Malone begged.

Every nut and bolt in the venerable chariot was protesting audibly. "I tried slowing down," Miss Withers said. "But it seems that black sedan behind us slows down whenever I do. And then it speeds up when I try to move ahead. Do you suppose—?"

"I do." Malone shook his head sadly. "Probably Phil Pappke's strong-arm boys. I should never have talked him into going bail for Nancy; he isn't known around City Hall as Filthy Phil for nothing."

"But it was Nancy Jorgens who jumped her bail. He should be annoyed at your client, not you."

"Well, I'm afraid that as partial surety for her I put up a building I own, out on the South Side. Unfortunately I won it in a poker game, so the title is cloudy. And it's been condemned anyway. Naturally Pappke got irritated when he found that out, after Nancy skipped town yesterday. In fact, Filthy Phil lived up to his moniker by giving me until midnight either to produce Nancy or the money—*or else.*"

"Midnight tonight?" gasped Miss Withers, passing a line of other cars and neatly getting back to her favorite position—directly over the white line.

"Midnight *last* night," Malone said. "On the other hand, this may not be Phil's henchmen at all. He's only one of many who want my scalp; he'll have to wait in line. Hildegarde, you see beside you a very unhappy man."

"You're not the first to be put behind the eight-ball by a woman," she reminded him. "Well, we're getting into Malibu now."

214

"Probably too late," the little lawyer moaned. "All we've got to do now is to get rid of that tail, then find out where Paul Bedford is hiding out—"

"Leave it to me," said Miss Withers. Then, ignoring his hopeful suggestion that they could inquire about Bedford at the nearest liquor store, she turned smack-dab into a parking lot just beside a small, squarish building which flew both the American and California flags.

"Hey, that's the sheriff's office!" Malone cried.

"Certainly. You'll notice that this move already takes care of the black sedan—it just went by, and very fast. Now if you'll give me a moment to fix Talley up—luckily he just had a clipping and looks quite silly enough to be anybody's pampered darling . . ." She put a rhinestone collar around the poodle's neck and affixed a green bow to his topknot. "Presents from Inspector Piper," she explained over her shoulder, as she led the bedizened dog out of the car and into the sheriff's substation.

Behind the rail sat a dough-faced, stolid man in a black uniform, engaged in reading a paperback titled *2,000 Questions from Civil Service Exams.* "Good morning, Sergeant," Miss Withers said brightly, keeping a firm grip on Talley's leash. And then she asked the crucial question.

The officer blinked. "The Bedford house? Why, it's closed up."

"No, it isn't, Griggsy," said a male voice from an inner room. "Bedford and his sister opened it up. They're camping out there—roughing it without even any servants."

"Oh, good!" exclaimed the schoolteacher. "Because I mislaid the address, and I'd hate to go all the way back to the kennels without delivering Miss Doris' dog."

"The number's 12 Loretta Lane," said the other uniformed man, appearing suddenly in a doorway. "You turn in about a mile up the pike, third gate from here, then take the first to the left, then left again at the circle." He smiled a Boy Scout smile. "It's not easy to find —maybe I could ride along?"

He was looking not at her but at the sergeant, who started to frown.

"Thanks, anyway," said Miss Withers hastily. "I'm quite sure I can find it." And she dragged Talley hastily away.

Sergeant Griggs returned to his *2,000 Questions.* Then he looked up. "Hey, didn't I see a flimsy go through on this guy Bedford?"

The other shrugged. "Not that I know of. Except that we were supposed to keep an eye on the place while it was boarded up. But the folks are living there, all right. They phoned in a big order to the Market Basket yesterday—I know because my kid brother delivered it. A raft of canned goods, caviar, champagne, brandy, smoked oysters, Westphalian ham—all sorts of fancy stuff."

"No fancier than that dog. A diamond collar yet!"

"Bud said they wanted a lot of candles and a Coleman stove and all the newspapers, too. Looks like the high-and-mighty Bedfords are planning to rough it for a while. Bud said they hadn't even taken the shutters off the windows except around to the south, on the ocean side."

Griggs was frowning. "That's funny! No servants, no utilities except the phone, calling in their orders. Maybe they don't want it known they're here! And maybe you shouldn't have been so helpful with that old

216

biddy—she might be the finger woman for a mob." He reached for the phone. "Your brother in high school now?"

"Yeah, Bud's a senior."

"I just wanted to ask him if there was any dog food in that order."

While his partner derisively hummed the boomp-de-boomp-boomp theme music of a popular cops-and-robbers TV show, Griggs made the call—he had been bucking for lieutenant for years.

But the damage was already done.

Malone, Miss Withers and Talley had found the rambling rose-pink house at 12 Loretta Lane, perched on the edge of the cliff high above a small private beach and the broad Pacific. It stood shuttered, silent, asleep. Yet, just as they were about to disembark, they heard the muffled but unmistakable sound of a pistol shot within. It was immediately followed by another shot, then by a choked feminine scream.

"Too late!" cried Malone, as they dashed up the side-walk.

Miss Withers knocked and knocked, and the little lawyer rattled the doorknob, without avail. "Break it down?" she suggested. He rammed it with his shoulder, then shook his head.

"You stay here!" he ordered. "I'll try the back." He ran off, followed by the poodle, who didn't quite understand the game but wanted to get into it.

"Well, I never!" said the schoolteacher, somewhat vexed. She banged on the door again, then tried to peer into one of the shuttered windows. "The dickens with it!" She raced to the back, around the garage wing, and came suddenly into the blazing sunshine and onto a wide, roughstone patio gay with grass and flowering shrubs, outdoor furniture and umbrellas, and an immense but empty swimming pool.

She arrived just in time to see John J. Malone with a naked girl in his arms.

"Excuse *me!*" Miss Withers cried, aghast.

But on second look the girl wasn't quite naked after all; she wore flesh-colored Bikini-type halter and shorts. Still, she was what the schoolteacher would have called "a scandal to the jaybirds," and her breathtaking beauty only made it more scandalous.

"Damn it, darling," she was almost screaming, "let me go!" The young woman squirmed like an eel, trying desperately to get away toward the flight of wooden steps that descended down the cliff to the little beach below.

Malone had a good grip; he not only held his prize but he shook her fiercely. "Listen, Nancy! Listen to me! I'm your attorney, remember? He tried to strangle you, and you shot him in self-defense—remember that!"

"Oh, you don't understand! Let me go!"

But Miss Withers understood. Nancy Jorgens had a nasty little pistol in one hand, and it was still smoking. Without hesitation the schoolteacher crept up silently and snatched it away. "There," she said. "Now will somebody please tell me—" But nobody did. Talley had the most to say, barking his head off with happy excitement.

The girl finally went limp in Malone's grasp. "Back inside," he said sternly. "I'm taking over now." And he half carried the curvaceous beauty through the French doors into the house. After a thoughtful moment Miss Withers followed, carefully closing the doors behind her, right in Talley's puzzled face.

From then on things remained nightmarish. They

218

were in an immense living room full of modern chairs and furniture and garnished with Picasso and Modigliani prints and metal mobiles—a room that smelled of perfume, of the sea, and of raw cordite. A thin rigid woman of around forty—obviously Doris Bedford, the sister—was standing near the fireplace. Not doing anything, just standing. A clock ticked away somewhere, and the waves crashed booming on the rocks below.

Paul Bedford, slightly overweight, slightly tanned, slightly dead, lay all akimbo at the farther end of the room near an open window, staring thoughtfully at the ceiling. A vagrant breeze drifted in uninvited and ruffled his curly, thinning hair.

"I didn't—!" screamed Nancy Jorgens, before Malone's hand clamped over her mouth.

"Now what happened here?" the little lawyer demanded, looking accusingly at Doris Bedford.

"Who are you?" she whispered, hardly moving her pale lips. She wasn't looking at the intruders or at the body of her brother—she wasn't looking at anything.

Miss Withers came to life. "Never mind arguing. What matters is whether—is if—" She steeled herself, then moved to bend over Paul Bedford. This sort of thing was not exactly her cup of tea; she preferred her murders at secondhand. A mental problem in applied criminology was one thing, but this . . .

"My brother is dead," said Doris hollowly. "You needn't bother trying his pulse or putting a mirror to his lips. He's dead, I tell you. And *she* shot him, just as I knew she would!"

"You—you weren't even in the room!" cried Nancy, twisting away from Malone again.

But the little lawyer caught her, and his hand clamped over her mouth. Then he shoved her into a chair so hard that her teeth rattled. "Shut up!" he whispered fiercely. "We *want* her to have been in the room, maybe! I said let me handle this!" He turned to face Doris Bedford. "I am John J. Malone, Miss Jorgens' attorney. Please tell us in your own words exactly what happened."

"Just what I feared would happen, if Paul didn't get far enough away from *her!* She came bursting in here uninvited—she must have swum out around the rocks and trespassed on our beach. That was while my brother and I were waiting for a very important phone call from Chicago to be put through to us. She insisted that she had to talk to Paul alone, so I went out. But naturally I could hear . . ."

"Then you don't claim to have witnessed the alleged crime?" began Malone in his best courtroom manner.

Miss Withers had had enough. "For heaven's sake!" she cried. "This man may *not* be dead! I don't see a wound or any blood. None of us is a doctor—where's the phone, quick? An ambulance—"

"Never mind the ambulance. Get . . . police . . ." murmured Doris Bedford. And then she crumpled to the floor in a dead faint.

Miss Withers tried to move in two directions at once. She didn't quite make it.

"Wait," snapped Malone. "Maybe all three of us should blow this joint fast—it's only her word against ours. Listen, Hildegarde—"

Hildegarde was listening—to the brief, *sotto voce skrr* of a siren outside, and almost immediately afterward to a hammering on the front door. "I'm not compounding any felonies," she said. "And I'm afraid my running days are over. You both stay put—I'm going to open the door."

220

"Yes?" she said politely to the man outside, her recent acquaintance of the substation, Sergeant Griggs. His round, perspiring face wore a look of worried deference.

"Excuse me for busting in, but—" he began. Then he recognized her. "Say, what's going on here?" At that inauspicious moment Talley the poodle came bounding through the flowerbeds, darting in past them through the open door, then stopping short at the entrance to the living room. He set up an ear-splitting barking, and by the time his distraught mistress could grab him and shut him up, the fat was in the fire.

"It's murder," she admitted to the officer. "You may as well come in. It's in there."

Griggs got as far as the door, and froze. "Migawd!" he cried, unbelievingly. "It's *wholesale!*"

Miss Withers was helpful. "I think Miss Bedford has only fainted," she said softly. "Her brother seems to be the victim . . ."

"If there was a victim," Malone spoke up. He was sitting calmly on the arm of Nancy's chair, one hand firmly on her bare shoulder. "My client has absolutely nothing to say at this time." It was not the exact truth—Nancy had "Ouch!" to say, reacting to his warning pinch.

Sergeant Griggs knelt for a moment over what was left of Paul Bedford. "Colder'n Kelsey," he said hollowly. "This is it, folks." Nobody said anything. Nancy Jorgens looked guilty, Malone looked guilty, and Miss Withers suspected that she looked guiltier than either of them.

For the sake of the professional reputations of Mr John J. Malone and Miss Hildegarde Withers, it might be well to draw the mantle of charity over the next hour. Everything had, as Malone aptly put it, "gone to hell in a handbasket." Paul Bedford was a stiffening corpse. His

221

sister had come out of her faint only long enough to point at Nancy and scream, "She shot him, she shot him twice!" and then had relapsed into a coma.

The police were everywhere, doubled and redoubled. "And three down, vulnerable," Miss Withers whispered to the little lawyer. "Bridge, you know."

"Nobody should burn their bridges until they come to them," he whispered back absently. "I wish you'd shut up and let me think." Typically, the retired schoolteacher had from time to time been making helpful suggestions about the way an on-the-spot murder investigation should be conducted, none of which Sergeant Griggs took in the right spirit. For some reason, the officer seemed inclined to consider Miss Withers as hot a suspect as the other two. That tied Hildegarde's hands, if not her tongue.

Nor was Malone in his best form, either. With a knowledge of women which, like Dr. Watson's, "extended over three continents," he must have had some doubts about his lovely client and the extent to which she had bedazzled him for her own ends. The ground was not firm beneath his immaculate Italian oxfords. Unfortunately, one of the first things the officers had done was to have everybody searched, and his pint bottle of snake-bite remedy had been summarily impounded. That was the last straw. He was in the depths, but he was still trying to think fast

Nancy Jorgens seemed the coolest of all. She had found a cigarette in a little box on a mosaic table beside her, and she lit it with a steady hand. Miss Withers was beginning to admit to herself a sneaking liking for the young woman. "There is more to that girl than meets the eye," she said to herself. "And at the moment there is certainly a good deal of her *to* meet the eye!" But

Nancy seemed magnificently unaware of her semi-nakedness.

Around the three of them the breakers of the law dashed higher and higher; the house was so full of uniforms that it looked like a St. Patrick's Day parade in Manhattan. There were doctors and coroner's physicians and a police crime-lab squad with cameras and fingerprint powders and tiny vacuum cleaners—and everyone was having a field day.

The three suspects had been herded into the play-room, near a dusty ping-pong table and an ornate but understocked bar, with one of the sheriff's deputies on guard and taking his duties very seriously. "I was just thinking—" began Miss Withers.

"No talking," the officer told her.

"But I was only going to say that it isn't sensible to lock my dog in the kitchen. He can open refrigerators and cupboards!"

"Quiet!" So the three of them just sat there. Doris Bedford had been taken tenderly to her bedroom and was now under the care of a doctor and a nurse; Miss Withers might have considered trying a maidenly swoon herself, but her curiosity had got the better of her. She had to see Malone talk his way out of this one!

After a time Sergeant Griggs stalked in on them, complete with notebook and pen. The case was his baby, and he made that perfectly clear. "This happened in unincorporated county territory," he told them. "So I'm in charge. I'm taking your statements—"

"One at a time, separately," put in Miss Withers. "I believe that's the correct procedure."

"Yes, one at a—be quiet! *You* first." He jabbed at Nancy. "Mac, take the other two away and sit on 'em."

"I object!" spoke up Malone. "I am John J. Malone,

223

.

Miss Jorgens' attorney-of-record. You will question her in my presence or not at all. Furthermore, if you question me I will give my name and address only. I was not a witness to the alleged crime, arriving on the scene only after whatever happened happened. Anything my client may have said to me is a privileged communication unless the court later decides it is properly part of the *res gestae* . . ."

"I said *QUIET!*" roared Griggs. He turned on Miss Withers. "Now you, ma'am—"

"This lady is also my client," Malone interposed. "I insist—"

"Nonsense," interrupted the schoolteacher. She took a deep breath. Then, not looking at the little lawyer, she said calmly, "Mr. Malone is mistaken when he says he is my attorney. He is just a friend of mine. I only drove him up here because he was in a hurry to see his client, Miss Jorgens, and thought she might have come here. Just as we arrived we heard two shots. Mr. Malone tried the front door, then told me to watch there while he ran around to the back of the house. I got tired of waiting and followed him, just in time to see him with Miss Jorgens on the patio. We three came inside immediately through the open French doors and found the body—"

"Okay, okay!" said Sergeant Griggs, scribbling. "But not so fast."

"We saw Miss Bedford standing near her brother's body. She said something about the girl's having shot him—"

Malone was so busy giving Hildegarde withering glances that he had momentarily forgotten Nancy, who spoke up with the determined insistence of a balked child. "She wasn't even in the room, I tell you!"

"But you do admit shooting him, don't you?"

224

"This is absolutely improper!" cried Malone desperately. "You are putting words in her mouth. And if there was any shooting it was solely in self-defense!"

"That would be just dandy," remarked the Sergeant dryly. "Only in self-defense nobody but nobody shoots an unarmed man in the back!" They froze at that. "There wasn't any wound or any blood on the front of the corpse, or I would have noticed it!" Griggs added triumphantly.

Nancy cried, "Oh, no, no! I—"

"Miss Jorgens," Malone interrupted, "denies everything!"

Griggs seemed at the point of spontaneous combustion; Miss Withers fancied she could already see smoke coming out of his big red ears. But at that moment they were relieved by the sound of a heavy knocking at the door. The officer who had been called Mac opened it, listened, then beckoned to his superior. Griggs hesitated, gave the suspects a warning glance and went reluctantly out. Mac stayed in the doorway, more interested in what was going on in the hall than in the room. Malone managed to catch Hildegarde's eye and whispered reproachfully, "Nice going, Miss Blabbermouth!"

"I'm afraid I've only just begun," the schoolteacher whispered back, feeling rather like Benedict Arnold. But she was convinced that what had to be done had to be done.

Meanwhile, the cause of all this commotion sat perfectly still, her lovely legs crossed, her pale hair unmussed. Nancy was like a child who had idly dropped a lighted match in the underbrush and now was only a mildly interested spectator at the holocaust. Perhaps she had not chosen the almost invisible bathing suit as the perfect costume in which to be arrested, but it certainly gave her a definite edge—with the opposite sex, anyway. If Griggs had known his business, Miss Withers was thinking, he would have found a robe or a blanket and made the girl put it on, so he and the rest of the officers could keep their minds on their work.

But their inquisitor came back, too soon. With him now were reinforcements in the shape of a number of sober-faced gentlemen in casual sports attire who were still obviously detectives or officials; one of them Miss Withers thought she remembered from the recent McWalters murder affair. He was a man named Dade, who was supposed to be something important in the D.A.'s office downtown. He had given her little or no trouble then—but that time she had been on the other side of the fence. Now he did not even nod.

In addition there was a pudgy civilian in sober "eastern" clothes, who wore an expression of unadulterated glee on his pale, slightly greenish face. "Well, Malone!" said the great Harbin Hamilton. "It is a pleasure, a great pleasure, to meet you like this!"

The little lawyer was obviously staggered. All he needed right now was the unwelcome sight of the Deputy D.A. of Cook County. "Hello, Harbin," he managed to say. "So you had to fly out and get into the act! You look even unhealthier than usual—rough trip, I hope I hope?"

"It was worth every bit of it, shyster," said Hamilton.

"All right!" cut in Sergeant Griggs, still trying to keep control of his first big murder case. "Never mind the personalities." He walked over and put his thick hand on Nancy's bare shoulder. "Nancy Jorgens, I arrest you on suspicion of murder!"

Nancy took his hand and removed it, as if it had been

a damp clam. "Am I supposed to say something?" she asked coolly.

"Play it your own way, sister. The doctor says you missed Bedford both times, and the bullets went out through the open window behind him. But you were the cause of a fatal heart attack, so it's exactly the same as if you'd taken dead aim. We know all about the trouble you had with him back in Chicago—"

"She tried to shake him down with a phony lawsuit, and when that failed she forged his name to a check for $25,000; she's under indictment for that now!" put in Harbin Hamilton helpfully. "And having jumped her bail, she's a fugitive from justice." He took a step toward Nancy. "We know you had a gun with you when you came out here from Chicago. You were aware that Bedford was hiding out with his sister—hiding out from you. You located him at this beach place, you knew you couldn't get in the front way, so you swam around the rocks to the private beach and came up here to have it out with him, then—"

Malone drew a deep breath. "A clever concatenation of pusillanimous, suppositional, hypothetical fabrications. I demand—"

"Shut up," Griggs said. "You have no privileged status here as an attorney. Mr. Hamilton has a bench warrant for you, on several charges of conspiracy. But murder takes precedence." Griggs's hand came down heavily on Malone's padded shoulder. "The charge is accessory after the fact and concealment of evidence—the pistol."

"What pistol? The presence of a weapon here has not been established!" But the little lawyer was standing on the thinnest of legal ground.

Griggs motioned to Miss Withers. "This lady here says she heard two shots, just as you arrived. The room stank of cordite when I got here. That's enough evidence for me—and we'll find the gun!"

Harbin Hamilton was obviously enjoying every moment. "That seems to settle you, once and for all," he told Malone. "And your girl friend, too." He nudged Sergeant Griggs. "What'll we do with the Withers woman? She's in on it too, isn't she? I seem to remember her being in cahoots with Malone once before—"

"Listen!" cried Nancy suddenly. "I can't stand any more of this. If I sign a confession will you let these people go? Mr. Malone and Miss Withers haven't done anything!" Her voice throbbed.

Sergeant Griggs was brightening, but Malone cut in. "I will not permit it!"

"I won't either," said Hamilton. "A confession to first degree murder can't be pled anyway. And we don't need a confession."

"That's right," agreed Griggs. He turned to the schoolteacher, who could already hear those iron doors clanging behind her.

"I'll go," Hildegarde said, "but I'll not go quietly! As a matter of fact, there are a number of things I must call to your attention. In my opinion, you're going about this investigation in entirely the wrong way, and—"

Just then Mr. Dade, the sober-faced gentleman from the D.A.'s office, drew the sergeant aside and whispered to him. Griggs listened, looked surprised and nodded. "Thanks for tipping me off, Mr. Dade," he said. Then he turned back to Miss Withers, who had her fingers crossed behind her back. "As for you, ma'am—I hear that you've meddled in police business before, and managed to make an unholy nuisance of yourself. On the other hand, you've helped us this time by making a statement. So if you'll wait while it's typed up—"

"But I'm certainly not going to leave right now!" she broke in. "I'm needed here! I've probably had a great deal more experience in murder cases than any of you, and I'll be happy to advise you!"

"You'll get out now," interrupted the sergeant wildly. "The statement can be signed later. And take that screwy-looking dog with you!"

Miss Withers looked as crestfallen as the traditional old maid in the limerick, who went to a Birth Control Ball. "Well, I *never!*" she huffed. But the party was over. Nancy was led away, belatedly covered with one of Doris Bedford's beach robes. Malone, at Harbin Hamilton's spiteful insistence, went through the ignominious experience of being handcuffed. The schoolteacher found herself being propelled firmly toward the door, but she did manage to flicker a reassuring wink over her shoulder in his general direction. Malone didn't see it, or perhaps he didn't wish to see it.

It just wasn't Miss Withers' day. To add to her troubles, just as she'd feared, Talley had pawed open the refrigerator and made smorgasbord of its contents. Leading him outside, she had to run the gauntlet of the press —evidently the Bedford murder was already front-page news. The photographers flashed cameras at her, and the reporters demanded statements.

"Stand back!" she warned them, holding Talley firmly.

"Does he bite?" one newsman asked.

"No, but he throws up!"

Somehow she made her way back to the little coupé and got it started. Talley, quite unused to lunching on smoked oysters and caviar, climbed slowly onto the back seat and curled up to sleep. Miss Withers felt rather like curling up too. Malone, one of her best friends, had come to her in his greatest hour of need, and now she was abandoning him to the jackals. She alone was free —but free to do what? The case against Nancy, a girl perhaps more sinned against than sinning, was utterly damning—and Malone was in it up to and including his ears.

And to make everything absolutely perfect, Miss Withers had not got ten miles down the coast on the way home before she saw the familiar black sedan tailing her. It hung on, perhaps an eighth of a mile back, as implacable as death and taxes. The schoolteacher's immediate reaction was a rush of righteous wrath to the head—but she remained cool, concocting a plan that was fiendishly simple.

"I think, Talley, we've been pushed around just about enough for one day!" She speeded up, dashing on down the highway until she saw a side road leading inland up one of the narrow canyons. Rashly she turned up it —a winding, two-lane road with looming cliffs on one hand and a dizzy drop-off on the other. The black sedan followed.

She gave a last burst of speed before taking one of the sharpest blind curves, then jammed on the brakes and stopped short, with the little coupé swung across the road.

The big sedan had excellent brakes, but no driver on earth could have seen that improvised roadblock in time. Rubber smoked and screeched—and then there was a resounding crash. Miss Withers' ancient Chevy rolled sluggishly over—and then disappeared. Topanga Canyon echoed a few seconds later to another, a very final crash, from far far below. . . .

"Why don't you look where I'm going?" demanded

Miss Hildegarde Withers, leaning precariously against the face of the rock cliff and holding Talley with both hands. "If we hadn't jumped in the nick of time—"

She addressed the two men in the front seat of the sedan, both of whom were pale and shaking. "Lady!" cried the driver, a middle-aged man in a chauffeur's cap. "I didn't—I'm only a hire-drive car—"

"Well-insured, I hope?" She turned to the other, a bulky young man in a sports shirt, whose five-o'clock shadow was hours ahead of schedule. "And you, I suppose, are Filthy Phil Pappke?"

"I'm his brother William, and no cracks! I don't know where you come in, but you got Phil all wrong. He's a businessman, an investor like—and he's got a lot of money invested in a tomato name of Nancy Jorgens because he went her bail and if she isn't back in Chi by tomorrow, it's forfeit. I was just tagging Malone, figuring he'd maybe be a lead to the dame."

"The dame is beyond your reach, and so is Malone. They're arrested."

"Ouch! Those police cars I saw—say, maybe it's okay and she gets sent back to Chi!"

"Nothing is okay. They'll be held here—for murder." Willie scowled, and started to mumble something about his brother's not going to like this. "Be quiet," she told him. "An accident to Malone isn't going to save your brother his money. Driver, just how serious is the damage to your car?"

"She'll still run, I guess."

"Then the least you can do is to drive me home!" She climbed in, the dog in her arms. "Willie, on the way back you and I are going to have a heart-to-heart talk!"

Willie protested that he had to get to a phone right

away and call his brother, but she told him that he was welcome to use hers. "Because I want a word with Filthy Phil Pappke myself!"

A little later Willie made his telephone report, which consisted mostly of listening to staccato sounds over long distance, until the schoolteacher got tired and took over. "Hello, Mr. Pappke? This is Miss Withers, the lady whose automobile was demolished by your shenanigans. Lucky I wasn't killed. What? Well, perhaps it isn't illegal to have somebody shadowed, but it is illegal to annoy a lady, in or out of a car. I intend to see my lawyer at once—that car was a collector's item and it had sentimental—"

"Listen, whoever you are! All I want—" came the protesting voice.

"All you want is to save $25,000! And let me tell you that your only chance in this world is to help me get John J. Malone out of jail, because he can straighten this out if anyone can. The moment his bail is set, you'd better have a man there with the money. What? I don't care how you feel about Malone; the point is that you've got to cooperate with us now—or else! Think about that—and while you're thinking, think about my lawsuit!" She hung up.

"That ain't the way to handle my brother Phil," Willie Pappke told her.

"The only way I would handle either of you is with a pair of ten-foot tongs! Now get out of here, I have work to do." Willie got.

Work to do, indeed? But what work, and where to begin? Malone had brought her a hopeless mess, and now it was a thousand times worse. But give him the benefit of the doubt. Suppose that in spite of his having brought a paternity suit involving a baby named after

232

him and paid for by him, he had acted in good faith. In desperation would he have been a party to forgery, even forgery which might have seemed morally justifiable? Yet Nancy was a breath-taking blonde, and breath-taking blondes were Malone's worst weakness—or one of his worst weaknesses.

As these unpleasant thoughts were bubbling in Miss Withers' mind, she was studying the legal papers in the little lawyer's briefcase—after first putting the one remaining bottle safely away. She read through the trial transcript and the transcript of the forgery prelim. She studied the photo-enlargements of the handwriting on the questioned check. The signature of Paul Bedford looked perfectly good to her, but pinned to it was the verdict of three famous handwriting experts who had all pronounced it queerer than a three-dollar bill.

The forgery and the fact that Paul Bedford had obviously died at Nancy's hand were unarguable. Still—

In the midst of her speculations another call from Chicago came in. It was Maggie, this time in tears. "I just this minute heard!" she was crying hysterically. "It's on the press tickers. Oh, I *told* you to keep him away from *that woman!*"

"Wild horses couldn't. Be quiet, Maggie. We've got to work fast. At the moment I'm quite ready to clutch at straws. But I'm happy to announce that we now have the cooperation of a very powerful, if somewhat unethical, ally. Yes, Filthy Phil Pappke. What? No matter how, I put the fear of lucre in him. The first thing you've got to do is to find out who the Bedford family doctor was, and arrange to have Mr. Pappke have somebody do a little strong-arm stuff. And stick by a phone. I may think of something else."

Five minutes later Miss Withers was headed downtown in a taxi, her first stop being the Hall of Justice in Los Angeles. That vast grim mausoleum of humanity's hopes and dreams was crowded, but nobody in the place could tell her if Malone had yet been brought in and taken to the jail floors; even if he were there, she couldn't get into the special jail elevator because she was neither his attorney nor his next-of-kin, though she made a stab at pretending to be the latter.

Well, that was that; she would have to proceed solo. On a sudden inspiration she stopped at the Information Desk and struck up a conversation with the elderly officer in charge. "Oh," she said, pointing to a man nearby, "isn't that what's-his-name, the famous handwriting expert who always testifies for the prosecution?"

"No, ma'am," said the officer. "That's just some two-bit lawyer. He doesn't look a bit like J. Edgar Salter. Salter's a thinner man, with a bald head and glasses." She thanked him as she left, with the name and description committed to memory. Mr. Salter had offices on Hill Street, she discovered by looking in a phone book; but she drew a blank on the call—he was in conference and could not be disturbed.

Which daunted the schoolteacher not at all. "I must go roundabout, as the Boyg advised Peer Gynt," she said to herself. And without more ado she hurried over to the Public Library, a vast pseudo-Moorish edifice on Fifth. Libraries were usually her last resort; there in the musty stacks was everything anybody in the world would want to know, if he only knew where to look.

She stayed until closing time, then stopped at a late-open bookstore to make one small purchase, and finally took a bus home. It had been a long, long day.

She had barely fed Talley, prepared a peanut butter sandwich and a cup of tea for herself, and changed into robe and slippers when the doorbell rang. This, she knew, would be the police, coming to get her statement. Or maybe to arrest her, the way luck was running. She braced herself for the inevitable, and opened the door. "Good heavens!" she cried. "This is where I came in!"

It was John J. Malone, looking the worse for wear. He entered, shoulders sagging, and sank wearily into her easiest chair. "I promised myself," he said slowly, "that next time we met I would bop you one, lady or no lady."

"I was afraid you'd misunderstand. But at least one of us had to be free and up and doing. Don't tell me you broke jail? Or did Filthy Phil actually send someone to put up your bail?"

He shook his head. "Released on my own recognizance," he said. "When they got me downtown, it turned out that several of the big wheels in the D.A.'s office knew me by reputation. And I guess Harbin Hamilton threw his weight around too much; he forgot that this wasn't Cook County. The D.A.'s office let me loose as a professional courtesy—but I'm still in a jam. And there's certain extradition back to Chicago even if I squirm out of this. Meanwhile there's Nancy. I don't know what to do about her!"

"I suppose you pondered over it in every bar on your way here?"

"Only two! I was in the U.C.L.A. Law Library, reading up. But I don't see a single loophole. Nancy may not get the works, but she'll get ten years at least."

"And in spite of everything, you're still in love with her?" John J. Malone nodded dismally as she went on. "Well, then! If you love her you don't have any choice but to believe her!"

"Yes—but we both heard those two shots, and I caught her trying to escape with the gun in her hand. Wish I knew where that gun disappeared to."

"I know, but skip it. What comes next, a grand-jury hearing?"

"Arraignment, two o'clock tomorrow—a formality that will take ten minutes. Nancy and I appear, the judge sets the date for the prelim and the amount of bail—any amount of which will be too much."

"Tomorrow! Oh, dear." The schoolteacher cocked her head. "Look, Malone, I have a wild idea. You know those meetings they have among scientists and researchers when everybody takes turns suggesting the wildest idea that comes into his head? Brainwashing, they call it—"

"Brain-storming," he corrected. "But by all the saints—"

"Let's try it, please! If you'll play I'll even show you where I hid your bottle!" He gave in promptly. "Very well," she began. "We'll release our mental brakes. Let me think. Nancy is completely innocent—it's a frame. Doris forged the check!"

"She wouldn't know how, and she wouldn't dare hire anybody—"

"You're not playing! Say something, no matter how fantastic!"

He sighed. "Doris hated Nancy. She not only forged the check to frame her, she thought that all her brother's money should be hers, so she killed him when he complained about her cooking. Wild enough?"

"Now you're swinging! Doris poisoned him with her cooking!"

"No, she used something that wouldn't show in the autopsy—a huge dose of adrenalin or digitalis. Or maybe

236

he's the real murderer, he killed himself out of pure meanness!"

"Maybe Harbin Hamilton forged the check . . . ?"

So it went, for an hour. At last they ran out of not only the improbable but also the impossible.

"It's no earthly use," Malone said dismally. "We're not getting anywhere. You and I both know that Nancy fired the shots that indirectly killed Bedford, and as for the forgery—"

"Stop thinking like the police! What is the unlikeliest possibility of all? There must be one factor in this case that has led everybody astray because we've been tricked into looking at it wrong side up or endways!"

"But we just haven't enough to go on!"

"I'm not so sure. I have a couple of irons in the fire, or where I could possibly start a fire." And she told him all about her afternoon. "If we could only find out a few things about Bedford's medical record—and what books he has in his library."

"So what? The prelim won't be for a week or so, and the trial not for months, and all that time Nancy will be in jail. You couldn't even get in to see this guy Salter, and if you do he'll just back up the other experts." She shook her head firmly, but he went on. "And you've missed the point in trying to sic Maggie onto Filthy Phil. Even if he will cooperate because you have him over a barrel, what's the use of roughing up the Bedford family doctor, and breaking into the Bedford house?"

"Just brain-storming," she admitted. "But I want to know more about certain things than anybody else knows. A shot in the dark will often scare something out of the bushes." Miss Withers yawned.

"Well, I don't know about you, but I'm going to bed and sleep on it. You're welcome to the couch here."

But Malone had promised the boys at the D.A.'s office to check in at a certain downtown hotel, just to make it look good. He departed, not forgetting his bottle. And he was no sooner out the door than Miss Withers was on the long distance phone to Maggie again, with new instructions. "Try to go along on the job yourself," she urged. "Here's what to look for. . . . What? Well, wouldn't you risk it if it will save Malone's neck? . . . There's a dear!"

All of which ended a memorable day. The schoolteacher even omitted her usual hundred strokes with the hairbrush, and crawled wearily into her maidenly couch, murmuring instead of a prayer—"Tomorrow is another day."

And so it was—a day that neither of them was ever likely to forget. They were both too busy in the forenoon to have a conference, except briefly by telephone. The telephone was also hot all the way to Chicago, where Maggie, the world's most devoted secretary, and Filthy Phil Pappke, surprisingly enough the world's most cooperative conspirator, were equally busy. That part of the story neither of them will talk about—at least, not until the statute of limitations runs out.

Both Miss Withers and the little lawyer were in Department 30 of the Hall of Justice, eighth floor, well ahead of time. There were only a few bored attendants in the courtroom. The plaque on the bench read *Herbert Winston, Judge,* but there was no sign yet of His Honor. Malone, very much in his element, plumped his briefcase confidently on the counsel table. Miss Withers took a seat in the front row and prayed.

Policemen, sheriff's deputies—among them Sergeant Griggs, of course—came in leisurely. Then two deputies, looking like lady wrestlers in spite of their trimly feminine uniforms, arrived with Nancy between them. Even the drab jail uniform could not cancel Nancy Jorgens' luscious measurements, but her eyes were haunted. She flicked a wan smile over to Miss Withers as she was led over to wait in the empty jury box, but her eyes were for Malone. He rose eagerly and started toward her.

"No, you don't!" came a harsh voice. Enter Harbin Hamilton, with several of the D.A.'s staff—one of them Mr. Dade, to whom the Chicagoan turned excitedly. "I protest against this man's trying to have a conference with his fellow conspirator!"

Dade smiled, a little stiffly. "Well, Mr. Malone is a member of the bar, and it's customary—"

"He is here as an *accused*—he has no attorney status!"

"Whether or not he is representing Miss Jorgens, there's nothing to prevent him from acting as his own attorney, is there?" Dade walked over and formally shook hands with Malone. They talked briefly, but in so low a tone that Miss Withers could only hear something about a "plea" and see Dade shake his head slowly.

More people were coming in; it was evidently close to zero hour. The hands of the clock showed ten past two, and Miss Withers found herself trying to hold her breath. She let it go as she saw Doris Bedford enter, wearing an unbecoming mutation mink, and seat herself on the aisle. Half a dozen other spectators also drifted in, by ones and by twos. One of them, a tall, bald, very lean man in a charcoal gray suit and glasses, seated himself directly behind Miss Withers. But she barely noticed. Everybody was springing to attention;

239

cigars and cigarettes vanished, and Judge Winston, robes and all, appeared and sat down on the bench. He looked rather like an animated prune.

They were finally under way, for better or for worse. It was all a blur to Miss Withers, though later she remembered Malone's air of absolute confidence—it should have won him an Academy Award nomination.

Court was in session: *The People versus Jorgens and Malone.*

"We intend to plead guilty, Your Honor," Malone started.

Harbin Hamilton stood up from his chair beside Mr. Dade and objected on the grounds that Malone had no status. The Judge looked at Dade.

"Mr. Malone, I don't believe you've been admitted to the bar of this state," Dade said. "Your status is that of co-defendant."

"Prisoners are entitled to counsel," interposed the Court. He looked slightly annoyed. "For your information, Mr. Malone, the State of California permits *only* a plea of not guilty in capital offenses. We are here merely to set the date for the preliminary hearing and to discuss bail—"

"Yes, Your Honor. But—"

"Nancy Jorgens, are you represented by counsel?" asked the Judge.

Nancy shook her head. "Not if Mr. Malone isn't—I won't have just anybody! I can be my own attorney too, can't I?"

"It is so noted," said Judge Winston. "Proceed."

Dade said, "As for bail, the law is clear. A defendant charged with an offense punishable by death cannot be admitted to bail when proof of guilt is indicated. It seems to be the case here—"

240

"Just a moment!" interrupted Malone. "Your Honor, I think that is open to argument. I have a request to make. If my learned colleague has no objection, I'd like to ask for a short recess in your chambers. I believe it may save the state the expense of a long-drawn-out trial."

"Well, I object!" boomed Harbin Hamilton. But one of the D.A.'s men touched his shoulder, and reminded him that he himself had no status. Mr. Dade looked somewhat confused.

"Mine is a reasonable request," Malone pointed out. "I am sure that in a few minutes we can come to an agreement." He looked at Mr. Dade, who frowned, then shrugged.

Judge Winston hesitated. Then he too frowned— Harbin Hamilton was audibly mumbling something about "the most ridiculous travesty of justice . . ." *Cr-r-rack!* sounded the gavel. "I will have order in the court!" roared the Judge. "Mr. Dade, will you speak on this most unusual request?"

Dade wavered, then a slow smile crept across his face. He had quite evidently had a good deal of Mr. Harbin Hamilton in the past twenty-four hours. "No objection whatever," he said, smiling.

"So ruled," said Judge Winston. "Court will recess until quarter of three." He started to rise, then sat down again. "By the way, gentlemen, there is no need to crowd into my chambers. I suggest you hold the discussion right here, and I'll listen. Clear the court of all but the interested parties."

Everybody looked at everybody else, then everybody looked at Malone, who was out on a long limb and knew it. He gave Nancy a big reassuring smile, then slowly and dramatically came over and held the gate open for Miss Withers, seating her formally in one of the at-

241

torneys' chairs at his end of the counsel table. She gave a quick look behind her and saw that Doris Bedford was coming forward, with a strange glint in her eye. But there was someone else—the man in the charcoal gray suit. "That's him!" whispered the schoolteacher to Malone, her excitement smothering her grammar. "But heaven knows if he's on our side or theirs!"

Malone nodded, waiting for the last of the casual spectators to be hustled out of the room by the officers. "May I proceed, Your Honor?"

"Go ahead," said Judge Winston. He took out a pipe and lit it, his face showing a hint of amusement.

"Your Honor, Mr. Dade, gentlemen—ladies and gentlemen, I should say," began Malone. "I asked for this chance, quite aware of the fact that I am sticking my neck out a mile, because I believe wholeheartedly that the sole purpose of any court is to serve the ends of justice. I intend to prove that bail *is* admissible in this case. Miss Jorgens has been charged with having willfully and with premeditation caused the death of Paul Bedford by heart failure while attempting to commit a felony—in this case, the attempt to take his life with a pistol. Is that not the situation, Mr. Dade?"

"You can hardly expect the State to lay bare its case at this time," Dade pointed out. "This is not the prelim."

"Quite right!" Malone set a cigar afire. "I'll just go on and state what I think your case is, and you can correct me if I'm wrong. You will contend, when this case comes to trial, that my client had a grievance against the deceased—"

"I'll say she had!" cut in Hamilton. "This woman committed one crime, maybe two, in Chicago. Bedford had her arrested and charged with forgery; she was in-

242

dicted and skipped her bail!" At this point Mr. Dade said acidly that he understood all that to be true, and furthermore—

"I'll stipulate, if you like, that Miss Jorgens did bring suit against Paul Bedford, claiming him to be the father of her child." Malone waved his hand. "And I'll stipulate that she did utter a forgery or what appears to be a forgery. But would she have brought that check to me to cash if she had *known* it was a forgery? And would I have cashed it for her if I had even suspected it wasn't legitimate?"

Nancy was staring at Malone with a look in her big beautiful eyes which almost brought tears to Miss Withers'. "I agree," Malone went on, "to stipulate some more of Mr. Dade's case. Nancy Jorgens did borrow a pistol, and she did bring it with her to California—a pistol, remember, that had been one of the props in a play. She was on the trail of Mr. Bedford, who had prudently taken to his heels at the first word of her getting out on bail. She did go to his family's beach house, she did lie in wait for him, she did finally enter and confront him, and she did then and there, in the middle of an argument, fire that pistol twice!"

There was absolute silence in the courtroom. "Now if I were presiding instead of being part of the audience," spoke up Judge Winston, "I'd expect an objection from somebody—maybe from the lady!"

"It's the truth," said Nancy Jorgens very calmly.

"Mr. Malone is making a strong case—for us!" Mr. Dade commented.

"Am I? But I contend that there is absolutely no basis for a murder charge. Unfortunately, the weapon has disappeared. . . ."

"I'm responsible for that," Miss Withers spoke up.

"The girl was struggling in Mr. Malone's arms, and I took the gun away from her and threw it into the ocean, where it couldn't do any more harm."

That was a minor bombshell.

Mr. Dade looked hard at Miss Withers, then remarked pointedly that it looked as if he might have some additional charges.

"But that pistol was just a stage prop!" Malone picked up again. "Such guns, for obvious reasons, fire only blanks! It is too bad that Miss Withers, with the best intentions in the world, put it beyond recall—"

"It ain't!" spoke up Sergeant Griggs. "That's what I come downtown to tell somebody. We found the gun this morning at low tide, half buried in the sand. I got it here—and it *is* a phony!"

The sergeant displayed the gun.

"Maybe she didn't know it wasn't a real weapon!" said Harbin Hamilton eagerly.

"I think anyone in show business would know that," Judge Winston suggested quietly. "Mr. Dade, does this change your attitude on the question of possible admission to bail?"

Dade hesitated—and then Harbin Hamilton, who quite evidently believed that an attorney should keep not only an open mind but an open mouth, cut in again. "What if the girl was only trying to scare Bedford—she scared him to death, didn't she? And any death caused during the commission of a felony is homicide—even, I believe, out here in California! And since Nancy Jorgens had been intimate with the man, certainly she must have known he had a weak heart!" He turned to Doris Bedford, bowing. "You knew it, didn't you, Miss Bedford?"

"Yes," said Doris. "Of course. But why are you wast-

244

ing all this time? She killed my brother, and I object to this incredibly asinine attempt to get her free! I tell you one and all, I'm going to use every resource in my power to see that this case isn't glossed over."

Mr. Dade held up his hand. "The State of California has even more resources than you, Miss Bedford. We are merely trying to get to the facts."

"Of course she knew Paul had a weak heart!" Doris snapped back. "I tell you, she wanted him out of the way so he couldn't be the complaining witness against her at the forgery trial—"

"Thank you," said Dade, shaking his head at her. "But we'd better get on—I'm afraid we are trying the patience of the court. Mr. Malone, I don't see your purpose in all this. We are not now involved with whatever happened back in Chicago. Your eloquence hasn't changed my mind so far as Miss Jorgens is concerned. We still refuse to admit her to bail. As for you—I admit that all we had against you was concealment of the gun, and now we have somebody else confessing to that. We'll consider admitting you to bail, or perhaps dropping the accessory charge entirely."

Malone, the schoolteacher realized, had now got himself *out* of trouble—but he had got Nancy and herself *in* even deeper. However, the little lawyer wasn't finished. "Mr. Dade," he said slowly, "I want you to reconsider your charges against my client. She meant only to throw a scare into Bedford—as a matter of fact, she had some wild hope of getting him to write out a statement clearing her of all charges. And when he just laughed at her, she let go with the blank cartridges. Is that *murder?*"

"She knew it would probably kill him!" Hamilton interrupted again.

"No! Because Paul Bedford *himself* didn't know he

245

had a bum heart! I have here a telegram from J. Willoughby Howe, the Bedford family doctor, in which he states that at Doris Bedford's insistence the bad news was kept from her brother, an ex-athlete who knew all about athlete's heart and therefore might worry himself to death over it." Malone tossed a yellow piece of paper to Dade. "We are prepared to bring Dr. Howe into court at the trial—"

"Dr. Howe would never say that!" shouted Doris wildly. "He gave me his solemn promise . . ." Then she bit her lip.

"I think perhaps the doctor yielded to *persuasion*," said Miss Withers, at the moment forgiving Filthy Phil all his trespasses. She had been silent longer than was her custom, but it still wasn't quite her time to get into the fray. "Why doesn't somebody ask Miss Jorgens herself?"

Nancy stood up. "I never dreamed—I never meant to kill Paul. I'd always hoped that some day he'd acknowledge his son. I once loved him, or thought I did. I'm sorry I caused his death, but I never in the world meant to kill him!"

Malone nodded his approval. "Well, Mr. Dade?"

Dade was in conference with his associates. Harbin Hamilton, who had been obviously left out, rose suddenly. "I see what is happening!" he stormed. "Go ahead and drop your charges here. I'll drag the woman back to Chicago, and the high-and-mighty Mr. Malone with her. She'll get twenty years for the forgery, anyway!" He caught the Judge's eye, and sat down suddenly.

"I'm coming to that forgery," said Malone very softly.

"But we're not talking about that case!" Dade protested. "We're supposed to be just discussing bail, and our time is about up."

"It is," said His Honor. "Gentlemen, I enjoy a break in the routine as much as anybody else, but—will you please conclude, Mr. Malone?"

"Yes, Your Honor. I need only a couple of minutes, most of which I'll turn over to somebody else. This lady beside me is Miss Hildegarde Withers, who has had some experience in criminology—"

"I know," said Mr. Dade with a stiffish smile. "The McWalters case. She committed justifiable mayhem."

"A simpler case than this one," said Miss Withers, bobbing her head. "Anyone in my profession—and I was a teacher in public schools for over thirty years—has to be interested in forgery. We run up against it in examination papers and on report cards. What bothered me from the very beginning about this affair was the fact that every handwriting expert agreed that Paul Bedford's name was forged to that check, yet—"

"And you can't get away from that!" Harbin Hamilton was irrepressible. "Don't forget, nobody had anything to gain from that forgery except Nancy Jorgens, and presumably her accomplice Malone! The forgery and the murder are tied up together!"

"But I never *dreamed* it was a forgery!" Nancy spoke up. "It looked exactly like Paul's signature, and I thought he'd had a change of heart! I couldn't believe he was all bad."

"If she didn't forge it she knows who did," the Chicago D.A. insisted, too loudly. By this time both the Judge and Dade were glaring at him. But he went on. "Ask her, some of you!"

"I believe I still have the floor," said Miss Withers. "You could ask me, but I'm afraid you wouldn't accept my answer. But there is somebody in this room who does know—"

Doris Bedford suddenly rose. "I do *not*—" she blurted out. Then she sat down again, realizing that nobody had been talking about her. Miss Withers was pointing at the man in the charcoal gray suit, who now came up to the counsel table with a big roll of papers. He nodded casually at the Judge, and at Dade.

"I was about to say, when I was interrupted by a lady who doth protest too much," continued Miss Withers, "that there is somebody in this room who knows all about disputed signatures. Most of you have probably heard of J. Edgar Salter, the author of *Handwriting Investigation,* the last word in its field."

"We'll stipulate him as an expert," agreed Mr. Dade, smiling. "But which case are we talking about, will somebody tell me?"

"There's only one!" Malone told him confidently. "You wait and see."

"I've heard of Mr. Salter," said Harbin Hamilton. "And nobody is going to tell me that he doesn't think that check is forged!"

All eyes were on Mr. Salter, who shook his head, then nodded. "Precisely," said Miss Withers. "But just *why* is it a forgery?"

The famous expert spread out his papers on the table, holding them up in turn. "Because," he said, "in these blowups, enlarged one hundred times, it isn't hard to see that the degrees of pressure used on the pen vary greatly. That is never true of a genuine signature."

"Wait!" said Malone. "You mean that you can tell by looking at a photograph of a signature just how hard the writer pressed down?"

"Almost to the ounce of pressure," Salter said. "It all shows up, right here. See this—and this? Why, we can even note the pulse beat!"

248

"Funny," said the little lawyer, "that the people in the bank who refused the check happened to notice it at all—since it hadn't yet been photographed and enlarged!"

"Unless somebody had phoned them and tipped them off!" Miss Withers said helpfully. But this time Doris Bedford did not rise to the bait; she sat with her lips pressed tight together. The schoolteacher turned back to Salter. "Why not go on, and tell them what I asked you?"

The man was amused. "This is one for the book," he chuckled. "Miss Withers got into my private office on the pretext of asking me to autograph a copy of my book, a lure which no author can resist. Then without warning she sprung a new one on me. I confess I laughed out loud. Then I thought it over and made some experiments with my own signature, and—well, what I found out rather staggered me!"

"Go on!" said the Judge.

"The lady had asked me—would it be possible for a man to *forge his own handwriting?* By that I mean, to write his name so that it would present all the typical signs of having been forged. And, so help me, it is!"

The courtroom was hushed. "Now does this begin to tie up?" Malone whispered to Mr. Dade. Then he turned to the expert. "And is that what happened in this case, in your opinion?"

"Well, it could have, certainly. But—"

"That's enough!" Malone boomed. "It was a fiendish frame! *De mortuis* and all that, but I submit to you that Paul Bedford, intent on getting rid of a girl whom he had wronged and who was a perpetual menace to him, *forged his own name* on a check and mailed it to her

249

so he could have her arrested and sent off to prison! Paul Bedford is the real villain in this case!"

"You can't speak those lies about my brother!" screamed Doris.

Miss Withers decided it was time to leap in. "I happen to know where Bedford picked up his knowledge of handwriting. He collected autographs of the signers of the Declaration of Independence, among them a disputed Button Gwinnett signature that was the subject of a book which is in most public libraries: *The Gwinnett Letter and Other Queers*. Naturally it goes into the forgery question rather thoroughly."

"My brother never went *near* a public library!"

"Perhaps not, Miss Bedford. But since the book was based on something in his own collection, I thought it likely he'd own a copy."

"Well, he didn't!" The thin woman was almost at her wits' end.

"I suggest that you go back home to Winnetka and look on the shelf just under the big window in your brother's study. Third from the north end—a slim red book. I have it on excellent authority, though I'm not at liberty to say whose."

Doris Bedford opened her mouth, gasping like a fish, but no words came. Harbin Hamilton was also silent. The Judge's prunelike face broke into an expression of utter rapture. "I'm going to write my memoirs and get this in," he announced, sighing happily.

But the Assistant District Attorney was shaking his head. "Yes, Your Honor. All very interesting. But all this isn't proof—it isn't even evidence. Mr. Salter only says that it *could* have happened—nobody can differentiate between an actual forgery and a simulated one!

I believe he was going on to say that when he was interrupted by our enthusiastic friend here."

Malone shrugged, obviously an archer who had shot all his bolts. "Is that all you have to tell us, Mr. Salter?" he said slowly.

The expert shook his head. "I was just going to call your attention to the signature again," he said. "See here? This—and this—and this are the pulse beats—little jumps. Except that the markings in this case are unusually irregular."

"Irregular!" echoed Malone. "The pulse—that's the heartbeat! Who would be more likely to have an irregular heartbeat than a man who had heart trouble?"

"And what would be more natural than for a man with a cardiac condition to have it show strongly when he was tense and engaged in committing a crime!" added Miss Withers. "Isn't that so, Mr. Salter?"

"Well—" said the expert. "I never heard of diagnosing cardiac trouble by studying handwriting, but—I guess I'll have to run a string of tests and maybe revise my book."

"Your move, Mr. Dade," said Malone. He began whistling "St. James Infirmary" under his breath.

Harbin Hamilton tried once more. "This isn't evidence!"

"And court is not in session," snapped the Judge. "I wish it were, so I could fine you for contempt! Mr. Dade?"

The room was by now in a turmoil, and Malone and Miss Withers were almost dancing a jig. The Assistant District Attorney's face was in something of a turmoil too—a study in mixed emotions. "I—I'll admit that the provocation seems to have been most unusual," he said.

"My learned friend here has just about ruined Mr. Hamilton's case back in Chicago, I'd say. But we are faced with the fact that a man was killed—"

"He died accidentally!" Malone pointed out quickly.

"Under the circumstances," continued Dade, "I think we can agree on a lesser charge in this case. Maybe manslaughter. Maybe something . . ."

"Make it anything at all!" Malone challenged. "Come now, Mr. Dade. After what Bedford pulled on Nancy Jorgens, do you honestly dare to go before a jury because he dropped dead when she tried to scare him? They wouldn't leave the box, and you know it!"

"And as for me," said His Honor, "I'll guarantee that, no matter what charge is brought, I'll release the prisoner here on her attorney's own recognizance until the trial, if the wheels of justice have to be gummed up with a trial at all!" He beamed paternally at Nancy, whose eyes were shining. The gavel cracked again. "Court is in session!"

Everybody came to attention.

"Your Honor," said Mr. Dade, resignedly but not too unhappily, "in the case of *The People versus Jorgens and Malone* the prosecution drops all charges against the defendants."

There was a buzz through the courtroom. "Release the prisoners," ordered Judge Winston. "Or is there still a charge against them?"

Harbin Hamilton drew himself up to his full height. "No, there isn't!" he roared. "But I'd like five minutes in which to express my opinion of the way court is conducted here, and—"

"You are in contempt," said the Judge gleefully. "One hundred dollars, or ten days!" He smacked his gavel down so hard it broke.

Which made Malone's day almost perfect. It was all over, or almost. Nancy's release would be within the hour; presumably they were sending out for some clothes for her so she wouldn't stop all downtown Los Angeles traffic. Miss Withers and John J. Malone went down the corridor, arm in arm. "You know," he said, you were wonderful, Hildy—you and your brain-storming!"

"It was you who gave me the idea about the forgery while we were running wild with our crazy guesses, when you said maybe Bedford was the murderer and killed himself! He didn't commit that crime, but he did commit the other!"

"So we wind up with no murder and no murderer." Malone grinned.

"Isn't that all right—in a love story?" She broke off as they ran into Doris Bedford and Harbin Hamilton, waiting for an elevator. It was one of those moments— and then the Chicago D.A. stepped forward and held out his hand, smiling a smile that must have hurt. Another nominee for Academy acting honors, Miss Withers thought.

"No hard feelings, Malone?"

"Believe me, it's a pleasure—" Malone began. But Doris Bedford forced herself between them.

"Don't think *I'm* not going to see my lawyer," she blurted out.

"My lawyer can lick your lawyer any day in the week!" snapped Miss Withers, proudly clinging to Malone's arm. "And just to make your day complete, Miss Bedford, may I remind you to notify your bank to honor that check?"

"Wait a minute!" Hamilton protested. "No check written by a deceased person can be honored—"

"Correction," said Malone. "The check was presented to the bank while Bedford was still alive. They've got to pay, or face suit." At that moment the elevator arrived, and Miss Withers and the little lawyer got in, leaving the other two playing Human Statues. "Wait until I tell Nancy this!" gloated Malone.

"I'm not waiting," Hildegarde said firmly. "You two have a right to be alone in your big moment."

"But I'm not good enough for her," Malone said, surprisingly. "Look, Hildegarde—if I do get up nerve enough to propose to her, you gotta be there!"

"It had better be matrimony that you propose," Miss Withers warned him. "And don't think I won't be at the wedding, complete with shotgun!"